MW01169525

Credits:

Edited by Linda Ingmanson

Cover Design by Deranged Doctor Design

Trident
Rescue

Enemy CONTACT

ALEX LIDELL

OTHER BOOKS BY THIS AUTHOR:

TRIDENT RESCUE (Writing as A.L. Lidell)
Contemporary Enemies-to-Lovers Romance
ENEMY ZONE (Audiobook available)
ENEMY CONTACT (Audiobook available)
ENEMY LINES (Audiobook available)
ENEMY HOLD (Audiobook available)
ENEMY CHASE
ENEMY STAND

IMMORTALS OF TALONSWOOD (4 books)
Reverse Harem Paranormal Romance
LAST CHANCE ACADEMY (Audiobook available)
LAST CHANCE REFORM (Audiobook available)
LAST CHANCE WITCH (Audiobook available)
LAST CHANCE WORLD (Audiobook available)

POWER OF FIVE (7 books)
Reverse Harem Fantasy Romance
POWER OF FIVE (Audiobook available)
MISTAKE OF MAGIC (Audiobook available)
TRIAL OF THREE (Audiobook available)
LERA OF LUNOS (Audiobook available)
GREAT FALLS CADET (Audiobook available)
GREAT FALLS ROGUE

GREAT FALLS PROTECTOR

∼

SIGN UP FOR NEW RELEASE NOTIFICATIONS at https://links.alexlidell.com/News

DANI

"May I help you?" The male receptionist behind the circular ivory reception desk at Mason Tower rises to greet me, his curly hair tamed with more product than I use.

"Yes, I'm Danielle Nelson, the executive evaluator," I say, laying my card down on the counter. "I have an appointment with Madison Mason."

"Of course, let me call up for you."

While the young man goes about checking me in, I sit on the edge of one of the reception area's leather chairs, taking in the lobby's Greek Revival-style architecture and wondering just how big a mistake I'm making by being here. As an executive evaluator, I help clients determine the suitability of key personnel for critical positions. Is the potential new CEO mentally and emotionally stable enough to hold up to the stress and pace of the position? Does the aggressive head of security harbor deep-seated biases? Will an actor's sudden fame negatively impact his work ethic and commitments? As a psychologist, I find the work fascinating. As someone who was raped in high school and then assaulted by an evaluee last month, I'm not sure I can keep doing it anymore. Not sure I *should* be doing it anymore.

"You can go right on up, Ms. Nelson," the receptionist calls cheerily. "Ms. Mason's office is on the twenty-first floor. Just head to the very top."

Gripping my messenger bag, I traverse the lobby, my own reflection in the glass walls keeping pace with me. Fortunately, the elevator that opens with a ding for me is glass too. A month ago —before Brock Talbot, CEO went after me that is—I wouldn't think twice about elevators, but it's different now. Although Talbot failed to get sexual, the violence itself dredged up too many demons. Bottom line, tight spaces make me so uncomfortable now that even an elevator feels like the closet where that high school senior had trapped me in years ago.

Taking a deep breath to calm my racing pulse, I push the button for the twenty-first floor and feel the right decision settle around me. Whatever job Mason Enterprises is about to offer me, I'm going to have to turn it down. I need a break. Maybe not forever, but for a time. Also, I'm not going to force myself into an elevator ever again. Twenty-one floors is nothing I can't handle on foot.

Taking regular, deep breaths, I focus on the gorgeous building. Inside this New York skyscraper is an open atrium with real fruit trees dotting each floor and flowering vines connecting the levels. When the elevator lets me out at the skylit penthouse, I find a woman in an impeccable dove-gray Donna Karan pantsuit waiting for me.

"Ms. Nelson?" The woman extends her hand, her voice somehow combining power and warmth with each note, her gray eyes matching her suit. "I'm Madison Mason. It is a pleasure to meet you."

"Please, call me Dani." Shaking Madison's hand, I follow her into her office. In her early fifties, the CEO of Mason Petroleum, one of the Mason Enterprise child companies, is as slender and lovely as everything in this building seems to be. Instead of sitting down behind her maple desk, she takes a plush chair right beside the one she offers me and leans toward me.

"The trees and greenery here are gorgeous," I say both to break the ice and because they really are. So is everything here. Even the odd working materials spread across Madison's desk seem premium, from a letter on gold-embossed stationery from Garibaldi Leasing to a flower-shaped paperweight that seems to open to the sun's rays streaming through the window. "The architect must be something special."

"I'm a big believer in supporting green initiatives," Madison says, accepting a glass of water from a young woman who has just appeared with a tray of refreshments and motioning me to do the same. "We have lots of the same greenery on our roof, but up there, we have some vegetable gardens too, as well as solar panels to reduce our carbon footprint. It's increased our efficiency by a good fivefold and lowered our energy bills. So it's a win-win. Are you a nature person, Dani?"

"My family is somewhat nature obsessed, actually," I say, finding it very difficult to dislike the woman—which will make it that much more difficult when I have to turn down the job. "I started hiking and rock climbing about the same time I started walking, and we grow both food and medicinal plants. My parents used to run an apothecary shop with natural medicines, in fact." I take a sip of water to stop talking. It was a large corporation like this one that got them shut down, and I don't want the bitterness to slip into my voice. Madison's business has nothing to do with medicine and is plainly going to some lengths to protect the environment.

"How lovely." Madison's perfect smile is the same as it was all along. Either she wasn't particularly interested in my answer or knew it before she asked.

I shift uncomfortably and get to the point. Even though I'm no longer open for business, it seems polite to hear her out.

Sometimes problems don't require a full evaluation, and if a consultation won't suffice, I may be able to recommend someone else for the job. "What led you to calling me, Ms. Mason?"

"I didn't call you. The Mason Enterprises board of directors called you." She smiles uncomfortably. "I'd like for that to be clear up front."

"You disagree with my being here?"

"Not at all. It's just that this situation is quite delicate."

It always is. I nod encouragingly.

"Elijah, the CEO in one of our satellite locations over in Denton Valley—Mason Pharmaceuticals—is displaying troublesome behavior. He doesn't seem to understand that it can't all be about money, that breaking the backs of your employees—and your community—is bad business." Madison crosses her legs, the diamonds in her ears catching the light.

"He chews them up and spits them out so regularly that the HR department has nicknamed that location a revolving door. I'm as much for the bottom line as everyone on the board of directors, but we can't be bulldozing down people's homes to expand our footprint any more than we can bully the employees as if they were, well, boot-camp recruits. Which brings light to another problem. He likes to buy out entire city blocks and displace their workers, as if we need to *increase* both the unemployed and homeless population. It's almost like a fun side hobby for him, one he's ruthless about.

"Bottom line is that I fear Elijah's values don't align with Mason Enterprises' as a whole and will lead the company to future peril. But as you can imagine, *feelings* aren't evidence the board of directors can consider. However..."

"However, a psychological assessment naming this leader a liability is a different matter," I finished for her, holding up my palm. This Elijah sounds like the kind of man who needs to be dethroned, but I'm not an ends-justify-the-means kind of girl, even if I were willing to take another case. "I have to be honest,

Ms. Mason, I'm not a hired gun who looks for dirt. There are a few private investigators I could recommend, but if you're only willing to accept a red-light profile, I can in no way agree to that. Overtly or by implication."

Instead of recoiling, Madison smiles more broadly. "You are as professional as your references say, Dani. There's nothing I'd like more than to learn that I'm wrong. That Elijah is a reasonable man and this whole mess is just a misunderstanding. You see, this is the delicate part—Elijah isn't just a troubling CEO of one of our affiliates, he's also my son. And I'm…" For the first time since I've met her, Madison's perfect composure falters into a wince.

"I fear that he's going to do something we will all regret, and not just from a business perspective. He's always had a propensity for violence and bullying. I had even enrolled him in military school in hopes that the discipline would help him set healthy boundaries, but unfortunately, that backfired. He did continue with the service, but by the time he returned from overseas and took charge of Mason Pharmaceuticals, he—I hate to say this about my own flesh and blood—he turned into an absolute *tyrant*. The combination of the military's *shut up and do what I say* with the type of money and power that circulates through Mason Enterprises can be a toxic combination for some. And Eli is one of those people."

A familiar wave of dread washes over me, the scent of déjà vu filling my mind. A domineering man who thinks his position and money entitle him to do whatever the fuck he wants. Frankly, Eli sounds like another Talbot—and that bastard is still sending me threatening letters.

I clear my throat. "I'm so sorry about the difficulties you are going through with Elijah, however—"

Before I can finish, Madison plucks a notepad from the table, writes a number on the uppermost sheet and hands it to me.

"This is how much the job will pay, Dani, should you choose to accept it."

I blink at the several zeroes on that number. More zeros than I've ever been paid previously. With a payout this significant, I could stop the bank from foreclosing on my parents' home, pay off my student loans, *and* ensure my baby sister Amber can afford college. All that just for doing what I believe in—provided I can relocate that spine I lost after Talbot. I glance back up at Madison Mason. She does sincerely seem caught between a rock and a hard place. *Wyrd.* Has Talbot shattered so much of my spirit that I can't pull myself together for one last job? "Wyrd," I murmur.

"Is 'weird' good or bad?" Madison inquires politely.

I blink at her, unable to help a rueful smile. "Wyrd?" I slow down the enunciation so it sounds like 'word.' "It's just an expletive. Something from Old English I picked up somewhere."

"Ah." She smiles again, the silence settling back around us.

I still don't know what to say.

"I understand this may appear like a lure into a family quarrel," Madison says apologetically, as if clearly sensing my discomfort. No, let's call it what it is. My cowardice. "But there are innocents to be considered, and—"

"That's not a problem, ma'am." Just my own fucked-up memories filling the place where my spine belongs. Sitting up straighter, I decide I'm not letting some phantom of a man from the past stand between me, my ethics, and my family's well-being. "I was just thinking that if I were Elijah, I'd never agree to the testing. This isn't a blood draw where you can hold someone down and take a sample by force. I need to talk to him. Watch him. It's extensive, and, frankly, it's intrusive. Like I said, if I were Elijah, I'd just refuse to cooperate."

She laughs. "I would too. Fortunately, the Mason Enterprise bylaws require all senior employees to submit to a psychological suitability evaluation at the board's request or risk being removed from their position. I secured the board's directive before ever dialing your number. Elijah is many things, but stupid is not one of them. He'll cooperate. Well, he'll appear to cooperate. I can't promise he won't lie through his teeth."

"I'd be shocked if he *didn't* lie," I say, proud of how confident my voice sounds, my heart speeding slightly as I step full force into the project. "I'm trained to deal with that, however. It seems I'm flying out to Denton Valley."

Madison Mason's flawlessly made-up face lightens considerably as she pushes to her feet. As I step away, she reaches out to touch my forearm, her fingers pressing into my skin. "Please know that I love my son," she says softly. "But he has a cruel streak, enjoys using his title and position to exert his power over others. That's not who we need overseeing the development of medicines and cures. Sometimes compassion needs to count as much as the bottom line."

I cover her hand, squeezing gently. "I'll do what I can."

"There's one last thing," Madison says. "This might seem like splitting hairs, but it's important. I'd like your word that no one, most especially Elijah, will ever learn that you and I met."

I frown. "You want me to present Elijah with an evaluation order from the board of directors while claiming I've never met anyone from Mason Enterprises?"

"No, no, of course not." Madison laughs. "I simply don't want it known that I was the specific board member you met with. I'm his boss, but I'm also his mother. Like I said, that complicates things."

"I understand. So long as I have the right paperwork, there's no operational need to disclose logistics."

"I have your word, then?" Madison presses.

"Yes," I assure her. "You have my word."

2

ELI

*E*li Mason leaned back in his black leather office chair until it squeaked, his ankles crossed, Liam's voice on speakerphone recounting the details of last night's bachelor party. The speakerphone part was especially convenient since without a video component, Liam wouldn't see Eli going over the latest financial report as they spoke. It wasn't that Eli's buddy was a stranger to long hours, but he had a protective streak that sometimes got downright irritating.

"Your brunette friend looked melted and poured into those ripped jeans of hers." Liam's voice had an admiring edge to it. "With that level of snugness, I wasn't sure you'd manage to get them off without trauma shears."

True story. It had been a bit of a challenge. "No comment."

"None needed. She had her tongue down your throat before you ever even left the Vault." Liam chuckled as he spoke, and again, he wasn't lying. Kiki—or had it been CeeCee—had been good to go. Quite good, in fact. North Vault, the club Liam owned, was the textbook definition of a place designed to pick up women. Or, as in Eli's case last night, to have women pick *him* up.

And he'd loved every fucking minute of it. Emphasis on the *fucking*.

Unfortunately, after engaging in some sweaty horizontal time together, Kiki—or CeeCee—had gotten saucer eyes over the expensive leather living room furniture and the thick cashmere throw the interior designer had tossed over the back of the sofa and started talking about *next time*. After she'd dragged a finger over his Rolex watch while it was still on his wrist, Eli couldn't get her out of the house quickly enough. Not that Liam needed to know that.

"She was an enjoyable diversion." And that was all she'd ever be. It was all any woman would *ever* be. Eli turned a page on his report— a detailed companion to the blueprint for a new commercial-residential space he was trying to build. If he could claw the city block from Garibaldi, the slumlord who currently owned the space. It was a personal project, and Eli looked forward to buying the bastard out before the tenants in the so-called apartments ended up in the hospital. Hell, some of those places had live wires and kids. "Listen, asshole, just because Cullen is getting hitched, doesn't mean you need to be nosing into my private life like a teenage girl."

"I'm not. I just think you need a good lay or five," said Liam just as someone at Eli's door cleared her throat.

Cutting the line, Eli whipped his head around to find a redheaded stranger now striding boldly—and without invitation —into his office. He didn't recognize her heart-shaped face or the pale jade-green of her eyes. Distantly, the thought occurred to him that she was visually stunning as she positioned herself haughtily in her pressed tan suit jacket and pencil skirt, but that didn't matter. What mattered was that she'd apparently gotten past his fucking worthless intern with no difficulty whatsoever.

"You better be a stripper," Eli informed the woman, snapping his chair upright. "Because that's the only circumstance under which I'd be happy to see you unannounced."

"Most definitely not a stripper." Reaching into her messenger bag, the woman pulled out an envelope with the seal of the Mason Enterprises board of directors on the outside and held it out to him. "I'm Danielle Nelson."

"Too bad. I'd rather you'd been a stripper," Eli said, taking the envelope.

He was going to kill Zana, his college intern who hadn't been worth her salt from day one. He'd tried explaining her duties, at which point she claimed to already know everything she was supposed to do, only she didn't actually do any of it. He'd then tried to assign her a mentor in the form of one of his most successful executive assistants. Yet Zana had refused to take direction.

Now she'd left him no choice but to scream some sense into her. Deep down, he knew he probably should've fired her well before now, but like him at that age, she had no one at home to set her straight. Zana needed the money as much as she needed to learn responsibility. He wasn't ready to give up just yet, no matter how much he longed to wring her neck. Not that he could deal with her right now.

Not with Red sashaying her gorgeous hourglass figure around his office as if she owned the place. She eyed the world map, made of indigenous stones, he'd had commissioned, filling half of one of his walls, the grandfather clock in the corner, and last but not least, the plans for his city-center project spread across his desk. Her jade gaze seemed to assess everything with an auctioneer's scrutiny, and he felt a sudden impulse to push her bodily out of his domain.

"Are you going to read the letter?" she asked finally.

Eli fingered the envelope in his hand, trying very hard to keep his rising anger in check. His first rule to all his employees was that no one was allowed into his office without his express permission. If he hadn't been so angry, he might've laughed at the quote that floated through his mind. *Dammit, Zana, you had one job!*

"Well?" the woman prompted again.

"You barged into my office. The least you can do is explain yourself."

"Very well." Turning toward him, Red crossed her arms under her breasts, her fingers long and slender. "As I said, my name is Danielle Nelson. I'm a cognitive psychologist, and I'm here to evaluate your fitness to conduct business on behalf of Mason Enterprises. The documents I've prompted you to review twice now explain the scope of my authority. I find it best if my evaluees read the directive from their parent company first, lest they think I'm making up requirements or violating a right they believe they hold. I would prefer you discuss any legal matters you feel are at play with your board of directors before we start."

Narrowing his eyes, Eli ripped open the envelope and scanned the contents in stony silence, growing more and more livid with each successive word. She wasn't here to inspect his business practices. No. She was here to evaluate *him* personally. To throw a series of tests meant to see if he was mentally and emotionally competent enough to be the CEO of Mason Pharmaceuticals, a position he'd held for three successful years.

What the actual fuck?

Looking up incredulously, he saw the woman raise a condescending eyebrow, as if they were in some pissing power contest.

"This need not be an adversarial process, Elijah," she had the audacity to say next. "As you can tell, we'll be working closely together for some weeks. You may even learn things about yourself you find helpful. Things that make you a better leader. Did I say something funny?"

Eli snorted. "I'm just looking forward to a shrink improving my leadership skills. If I knew it was as simple as spending a few weeks with you, I could have skipped the years of being a naval officer and a SEAL. You must be a national secret."

She sighed. "Elijah—"

"Mason."

"I beg your pardon?" For the first time since walking in, Red seemed taken aback.

"My friends call me Eli. You may call me Mason. That's my last name. There is a cheat sheet for spelling it right over the entrance to the building."

"Right. You can call me Dani." She glanced toward one of the chairs, plainly waiting for an invitation to sit—though it was a fucking miracle she hadn't bothered to simply rearrange the furniture to her liking.

Eli ignored the glance. He was in as much mood for pleasantries as he was in a mood to give Zana the intern a raise. Having previously skimmed over the letter from corporate, Eli now spun his chair toward his desk and reread the directive more carefully, clicking the top of a ballpoint pen over and over. When he got to the bottom and found no loopholes, his jaw tightened.

Eli didn't shout at the bearer of the ridiculous news, but with one harsh flick of his thumb, the pressure he exerted on the pen casing snapped the thing right in two. The cracking plastic made a louder noise than he might have anticipated, the ink splattering over the letter and the cuff of his starched white Oxford shirt.

Danielle Nelson flinched, her face paling.

Eli's fury dipped into more of a simmer as he glanced up at the woman who'd gone from frozen ice queen to visibly frightened. He regretted losing his temper, but if she was going to bolt at nothing more than a broken writing utensil, it didn't bode well for any further interactions between them.

Not that anything *could* go well after such an unwelcome introduction.

Seeming to steel herself, Dani finally invited herself to sit down. "F-first of all," she said, her voice going from quavering to steady. "I will be shadowing you during your business dealings over the next several weeks. I'll be conducting regular interviews with you, and then I'll drop by frequently for unannounced observations. As far as anyone else will know, especially the public, I'll be seen as a representative of the board. This will maintain both your reputation and that of the board of directors. Do you understand, Mr. Mason?"

It took all of Eli's military training to keep his features in check. This was wrong on so many levels. Not only was Mason Pharmaceuticals his by rights—his deceased grandfather had bequeathed this arm of the family business to him in his legal will —but Eli had proven his acumen many times over since returning from his tours of duty.

Under his leadership, profits had increased by twenty-five percent, and his price cap on their prescription medications meant their brand of distributors became the most trusted among doctors and patients. If that wasn't a ringing endorsement, he didn't know what else possibly could be.

The real question was whether this evaluation was truly about Eli's performance as CEO. Despite the signatures of all five members of the board of directors on the order, Eli smelled his mother's machinations behind this mess as plainly as if she'd sprayed the high quality paper with her perfume. Madison was always looking for new ways to punish Eli for killing his twin sister—the murder he'd committed while still in the womb when he'd apparently taken up too many nutrients to let his other half thrive.

So what was this—another of Madison's rigged games or an objective inquiry? The latter could be passed, the former could not. Eli scanned the order again, examining the signatures on the bottom. However this got started, they had to have had a majority. Alfonso DeJesus, the one board member who Eli had a decent relationship with, hadn't given him a heads-up. Did that signify the man's support of this despicable turn of events?

"Who hired you?" Eli asked.

"The Mason Enterprise board of directors."

"And more specifically?"

"That was quite specific."

"Did Madison Mason hire you?"

"My paycheck is signed by Mr. Fettering, the chairman of the board, if that's what you are asking." Danielle Nelson stood and rested her palms on his desk. She had delicate fingers, the tips of her nails painted in a pale cream color, something he might've found attractive under different circumstances. He'd always had a thing for beautiful hands, especially the way they appeared when wrapped around his cock. But he was certainly not in the mood for such thoughts now. Instead, he joined the woman by yanking himself abruptly to his own feet, mirroring her position.

She backed up immediately as he towered over her from his side of the desk, seeming to feel a need to distance herself. Still, when she spoke up again, it was with a firm soprano voice.

"I believe I asked you if you understood the rules of engagement on this, Mr. Mason?"

But put a fork in him. Eli was *done*.

"You're dismissed," he barked out at her like the soldier he'd once been, avoiding answering her question. If she or the board thought him some idiot, they were each sorely mistaken. He didn't want her in his office anymore. He hadn't wanted her there even before she'd slipped in. Another spike of rage sizzled along his nerve endings toward his hapless intern.

"But—" Danielle protested, but Eli was so not in the mood for anyone to contradict him.

"What part of dismissed do you not understand?" he snapped, even more harshly than he'd spoken a moment ago. "If you need to infringe on my time, you can locate my intern, Zana, and make an appointment."

Not wasting any more of his precious morning on this threat to his competence and therefore his goddamn livelihood, Eli did an about-face and offered Danielle Nelson nothing but his back. Holding his arms behind him, he left her and the letter from the board behind and marched over to his floor-to-ceiling window to glance out at the view.

Denton Valley was in the midst of fall, the mountains ringing the valley green and orange along the bottom and a slate gray higher up where some were missing their winter caps of pristine white snow.

Fuck. The worst part was that this whole thing came completely out of left field. He'd had spats with the board here and there—what CEO didn't?—but Eli's people were doing good work inside these walls. The type of research that produced new vaccines and treatments for chronic diseases. He'd poured a lot of his heart into it along with sweat and hard work. So this? Why now? For once in his life, Eli didn't even know what he'd done to piss off the board.

Behind him, Danielle's heels clicked against the parquet pattern of his hardwood floors until he caught sight of her reflection in the window. He watched as the board's hired muscle straightened to her full height—one that was half a foot shorter than his own six foot two—thrust her chin in the air, and stormed righteously toward the exit.

3

DANI

I wait until I've crossed the threshold of Eli's office—and well out of his line of sight—before allowing myself to take the deep, stabilizing breaths I desperately need. That was intense. Or maybe Eli Mason himself is just intense, his leanly muscled six-foot-two body taking up all the oxygen in the room. I still feel the energy and power that emanated from him tingling along my skin, spurring my heart into a jog. With broad shoulders filling his crisp white shirt and washboard abs that were evident even beneath the tailored suit, the man is too beautiful for cosmic fairness. Except for his eyes. The cold gray steel in them is hard enough to cut stone.

For all his power, Eli Mason had spent the entirety of our first meeting erecting a wall between us. That isn't unexpected, but my sudden gratitude for the distance is. Getting close enough to discover who Eli is is my job, but wyrd take me... I'm afraid of what I'll find.

Getting my bearings, I pull myself together and settle on one of the blue benches in the reception area, taking note of the environment. This floor is sleek and modern, with cubicle walls of clear plexiglass, a navy-blue carpet runner and ergonomic office chairs. A massive depiction of a DNA double helix is painted on the wall. Everything neat as a pin. Unnatural. Like a military bunk made up tightly enough to bounce quarters off the blanket.

Nothing like the organic decor of the main office.

I'm in the middle of a note to find out whether the branding choice is incidental or a deliberate fuck-you to his headquarters when Eli Mason's deep voice booms over the intercom system.

"Zana Crusoe, report to the CEO's office, please. Zana to the CEO's office."

He sounds professional and clear over the PA, like a man used to speaking on the radio, though I think I detect a certain tightness in his words. *You've met the man for all of ten minutes and now you want to analyze his PA announcements?* I shake my head at myself. Eli has a heart-wrenching British accent—and yes, that alone makes me long to analyze his tone. But that doesn't actually mean anything.

In my peripheral vision, I catch sight of a young woman with spiky black hair and heavy goth-like makeup take a sip of soda and check her phone before starting toward Eli's door. She disappears inside the same room I'd just escaped from, only now I hear raised voices echoing from the space. Well, only one raised voice, really. Eli Mason's. His door must have some partial soundproofing since I can't hear any specifics, but the sheer force and volume of the yelling is enough to make me blanch.

When, a few minutes later, the door bursts open to expel a sobbing Zana, it's all I can do to keep from going in there and setting the asshole straight about acceptable human conversation. But correcting Eli Mason isn't my job right now. Dethroning his ass before he abuses more employees is.

Madison's confession about her son's bullying tendencies trickles back into my consciousness, and I can't disagree. Most often, people show their true colors by how they treat those who can neither harm nor help them in return. Like a young receptionist pitted against the CEO of an international conglomerate. Anxiety pecking away at my chest, I head for the stairs, just like I did on the way up. I'll have to come back, but for today, I've seen quite enough.

Returning back to the Marriott, I settle in behind the desk to open my laptop and type up the day's meeting and check on emails. The usual suspects populate my in-box, including two copies of *Natural Medicine Today*, which my father keeps forwarding to me no matter how many times I tell him that I get the same newsletter. I think he still harbors hopes that Amber and I will one day reopen the little natural-healing apothecary shop he used to run before Natural Products International put him out of business, but I don't see that business ever being viable again. Not with conglomerates like Eli's bulldozing mom-and-pop shops to push mass-market pharmaceuticals.

I'd seen the construction blueprint on his desk, along with the list of the small businesses that would be sacrificed for the venture. A florist, an independent bookstore, a small bodega, and a hot dog place. All of them looked like they'd been there for decades. Did they even know that one day soon, a too-cocky billionaire would show up and evict them? Would they survive, or go into bankruptcy like my father's apothecary shop had?

Sending the extra copy of *Natural Medicine* to the digital trash, I read over a note from Amber complaining about her gym class —she's sixteen and certain that the world is out to get her—and then open the welcome letter from the Ascenders Rising, the women's rock-climbing group I found in Denton. The group leader, a petite grinning girl appropriately named Jaz, sounds lovely, though in much better climbing shape than I am.

I'm about to click open my word processor when a new email flashes at the top of the cue, the From line reading *M. M.* Madison Mason's personal account, perhaps? The subject line reads, *Just a quick note.*

I click it open and freeze at the two short sentences.

Stop trying to play hide-and-seek with me, bitch. I'm not in the mood.

My throat closes, a chill surging up my spine vertebra by vertebra. The message is not signed, but I've no doubt that it's from Brock Talbot no matter what the From line reads. Fuck. How the hell did Talbot get my email address? I'd just opened this account a week ago. A honk from the highway echoes through the room, making me jump. Bolting off my chair, I palm the pepper spray canister I always have nearby now, and twist around to look at the whole room. No one there.

My heart still pounding, I rip away the floral bedspread to check beneath the bed, then yank open the window curtains, the closet door, the frosted glass panel in the shower. Nothing.

Of course there's nothing. Talbot is back in Boston, unhappy about my change of email. He's just the kind of strange person who thinks he's entitled to send nasty messages to anyone who crosses his path, so of course he'd find my blocking him a personal offense.

Putting my pepper spray down before I accidentally hit the aerosol button, I neaten the bedspread I'd thrown to the floor, grab a lavender sachet out of my purse, and sit cross-legged in the center of the floral pattern.

Lengthening my spine, I take a long whiff of the scent, just like my parents taught me to do back in high school when I was recovering from the senior who wouldn't take no for an answer.

I'm floating on a winding river, its shoreline covered in lavender bushes. Its current carries me along under a soothing blue sky. The sun shines down its warmth, healing me. Nothing can harm me here. I'm safe here. I am safe here.

IT FIGURES that when I return to Mason Pharmaceuticals the following day, I discover that the only neutral territory available is a tiny windowless conference room that looks more like an interrogation chamber or maybe a sand dune. The walls. The carpet. The chairs. Even the conference table sitting between us. Everything is beige.

Within moments, I feel the walls pressing in on me, perspiration snaking down my back and neck.

Eli raises a brow. "You're certain you prefer this to my office?"

Prefer? Ha. There's nothing I'd like more than to see sunlight streaming in through Eli's floor-to-ceiling windows, but I need the CEO away from a space he considers his den just now. Giving Eli my best fake smile, I pull out a chair and sit down. "This is perfect."

Taking a chair across the table from me, Eli turns it around and straddles it. Another barrier, just like the hardness showing on his handsome face. But I let it go.

"All right, Mr. Mason," I say, straightening my already straight pile of paperwork on the tabletop next to a pitcher of ice water and two empty tumblers. "Today I'll be giving you a modified Comprehensive Insights Assessment. This and all other evaluations will be recorded, and I'll send you a copy of that recording once each assessment is complete." I soften my tone. "This isn't intended to be a witch hunt. I promise I'll be as objective as humanly possible, and there's no one single answer that can 'fail' you. We're looking at the totality of the circumstance, not digging for some incriminating statement like a trial lawyer would."

Eli stares impassively back at me. With his reddish-brown curls, wide chin, and square jaw, it's difficult to forget just how devastatingly attractive the man is, but his personality makes up the balance.

"Would you like some water before we begin?" I ask.

"No."

I pour some for both of us nonetheless, a silent *see, I do care about your needs* gesture.

Standing, Eli takes the chilled glass and dumps it into a potted plant in the corner of the room. From the waxy look of the leaves, I think the thing is plastic. Right. Time to earn my pay.

"The purpose of this session is twofold. First, it's a way for us to get to know one another. Second, it gives me insight into how you see yourself," I explain. "I'm going to be giving you two terms. Choose the one you most associate with yourself. If you would like to tell me why or otherwise give context to your answer, I'd welcome the explanation. Do you have any questions?"

"No."

"All right. Are you ready?"

Eli stares at me and says nothing, just folds his arms over the top of the chair. He's wearing a navy-blue suit today, the fabric straining just slightly around his biceps. When, ten seconds later, he's still neither shaken his head nor nodded, I decide to push onward and place a small black voice recorder on the conference table next to me.

"Do you consider yourself to be more trusting or skeptical? Remember, there is no wrong answer."

"Skeptical."

No surprise there. "Proactive or reactive?"

"Pro."

"Deliberative or instinctual?"

"Both."

"What if you had to pick one? Think back to the last few decisions you made. What influenced you more, your gut feeling or analysis?"

"Both."

Come on. "Equally?" I ask.

"Yes."

Fine. I make a note to administer the battery electronically and skip to something that I'm hoping might encourage conversation. "Tell me what you think your greatest strength is as a leader of this company."

"Ask my accounting department."

I wait for him to elaborate.

He doesn't.

"So you measure the success of your position by the bottom line on the accounting ledger. Would that be fair to say?" Again, I hold on for several beats before deciding this isn't the hill I want to die on. "All right, we'll say that's a yes. How about your greatest weakness?"

"Impatience."

"In what ways are you impatient here at work?"

"When people waste my time." He says this with so much aggravation and what I can only interpret as menace that my pulse accelerates to an unhealthy degree. It's the first time he's answered with more than a word or two, and I find it intimidating. I find *him* intimidating. My hands tremble for a moment like they did back at the hotel room, and I firm up my grip on my papers and pen to keep this from becoming evident.

"What sort of relationship would you say you have with your subordinates?"

"I'm in charge of them."

"You're their boss." God, it's like pulling teeth. Teeth with impacted roots. "How do you demonstrate your authority? How do your subordinates tend to respond?"

"I tell them what to do. They do it."

"What do you do when your subordinates *don't* complete the tasks you assign?" I ask, checking my frustration. Hard.

"Correct them."

Yesterday's episode with the young assistant Eli ripped to tears flashes in my mind, making it hard to keep a neutral tone, though somehow I manage. "How do you correct them?"

"Efficiently."

Oh, for wyrd's sake. I feel my own patience fray at the edges, the words spilling out unchecked. "What specifically do you do, Mr. Mason? Do you fire them? Send them to class? Yell? Hit?"

"Yes," says Eli.

"Yes, what?"

"All of the above."

I click the recorder off, fury simmering through my blood. I've never lost my temper with a client before, but something about Eli Mason gets under my skin in a way that makes my head spin.

"Are you paying goddamn attention to a single word I say?" I demand, leaning forward toward the man. "I just asked you if you beat your employees and you said 'yes.' On a recording. Forgive me, Mr. Mason, but no one is stupid enough to say something like that unless they aren't paying a single iota of attention."

"You asked about subordinates. I answered." There's a harshness lining his voice, a cold anger that fuels my own. Eli Mason cannot possibly know anything about me, and yet he seems not only to despise me with every fiber of his being, but to ensure that I despise him in return. Even Brock Talbot hadn't done *that*, pretending instead like we were good friends—right up until he saw my report. Eli's gray gaze flashes at the recorder. "If you're not going to listen when I answer your questions, I suggest you listen to your recording after the fact."

I throw up my hands "Do you imagine antagonizing me will be somehow advantageous to you?"

No answer.

My heart pounds against my rib cage, and I long to pull out the lavender in my purse. But I don't. I pull myself together like the professional I am and click the recorder back on. "Please describe your management style."

"Efficient," he tells me, just as his phone rings. Without asking me if I mind, he swipes his finger across the screen to answer it.

"Mason." I hear a woman's voice saying something I can't make out, and I wonder if it's a girlfriend. Or a booty call. Whoever it is, Eli tells her he's on his way and, disconnecting the line, gets to his feet.

"This *assessment*...is over for today," he says, starting for the door as if someone had lit a fire in the room. "You found your way out once. I'm sure you can do it again."

4

DANI

Sipping my coffee, I smile at my parents' faces filling the computer screen. With his graying hair and kind eyes, my father is the first to speak.

"Dani, how are you, sweetheart?"

Better now that I'm hearing your voice. "Good. Just wanted to check in and let you know I'm here at the Marriott in Denton Valley. I got here about two days ago."

My mom frowns. "And you're only calling now?" She always insists someone who loves me knows where I am. "Danielle, you know better."

"She's a grown woman, Helen. You keep at her like this and she'll stop calling." My dad leans forward. "Colorado is a beautiful state. And you look ready to take on the mountains."

I run my hand over my tech T-shirt, unsurprised that my dad noticed. "I am. I found a women's climbing group. Going to meet with someone named Jaz this morning. She sounds very bubbly on email."

"If you find some common mallow, get a sample, would you?

Your mother and I would appreciate the seeds." My dad raises his finger. "That particular white-and-purple flower used as ground cover works incredibly well as an anti-inflammatory topical agent, as well as a natural astringent."

"I know, Daddy," I say, swallowing a bit of bitterness. This time two years ago, he'd want enough to sell at the apothecary. Now it's probably just for a personal garden they may not keep if the house is foreclosed on.

Which I won't let happen. Not with this paycheck.

"What's the new client like?" my mother asks. "I don't see why it takes you so long with each one. It's the same evaluation."

"The same evaluation, but not the same results, Ma. I still have to go through the whole thing."

"Bah. There's a certain personality that one needs to run a conglomerate," my mom says. "You have to be willing to squish everyone like a bug and not feel a damn thing about it. Not feel a damn thing about anything. Money is an anesthetic, you know."

I roll my mom's words around in my mouth, tasting them. It's not the first time I've heard her theories, but since I can't seem to get Eli Mason out of my head, I can't help trying her definition on for size. Willingness to squish? Check. Money is power? Check. Not feeling a damn thing? No... No, Eli Mason most certainly feels something. If only I can figure out what it is.

"Just be careful, honey, all right?" Dad says, his brows tightening as he studies my face. "We love you."

"I love you too." I pause, soothed by his familiar raspy voice. Afraid to hold the connection too long lest he notice how rattled I am, I flash a quick smile. "I'm meeting the climbers in thirty. I better go and hope not to embarrass myself. Colorado's climbers aren't kidding around."

I meet Jaz and five other Ascenders at the email-designated base camp beside a copse of blue spruce trees, their evergreen aroma wafting over us. The pureness of the mountain is invigorating, as if there's more air here than anywhere else on the planet. Giving me a quick welcome and introductions, Jaz launches into a safety brief that morphs quickly into one of the most detailed technique demos I've seen. With top rope belay systems already in place, we separate quickly into climbing pairs with Jaz moving between us to supervise.

"You want to go first?" Sky, a woman about my age with strawberry hair and a contagious smile, holds her climbing shoes in her hand. "I'm not wearing these while I belay. They hurt."

"So climb in your sneakers. It's an easy course," Jaz calls over her shoulder as she checks the harness and knots of a pair of beginner climbers.

Sky rolls her eyes. "Jaz thinks everything is easy. Mind you, she's a CityROCK champ, so for her it is. So, you want to climb first or belay?"

"She can't belay until I test her out on that," Jaz calls, giving me a grin to make clear no offense is meant. And I take none. The women here are clearly serious about safety, which is exactly the kind of climbers I want to be with.

Climbing first, I manage—barely—not to make a fool of myself on the rock face and return in time to see Jaz give me an approving nod. After I prove to her that I can safely belay a climber, she lets Sky and me practice on the rock face until the beginners tucker themselves out and head home while the three of us move to more challenging spots on the mountain. By the time midday rolls around, I'm drenched in a combination of sweat and contentment.

The three of us settle for a break at the top of a rocky outcropping, our legs dangling off the edge. Despite having just met Sky and Jaz, I feel a connection to them already, which is understandable given that over the past hours, we've literally held each other's lives in our hands.

"So, has Cullen talked you into a military wedding yet? The Tridents look amazing in dress uniforms. Just saying."

Assuming the glittery three-carat diamond on Sky's left hand is an engagement ring, I'm guessing Cullen is Sky's husband-to-be.

Sky snorts, her gaze peering out over the amazing view of the Garden of the Gods. The fall breeze brings us all some welcome relief from the heat. "He still doesn't understand why we can't just go sign some papers at the magistrate."

Jaz rolls her eyes and turns to me, her dark hair ruffling in the wind. "We're going to hike out to the Broadmoor Seven Falls over at Colorado Springs in about a month," Jaz says. "You ought to come with. We're bringing a picnic lunch. With adult beverages." She wiggles her brows at me, and I laugh.

"I'd love to, but I'm here for work, and the assignment should be over by then." Wyrd, I hope it will be over by then. A month is more than anyone should have to spend in Eli Mason's company. "What's a Trident?"

Sky chuckles. "When I came to Denton Valley, I was asking the exact damn thing, and now it seems strange whenever someone doesn't know it. Long story short, Cullen and three of his buddies all went to this military school called Trident Academy, became SEALs, and went off to do manly things. The nickname Trident Gods came back from the academy with them. It was supposed to be derogatory, but no one in town got the message. Plus, Cullen started an emergency medical search-and-rescue thing called Trident Rescue. All the guys had medical training overseas, and they wanted to keep up their skills and give back. So…"

"So Trident Gods." I shake my head. "So all the Tridents are medics?"

"Yeah, but more like volunteer medics. They all have real jobs, but when a call comes into the Rescue, they take it. Jaz's brother is a Trident too." Sky stretches her back. "So you have plans tonight? We're meeting up with Cullen and his buddies at the North Vault. It's nice. There's music, but not so loud you can't hear yourself think."

"I...I would absolutely love to." I grin, my spirit flying happily with the breeze. If I get to spend some time with Sky and Jaz, the month in Colorado might not be a total disaster after all.

5

ELI

*E*li knocked back his second shot of Jack, buffing away the sharpest edges of his week as he peered at the soothing blue surroundings of the North Vault and felt moderately less testy.

"You look like Sky made you try on tuxedos," said Liam, settling into the booth on the opposite side of him. Liam was always observant, but even more so at the Vault, probably because it was his. "Bad call yesterday?"

"A couple of teenagers with more bravado than brains." Eli swirled the liquid in his glass. The pair had decided they'd watch some YouTube videos on how to place anchors and paid the price when the safety system pulled out of the rock like a nail from drywall. "One got off with a broken leg, but the other cracked his skull. I tubed him before we airlifted him out but…" He let the words trail off. The kid had been fourteen, and even with all the machinery of modern medicine they had access to, he wasn't going to make it.

"Fuck." Liam shook his head. "It should have been my call to take too. I'm sorry to call you from work."

"You were right to." He didn't even want to think about Danielle Nelson right now. That was what it was, and Eli was going with an old adage: when all else fails, try the truth. The woman was going to get her answers. Whether she liked them or not was her problem.

Well, his too. But he couldn't control that.

"Where's Sky?" Eli changed the subject as Cullen and Kyan took their usual seats, both dressed down in snug T-shirts and dark jeans. He thought she was coming.

"She's with Jaz." A look of rare contentment flickered over Cullen's face, making Eli almost envious. Almost, because he wasn't actually looking for a woman for anything beyond a bit of a one-night diversion. He made no secret of it, just as the women who went out with him usually made no secret of appreciating his wealth. But so long as everyone enjoyed themselves, there was no harm, no foul.

And when did you last actually enjoy yourself? a voice in the back of Eli's mind demanded. He chased it away with another sip of Jack. Maybe if any of them looked like Dani, with her thick red hair and jade eyes that managed to somehow be both fierce and vulnerable at the same time, things would be different. Unfortunately, the Nelson body and Nelson eyes came with a Madison Mason for-sale tag. "You know, life would be so much easier if I were a masochist," he muttered into his drink.

Liam choked on his Diet Coke. "Trust me, you aren't one."

Eli rolled his eyes. "Don't be so literal, asshole." Since Liam actually indulged in the lifestyle, he sometimes took off-hand comments to their logical absurdity. Though the fact that Liam was nursing a soft drink instead of alcohol—meaning that he intended to play with a submissive later—should have warned Eli as to where his friend's mind currently was.

At least, unlike Cullen, none of the other Tridents had shown any inclination to hook up permanently. Eli certainly wished Cullen and Sky well, but given the heaven-on-the-outside hell-on-the-inside course his own parents' marriage took, Eli would rather take his chances in Afghanistan than on matrimony himself.

Seeing Cullen's face light up—and Liam's darken just as rapidly—Eli turned toward the door fully expecting to find Sky and Jaz striding into the Vault. There they were, laughing, and radiant and—Eli did a double take as he saw a third woman enter behind them. Red hair. Light jade eyes. Venom coursing through her veins.

Eli's cock twitched. Fuck.

"Hey, you," Jaz wrapped her arms around Eli, her small body pixie-like beside his large six-two frame.

"Hey, Jazzy-girl." Eli tried his best to conjure a smile for her, his gaze having trouble detangling from the judge, jury, and executioner that Sky and Jaz had unintentionally brought with them. Or maybe there was nothing unintentional behind it at all. Eli wouldn't put it past Madison to have given his pet psychologist orders to ferret out Eli's friends. But it still crossed the line.

"Everyone, this is Dani," Jaz said, obviously oblivious to the thoughts racing through Eli's head. "She went climbing with me and Sky today."

Did she?

"Dani," Jaz continued, "these are the Tridents. Cullen, Liam, Eli, and that asshole over there is my brother, Kyan."

Dani's eyes widened as her gaze met Eli's, the shock in them almost genuine. If you believed in coincidences—and Eli most certainly did not. Swallowing, the woman extended a slender hand. "A pleasure to meet you. I'm Dani."

For a moment, Eli considered letting the offered hand stay there, but his mother taught him better than to indulge in public displays of his thoughts. Appearances mattered. Appearances always mattered. And just now, for some reason, Dani wanted to pretend like she wasn't holding a gun to Eli's head. The only way to find out why was to play along.

"Mason. A pleasure." He shook the offered hand, finding Dani's surprisingly smooth and soft. At a slender five foot seven or so, she wasn't short, but certainly looked so beside the Tridents. Small and innocent and fragile. Yeah. Just like a fucking grenade. "What brings you here?"

Color rose to Dani's face, painting her cheeks with a faint blush.

"Eli!" Sky slid over to him, rising on her toes to plant a kiss on his cheek. "Thank you so much for picking up the call yesterday. The closest other bird was two hours away, believe it or not."

Unfortunately, Eli doubted that it would have mattered. Not that Sky needed to know that. "Any time, Reynolds."

"There was a bird emergency?" Dani asked, her intelligent gaze betraying more than idle curiosity behind the question. The woman was charting Eli's movements.

"A medical emergency," the too-helpful-just-now Sky answered before Eli could deflect the conversation. "A couple of young teens got pretty badly hurt on a climb and needed an airlift. Considering how we need a helicopter, it's pretty abysmal that the local EMS has, like, one pilot." She shook her head. "Luckily, Eli and Liam both fly. Oh, you should get them to take you up once before you leave. It's an amazing view."

"I'm sure it is," Dani muttered.

Yeah. Enough of this charade. "Let me show you some aerial pictures," Eli said, pulling out his phone as he motioned Dani to a more private table in the back. It was all he could do to keep from grabbing her arm and force marching her there, but fortunately, the woman followed along. She even managed to wrangle up a close-lipped smile.

"Mr. Mason," Dani started the moment they strode out of earshot. "Please listen—"

"No." Eli's voice came low and harsh, the cool tone sliding beneath the music. He was standing close enough to Dani that her lavender scent trickled into his lungs and made his pulse quicken. "You listen. You were hired to dig up dirt on me? Dig away. But that's where the line is. *Me*. You do not go after my friends, and you sure as hell don't go after their fiancée and kid sister. Pull a stunt like this again, and I'll personally stuff you into an aircraft and ship you back to Madison. And I'm not going to care what the board makes of that. Are we clear?"

"Yes," she said quietly. Her throat bobbed as she swallowed, and for a second, Dani looked like a startled rabbit instead of the predator Eli knew her to be. "Yes, of course."

Eli tilted his head, studying her. That felt way too easy. Another act? Another test?

"I had no idea that you knew Sky and Jaz, and I can assure you that if I had, I never would have agreed to come to the North Vault with them," Dani continued. "That was unprofessional, and I apologize."

Eli gave her a noncommittal grunt. He trusted the apology as much as he trusted anything from Dani and Madison, and unless he was going to lie—which he wasn't—he had nothing polite to say. Instead, he offered her a smile that he knew never reached his eyes. "In that case, allow me to give you a ride home and give everybody here an utterly wrong idea of how the night is ending."

"Won't that have the opposite effect?" Dani asked. "I mean, if we leave together, won't they expect us to… I mean next time, won't they expect to see us together again?"

"Of course not. I never see a woman more than once. And everyone knows it."

6

DANI

*M*y heart pounds as I return to Eli's office Monday, and for once, the prospect of sitting in the windowless room has nothing to do with it. I had fucked up. Accidentally. Innocently. But the result was the same: I've shredded what little trust I'd built with my evaluee, creating a problem that would take days to fix. If I could fix it at all. Eli Mason now believes I've been spying on him like some twentieth-century KGB agent, and for a man who clearly finds even the most nonthreatening questions an intrusion, the notion that I somehow "got to" his friends must feel like an underhanded attack.

I need to fix this. And fast. It would be unfair of me to evaluate Eli based on an artificial circumstance I've created.

My phone rings just as I stop to rest on a landing between the eleventh and twelfth floors of Mason Pharmaceuticals.

"Dani!" Jaz's voice, full of energy and life, bubbles through the line. "We missed you last night and wanted to make sure you knew about the Wednesday climb. We're going to take a different path this time, heading west instead of east. There's so much to see out that way. I know it's a weekday, but we're taking advantage of the late sundown and—"

"I can't." I don't bother trying to conceal the disappointment from my voice. The climb with Jaz and Sky, those wonderful soul-freeing hours on the mountains, are the one bright spot of my time in Colorado. Giving them up feels like cutting off a limb. But Eli is right, it isn't fair to him. And he's why I'm here. Not Pikes Peak. Not the wonderful women of the Ascenders Rising. "Believe me, I'd love to, Jaz, but I'm feeling under the weather. It wouldn't be safe."

"Oh. Was it something you ate?"

No. It was something I learned. You are closely connected to one Eli Mason, which means I can't hang out with you again. Possibly ever. "Maybe," I hedge.

"Well, hit us up when you feel better, okay?"

Yeah. I say all the right things before disconnecting the phone and stuffing it back into my purse, loneliness keeping me company all the way to Eli's floor. The truth is, it isn't just Jaz and Sky. With a business as big as Eli's, he likely has connections all over the place. Hell, he might own half the town. I should've known better than to assume his reach wouldn't extend beyond Mason Pharmaceuticals, and I've already gotten burned once.

ONCE I REACH my destination of the Mason Pharmaceutical C-suite, I find Eli's intern, Zana, with a cell phone in hand while a voice coming from the desk's speakerphone is explaining storage temperatures for some drug.

"So you do have the facilities for minus-three-degree storage on-site?" the woman on the other end asks.

"Uh-huh." Zana taps something into her phone.

"Excellent. I wasn't sure. What capacity can you store at once?"

"Not a problem at all."

"I'm sorry?" The voice sounds confused.

"Whatever you need, it's no problem," Zana says, hanging up before pressing Send on her cell. I catch the beep of a text message, the words *I'm going to suck you like a vacuum tonight, Boo-bear* flying off to someone on the other end and decide that I can get myself situated without the young woman's help.

Forgoing the windowless room, this time I decide to have the meeting in Eli's office. Unlike Madison, who'd come to sit next to me while we talked, Eli keeps the desk between us, his ballpoint pen clicking in his hand as he watches me pull out my papers and the recorder.

"Are we starting?" Eli asks, his eyes flickering to the Rolex on his wrist, his deep gray suit shifting with the coiled muscles beneath the expensive fabric.

I pick up the recorder, watching the man's muscles tense beneath his tailored jacket. Right. Instead of pressing the Record button, I flip the device over and pop off the back cover, taking out the batteries. "I thought we could just talk today," I say. "No recording, no report. Just regaining our footing."

Eli's gray eyes watch me impassively. "All right. Talk."

I lengthen my spine, reminding myself that it's me who is holding the proverbial gun to him, not the other way around. "Was the rescue call the reason you cut our last session short?" I ask.

"Yes."

"Did everything turn out all right?"

A shadow passes over Eli's face. "No."

Shit. So much for a good line of conversation. I'm careful not to phrase my next words as a reprimand, though wyrd knows he deserves one. "If you had just told me why you were leaving, I wouldn't try to hold you up. I just wanted you to know that. I know you have responsibilities, and I'll work around your schedule."

Silence.

ALEX LIDELL

All right. I can work with silence. I'm a trained psychologist, for wyrd's sake. Just because the silence is coming from a man who by all rights should be modeling men's underclothes, doesn't make it any less of a defensive strategy. "I wanted to tell you that I did what you suggested last time. I relistened to my questions and your answers. I noticed that you are careful with your words —more careful than I was. Specifically, the words employee versus a subordinate. What's the difference between the two?"

For the first time, I see a flicker of interest in Eli's eyes. A tiny little victory that I'm not above celebrating. *Come on, Eli, I can see you thinking. Say something. Say anything.*

"An employee is somebody who works for my company in exchange for money I pay them," Eli says. "If they don't perform, the worst thing that will happen to them is a loss of their job. A subordinate is someone under my military command. If they don't perform, they can lose their life. Or the lives of others."

I lean forward, gripping each of Eli's words, the way each is backed by years of pain and experience. This isn't a man who's watched *Full Metal Jacket* and learned the lines. It's a man who has lived them. "When you said yes to having struck a subordinate before—"

"I was a SERE instructor," Eli says, cutting off my full intent to phrase things diplomatically. "If you're unfamiliar with the program, google it."

"What did that feel like?"

Eli snorts without humor, but for once, there's no malice in it. "About the same as what it feels like to set a broken limb in the field when it's too dangerous to use sedatives." He clicks his pen, the *tic tic tic* of the spring sending an unsettling wave of nervousness through me. "My turn, since we're *just talking*."

"Of course." I open my hands in an inviting gesture, though something about his sharp gaze makes my pulse jump. Inevitably, he's going to want to know about my conversation with Madison, and there's nothing I can tell him about it. "What would you like to know?"

"Are my elevators not working?"

I blink. "I wouldn't know."

"No, I imagine you wouldn't, since apparently you prefer walking up and down fourteen floors. Why?"

I realize my mouth has fallen open and close it quickly. That is most certainly not the question I expected, the intrusiveness in it crawling under my skin.

Eli leans forward, the *tic tic tic* of his pen starting up once more. "I don't think you liked the room we met in last either. So small. Sunless. I could be wrong, though. Should I ensure we have all our meetings there?"

"No." I draw a deep breath, ordering my damn pulse to slow. In the back of my mind, I try to tell myself that Eli's going on attack is a sign of progress, but it sure as fuck doesn't feel that way just now. Clearing my throat, I check my voice to cool professionalism. "If you're asking whether I have claustrophobia, the answer is yes. However, that's a personal matter and not for further discussion. Are we clear on that?"

A corner of Eli's mouth twitches up, and he leans back in his chair. "Crystal clear. Maybe you should reinstall those batteries and get us back to business, then."

7

DANI

*T*he hairs on the back of my neck prickle, ice running down my spine. It's 7:00 a.m., and instead of heading out to grab an Uber to Mason Pharmaceuticals for the staff interviews I had Zana set up for me, I'm standing frozen at the railing of the Marriott's open corridor, watching the glass elevator rise through the massive indoor courtyard that's the signature of the hotel chain. There is a man inside, staring at me. Short, trimmed salt-and-pepper hair, expensive suit, loose jowls. I can't move. Can't glance away even as the elevator zips over my floor and keeps going up and up and up. Was that Brock Talbot I just saw, or just another middle-aged business traveler, like hundreds of others? Thousands.

Brock Talbot is two thousand miles away in Boston, I remind myself, my hands bone white where they grip the railing. My neck tingles, recalling the feel of Brock Talbot's hands as they closed around my windpipe. Grabbing my key card, I fumble sticking it into the slot lock on the hotel door. My shaking hands make four attempts before I can coax out a click and a green light that lets me inside.

Slamming the door shut behind me, I engage the dead bolt before putting my back against the door and sliding down to sit on the carpeted floor. My heart pounds in my ears, and there's a chemical taste of pure terror coating my mouth. Making it impossible to swallow. To breathe.

Straightening my spine, I force air into my lungs. Then lower, toward my belly. The door is cool behind my back. The floor solid beneath me. I imagine myself a steady tree, my roots sinking down into the earth. Grounding me. I'm at a hotel. I saw a middle-aged traveler in an elevator. That was it.

Fishing my phone out of my purse, I press the Home button until the screen comes to life—and then stare blankly at the screen. I don't know why I bothered. I don't have anyone to call. My therapist retired six months ago, and I never got around to finding a new one. I haven't been around any one place long enough to make friends. As for my parents, they know nothing about Talbot—they've had enough hardship in their lives without having to worry about me as well. Hell, they still think that when the high school jock, Gage, got me alone in a closet with athletic gear my sophomore year, all he did was rip my clothes to fondle my breasts.

Well, he *did* fondle them. Right before he raped me. But with a family as rich and powerful as Gage's, the first thing the principal did was read me the riot act about what happens to "false accusers" and the joys of rape kits. By the time I got a word in edgewise, I knew there'd be no point.

Gathering what's left of my wits back together, I pad over to my window and look out. Pikes Peak is visible in the distance, its uppermost summit still white with snowfall despite the higher temperatures down here in the valley. Though it's still early, everything outside is bright. Inviting. The mountains promise little chance of rain and even less of middle-aged men in business suits.

I take another deep breath, imagining that I can smell the

aspen trees. All right. New plan. Go in to do the interviews, then out to the mountain. Catch up on the notes in the evening. I may not be able to climb with Jaz and Sky without violating my professional obligations, but no one can keep me from the mountain itself. Hiking. Bouldering. Existing with nature. There's so much out there. So much life and balance and harmony. All that's missing is, well, me.

Getting myself back on track, I go down to the lobby and call a ride, using the wait time to google that term Eli had tossed out to me yesterday. SEAR instructor. A few taps and I discover no such thing exists in a relevant context, though the search engine conveniently asks whether I meant SERE. I shrug at my phone. Eli hadn't bothered to spell the acronym, so Google's guess is as good as mine, and SERE training does seem to be a big military thing. Survival, Evasion, Resistance, and Escape. If the title alone hadn't given me the creeps, the POW flag flying in the photos would have.

I continue my research as my ride arrives, using the trip to read through the description of the training, my skin chilling with every new fact. The man I'm here to evaluate used to actually torture soldiers for a living. Wyrd. How is this shit even legal? I swallow hard. No wonder Eli picked up on my claustrophobia. To him, it's probably blood in the water.

Tucking my phone away as the Uber pulls up to the building, I make my way up the fourteen flights of stairs and smile at Zana the intern, who is typing away furiously at her computer.

"Ms. Nelson! Good morning!" Zana tells me brightly. "I'm afraid Mr. Mason is off-site today."

I frown. "Yes, I know. I'm here to meet with some other folks." I let my inflection rise at the end, prompting the young woman.

"Oh. That's great." Zana returns to typing and giggles under her breath. A quick look at the computer screen shows several active chats, a TikTok page, and several articles on celebrity babies open.

Not my circus, not my monkeys. Maybe if I worked for a boss who used me for verbal target practice, I'd savor the day away from his company as well. I clear my throat. "Where should I meet with them?"

Zana blinks at me, her tone growing irritated. "Anywhere you'd like."

My stomach tightens. "Zana, you did schedule the interviews, right? The list I gave you yesterday?"

"Oh. You don't need an appointment. Just go on ahead."

You've got to be kidding me. I pull myself together and school my voice before speaking. "All right. Tell me who's here today and where they sit."

She stares at me. "I'm sorry, Ms. Nelson, but I'm Mr. Mason's assistant. I wouldn't know about anyone else's schedule. Or location. Maybe you can try the main information line?"

All right. No. Not all right. Taking the list of people I need to see out of my portfolio, I set it right in front of the intern. "I'm going to leave for the day. You, Zana, are going to go down this list, get in touch with every single person, and set up an appointment for me. You're also going to reserve a conference room. When I come in tomorrow, you will have the schedule printed for my use. Is there any confusion in my instructions?"

The girl gives me a glare. "Yeah, no problem," she says, adding "bitch" under her breath the moment I turn my back.

Well, that's a waste of a day. Or maybe not. I glance at Pikes Peak, my mood brightening. Looks like I'm going to get out on the mountain earlier than I thought.

AFTER A QUICK STOP back at the hotel to change and sprint through the lobby so quickly that the poor receptionist's "Have a nice day!" hits me between the shoulder blades, I'm back in an

Uber heading for one of Pikes Peak's backtrails. I don't want to see people today. Only the trees and mountains and the brilliant sky. Nature has always been my refuge, and with my attention on the mountain range, I can feel myself relaxing with every mile of pavement I leave behind.

"This here isn't a very popular place," the too-helpful Uber driver warns as his phone informs him we've arrived at the trailhead. "You'd be better off a few miles west. There's a visitor's center there and a small fast food place they call Canteen. Best fries in town."

"I'll manage." Shouldering my daypack, I step out into the scent of aspen trees and the feel of spongy soil beneath my feet. The air is so fresh here that I feel my body shedding toxins with each exhale as I head toward the craggy boulders and precipices.

About a half mile up the trail, I come across a detached rock formation about twenty-five-feet high with natural holds that are all but a welcome shingle with *Open for Bouldering* stamped on it. Setting my pack to the side of the trail, I put on my climbing shoes and attack the low holds to haul myself upward.

It only takes me a few minutes to conquer my first boulder, and now that my muscles are warm and singing, I'm ready for a bigger challenge. Conveniently, there's a perfect one two paces away. An infinity of perfect ones. For the next two hours, I lose myself in the climb, each new rock formation bringing its own flavor to the challenge—one is more porous, one is covered in blue-green lichen that smells slightly of the sea, one has veins of glittering quartz and fissures that make easy holds. Out here, there are no men in suits, no monosyllabic clients, no anything but the now.

I'm descending from my highest boulder yet—a forty-foot beauty with a great crack running down the middle—when the rock beneath my left foot comes loose beneath me. My toes skid, my heartbeat rising. I shift my weight to my hands, relying too much on upper body strength as I seek better footing. My arms tremble, my foot tapping against the stone in search of purchase. But there isn't any to be had. It wasn't just a small hold that crumbled, the entire damn ledge I thought was there is nothing but clumped dirt.

My fingers slip. I push my hips to the stone, a final desperate attempt to keep my balance. But it's too late. The world slows, my fingers fail as the stone I'm sliding down rips into my flesh. My breathing stops as I claw anything and everything I can reach, my body plunging faster and faster toward unwelcoming ground. Distant pain echoes through my body, pulsating behind the terror until…until a grand dull throb echoes through me and the world swims before going blank.

ELI

"*E*li, heads up." Pulling down her headset at Trident Rescue's dispatch station, Skylar threw a Nerf ball at Eli's head. "A female lost a fight with gravity near Riles Ridge. With-it enough to call 911, but can't walk. She thinks she slid twenty feet or so."

Eli brought his chair upright, bringing up a map on the computer screen. Not far from where the teenager had been injured. "Anyone with her?"

"No."

"Safety gear on-site?"

Sky winced. "Not even a rope. She was bouldering and—"

Eli cursed colorfully, cutting Sky off. What the fuck was wrong with people going to isolated places without basic damn safety precautions? At least the bloody teenagers went together.

"If you're done swearing, the Suburban is ready."

Eli shook his head, shouldering his trauma kit. "The access road exists on a map only. I'll take the ATV, but we'll need a bird if there's a spinal injury. Put one on standby for me?"

"It's not the bird that's hard, it's the pilot," Sky said, already on the radio. Hopefully, the precaution was unnecessary. Though if the woman wasn't at death's door, by the time Eli was through ripping her a new one, she might wish she was.

Maneuvering the ATV as close to Riles Ridge as he could get it, Eli dismounted and shouldered the trauma pack. The GPS went wonky here, and there was no substituting simply *looking*. The more times Eli visited Riles Ridge, the more he hated the place. Secluded and filled with gorgeous and unstable boulders, the place was Mother Nature's grand fuck-you to humanity. Though they looked like an easy, inviting climb, the boulders here held camouflaged muddy debris that formed during the spring rains. To an unwary climber, the things were as dangerous as an icy peak.

"Medic!" Eli called out into the wild to identify himself as he walked toward the first free-standing formation. "Where are you?"

"Over here!" a woman's voice called.

"That's not nearly as helpful a location marker as you imagine," Eli muttered to himself before raising his voice. "Don't move. I'll come to you. Tell me what you see and keep talking."

The woman proved good at following instructions, though there was something all too familiar about her voice. Which was absurd. Dani Nelson was back at Mason Pharmaceuticals harassing his staff. The least she could do was have the decency to stay out of his head when he was off here. But that was half the problem, wasn't it? He *couldn't* get Red out of his head, and the fact that his cock twitched painfully every time she walked into a room didn't help.

Eli still didn't understand why he'd gone out of his way to rub Red's nose in her claustrophobia. It had been a juvenile thing to do, an upgraded equivalent of pulling a girl's braid in elementary school. And yet he'd done it. Had enjoyed watching her shift off-balance for once, her cheeks flushing that beautiful color that offset the fiery red of her hair. But then, once she conceded the point, once Eli saw the quick flash of deep-seated pain in Dani's eyes, there was no longer satisfaction in it. Only fury at whoever gave her that fear. A desire to rip the bastard apart fiber by fucking fiber.

Catching sight of a black-and-white climbing shoe and skintight leggings peeking out from behind a rock, Eli zeroed in on his objective. A clingy bright-pink midriff-baring shirt came into sight next. The woman's stomach was flat and a bit defined and—if Eli wasn't of such low opinion of her judgment skills— he might've appreciated her sexy figure. There. Yes. That was more like it. Dani wasn't the only one whose body Eli could appreciate. Maybe a day out here was exactly what he needed to clear Red out of his system.

Or maybe it was all a fucking jest of the universe.

Stepping beyond the pines, Eli froze at the sight of the long bright-red hair, the face he was so determined *not* to see today. What the actual fuck?

Eli belatedly realized he'd spoken that last thought aloud. Well, good. Because really, that was the pertinent question. "What the fuck are you doing here, Nelson?"

"Trying to get away from you and—" She cut off in a gasp of pain, her jade-green eyes as wide and startled as his must be. The woman's gaze flitted down his body, taking in his uniform. She winced. "It didn't work."

"What happened?" Eli set down his trauma bag. He could already see swelling and discoloration around her left ankle and stains of blood soaking her leggings and shirt. She was alert and oriented, which was a good sign, but how bad the damage was was still a question.

"Lost my footing and fell."

"How high were you?"

"Twenty feet, maybe? I'm more solid than I feel."

Twenty feet. Without equipment, a partner, or enough skill to know that she didn't fucking know the terrain. All in all, Eli fully intended to inform her about it just as soon as he didn't need a clean set of vitals. Swallowing all the words on the tip of his tongue, Eli reached to take the pulse at her neck.

Dani's terror-filled shriek as she grabbed his wrist unsettled a whole flock of innocently resting birds.

"What the hell are you doing?" Eli asked curiously, ignoring the sting of pain as Dani's nails dug into his skin.

"What the hell are *you* doing?" she shot back.

"Trying to get a heart rate." He jerked his chin to her neck. "Carotid artery is there. Unless you want me to try your wrists, but with how you slid down the rock, there isn't much by way of unscraped skin around there."

"Oh." She blinked, releasing him at once. "Sorry."

"What did you think I was doing?"

"Nothing." Her jaw tightened. "Sorry, I'm shaken up. The world was going in and out of existence for a while there after I fell, and I'm still not fully with it."

"Right." There was nothing right about it, actually, but this wasn't the time or place. So much for a clear set of vitals. He took her pulse anyway. It was too fast. Of course it couldn't be anything but fast just now. He cleared her c-spine, then dug out a pair of trauma shears and sliced through the legging's thin material from hem to crotch.

"What did you do that for?" Dani gasped, pain and indignation filling her voice.

"I don't have X-ray vision, Nelson. If you are bleeding, I'd like a heads-up before you pass out." Eli opened up the second leg, peeling the stretchy wet material back from an ugly scrape along Dani's thigh. Not dangerous, but certainly painful. He pressed the crests of her hips and, finding the pelvis stable, slid his hand up toward her abdomen. As with her wrists and forearms, scratches littered the skin here too, disappearing beneath that pink shirt of hers.

Reclaiming his trauma shears, Eli cut the shirt—and everything beneath—right down the middle.

Dani's full beautiful breasts opened before him like a book, and it was all Eli could do to not look at the delicious, bunched nipples. Keeping his gaze very, very much where it belonged, he used some gauze and saline to wipe away the blood before palpating the ribs as Dani trembled beneath his touch.

Yeah. Getting hurt fucking sucks. Eli could have told her as much before she'd decided to disregard all the bloody safety rules. Dani Nelson got here through her own recklessness. She was lucky she'd smashed her ankle and not her skull. Or maybe it was Eli who was lucky. He didn't need another call like that just now. He didn't need another call like that fucking ever.

"What in the bloody hell and beyond possessed you to go climbing alone?" Eli demanded, not bothering to soften his voice. "Not just alone, but on a remote trail you know nothing about? You think that phone you called for help with is more resilient than bone? That it couldn't have been smashed as easily as your ankle?"

Her jade-green eyes flashed. "Didn't have anyone to go with me."

"You couldn't *find* someone?"

She closed her eyes. "I did. Two of them. We know how that ended."

Eli's hand froze, his pulse hammering against his ribs. He knew this game. Had grown up with it. It was *his* fault Dani went out alone, because in a state full of climbers, he'd declared the two he considered family off-limits. It didn't matter how many people lived in Colorado, or that there were safer, busier routes to climb, or that Dani didn't *have to* go to the mountain at all if she could not do it safely. It was still Eli's fault. Just like it had been Eli's fault that his twin sister was stillborn. He shouldn't have hoarded everything for himself, Madison had told him. He'd been a selfish bastard from before he was even born.

A wall that Eli had built brick by painstaking brick slammed down inside him, crushing his emotions to dust. He felt nothing as he pulled his hands away. As he palpated the injured ankle. Gently. Correctly. Ignoring gasps of pain.

"No broken ribs. Except for the possible ankle fracture, the rest is likely superficial," Eli said, getting to his feet and starting toward the ATV where he'd left immobilization gear. "You'll need some X-rays and a concussion workup. The deep abrasions will need care for infection and pain control. Stay here. I'll be back."

He made it all of five steps before Dani's shout halted him in his tracks.

"Eli!" The fear and panic saturating the woman's voice beat against his walls. When he pivoted back around, tears welled in the corners of Dani's eyes. "Are you going to just leave me here?"

BLOODY HELL, was that what she thought? Why not. It was his fault she was injured to begin with, wasn't it?

"No," he bit out sharply, then schooled his voice. "No. I'm just getting a SAM splint and blanket from my vehicle. I do not lie, Ms. Nelson. When I say I'll be back, I will."

She closed her eyes, which he took as acquiescence. By the time he returned a few minutes later, she was sitting up, shaking as she covered her exposed chest. As Eli's shadow loomed over her, Dani's arm flew up as if to protect herself from a blow. The motion was plainly instinctual, and one Eli himself knew all too well.

Fuck. Another brick in his wall loosened, and it took several breaths to pull it back into place.

"It's just me," he said, waiting until she acknowledged him before wrapping the blanket around her shoulders. "Let's get you to the ER, and then you don't have to see me again until morning."

9

DANI

*G*et me to the ER. Eli's words reach me through a fog of
anxiety. The ER as in the hospital. With bills high
enough to absorb everything I'm supposed to earn on
this assignment. With doctors more worried about malpractice
suits than common sense, whatever resident sees me for five
minutes is going to order every test on their computer checklist.
A few hours in that place and there will be no helping my parents
keep their house, no starter fund to send Amber to college.

Plus, even with the best of intentions, most *modern* practices
overtreat, throwing antibiotics around like candy and reaching
for the most complex newly manufactured toy they can find while
ignoring the natural remedy growing outside their window.

"No hospital," I tell Eli.

He looks up from the radio that he already has by his mouth.
Out here in the wilderness, Eli Mason looks nothing like the
business tycoon presiding behind his mahogany office desk. A
dark Under Armour shirt clings to his lithe body, underscoring
every measured motion. He reminds me of a leopard, never
engaging one muscle more than necessary to accomplish

57

anything. A powerful, self-confident, and infuriatingly smug leopard.

A leopard who is also my evaluee. And whom I'll again look in the eye without remembering how helpless and naked he saw me this afternoon.

Eli cocks a brow at me. "Yes, hospital." He pressed a button on the radio. "Sky, tell Denton Valley Memorial I'm bringing in a trauma patient. We'll stop by the Rescue to switch over to the Suburban."

"Understood."

Fury spills into my blood, pulsing so hard through me that it drowns out the pain. "I'm not joking, Mason."

Eli packs up his things, utterly unperturbed. "Neither am I."

Grabbing on to the trunk of a nearby tree, I pull myself up. I might not be as tall as he is, but the bit of height at least gives me some agency as I deal with the asshole. "Taking someone against their will is called kidnapping."

"True enough." Eli weighs me with his gaze, and—without so much as a warning—pulls me up into his arms. I'm not exactly small, but the man carries me with all the effort of moving a sack of apples around. And with as much emotion. As if some shield has snapped into place inside him, clouding Eli's beautiful, expressive eyes. He smells of fresh shampoo and male musk, his steps as even as if carrying nothing. Setting me onto the ATV, he gives me back the blanket that had fallen during the relocation. "Treating someone without consent is also assault and battery. Feel free to have your attorney send a copy of the charges to my legal department."

Eli mounts the ATV behind me, his arms encircling me on either side as the powerful beast beneath us roars into motion.

My heart and ankle both pound by the time we pull into the Rescue to change vehicles, my eyes on the edge of tears. New plan, I decide. Eli is right: I can't stop him from hauling me to the ER. He's too powerful, both physically and legally to be touched. But no one can stop me from signing out against medical advice.

"OMG, Dani?" Sky rushes out from the Rescue station as Eli and I pull into the parking lot, her presence adding insult to injury. "Why—"

"Stand down, Reynolds. I've already read her the riot act," Eli says, stepping between us and at least sparing me that conversation.

Sky gives me a sympathetic look. Apparently, she's heard Eli's riot acts before.

"I'll call you in so you can bypass registration," she offers. "I have your name and date of birth from the climbing club. What medical insurance?"

Fuck. I swallow.

Eli, who is unslinging gear, freezes midmotion. "Have them directly bill Mason Pharmaceuticals," he says without even looking in my direction. "Turns out she's a temp from corporate."

"Sure thing." Sky smiles her encouragement to me and walks back into the building while I feel that tear slip down my cheek after all. Apparently, I can bear Eli's bullishness more easily than his kindness. In someone else—in someone normal—I'd worry the gesture was a way to make me do what he wants, but with him, it's worse. So much worse.

Eli transfers gear with military efficiency, not a single motion or second wasted as things get stowed perfectly in their place, each piece of equipment latched down securely. Watching him work is like seeing a highly choreographed dance, knowing that each member of the ensemble does the same motions the same way every time the curtain opens. When I try to get myself into the passenger's side of the Suburban, the man snags me up without permission and installs me in place, latching me down with the seat belt with the same efficiency he treated the gear.

We say nothing to each other as he drives through the streets of Denton Valley, past tree-lined avenues and manicured lawns, pulling up into a designated spot in the Denton Valley Memorial emergency lot. Eli gets out of the car, and I use the moment to scrub my cheeks dry. I'd managed to keep my face turned away the entire ride, but that luxury is about to come to an end. This situation couldn't get any more twisted if it morphed into a Rubik's Cube.

Eli rolls me into the ER in a wheelchair, my face red enough to stop traffic. I don't even know why I care anymore. What's one more humiliation to add to the pile?

"Is this the trauma Rescue called in?" a nurse with a long braid asks Eli, her tone suggesting she knows the man well. Which she probably does. Hell, the man owns—or is in the process of acquiring—a third of the real estate in the entire town, so why wouldn't everyone know him? "Take bay three."

Eli nods and turns me into an alcove with a large number three printed above the curtained-off bed. As soon as my ass hits the crinkled paper, he does an about-face and goes in another direction, leaving me alone with the hospital's signature acerbic tang of rubbing alcohol and bleach.

Curling my hands around the sides of the uncomfortable mattress, I watch through the slit in the curtain as Eli heads down the main corridor of the emergency area, waiting to breathe a sigh of relief until he's officially out of sight. With Eli gone, I'm free to sign myself out without issue. Or just leave. Eli's covering the medical bill will keep me out of bankruptcy, but I don't want to accept charity if I can help it. Plus, hospitals give me the creeps.

Squaring my shoulders, I brace myself to put all my weight on my good foot, and slide carefully off the edge of the bed. Since I'm still half-naked and clutching a blanket for decency due to Eli cutting off most of my clothing, the first order of business is to find a pair of scrubs to borrow. Hopping awkwardly toward the wall, I wince as my scraped-up hands take my weight and move awkwardly into the hallway—just in time to hear my name.

"Dani! There you are!" It's Sky. Great. "Where are you going?"

"Uh…" My verbal skills abandon me. Awesome. Failing all else, I go with the truth. "I was looking for pants. Um, scrubs. Something that Eli didn't take a pair of trauma shears to. What are you doing here?"

"Coming to cheer you up, of course." Sky waves down the lady with the braided hair. "I know you're hurting right now, but don't worry, Michelle will make sure you get fixed up. She's one of the head nurses, and she's excellent. Here, let me help you back up to your bed."

Now that my exit route has been cut off, I have no other option but to obey the woman I'd once hoped to have as a friend yet now know will never be. My eyes burn dangerously, but I command myself not to cry. I've already cried too much. As Head Nurse Michelle checks me over, Sky asks her about the kids and gets a question about Cullen in return. I don't know any specifics because I'm not paying any attention. But maybe I should have been doing a better job of monitoring things, because I only realize they've stopped when they both stare at me expectantly.

"I'm sorry," I say, and isn't that the truth? If I could go back and change my decisions from earlier in the day, I absolutely would.

"I just asked if I could help you into a hospital gown," Michelle says. "That way, you won't have to hold on to that blanket when the lab tech shows up to take you to X-ray."

"Great." She and Sky both help me out of shredded clothing and into the unisex fashion of Denton Valley Memorial, stripping away what little dignity I have left. When I was growing up, my father always made it a point to see everyone who walked into his apothecary as a full, beautiful, unique person. The only thing that makes me unique now is the colored panties I have hanging out the back—the only piece of my clothing Eli hadn't sliced into uselessness. Small mercies. Not that the harried tech who comes to wheel me to X-ray notices—or cares—whether I have anything on at all. Wyrd. I could probably just have left my chart on the bed instead of me and the man wouldn't have noticed so long as he had a barcode to scan before unlocking the bed brake with his foot.

Efficiency in spades.

Sky stays with me as the intern, the resident, and then finally the attending come to ask the same set of questions and look carefully over the same sets of results. The final one, at least, condescends to share the verdict with me.

"You were very fortunate, Ms. Nelson," the doctor says, adjusting round spectacles along the bridge of his nose. "Moderate concussion. Enough scrapes and bruises to remind you of your adventure, but no fracture. That said, there's damage to the soft tissue in the ankle. I want you to stay off it completely for a couple of days, then add weight slowly. If all goes well, you should be back to sports in six weeks."

"Six weeks?" No way in hell.

"I'm sending you home with some Percocet for pain relief and a set of supplies to change the dressing on the laceration along the outer ankle."

"I don't like medication."

"Michelle will give you a tetanus shot before you leave, and given the amount of skin that was compromised, I'd like to start a wide-spectrum antibiotic as a prophylactic measure."

"No." I shut my eyes. Open them. Discover the doctor is still there, right along with his frowning entourage, all looking in bewilderment at the rare hospital-gowned creature who has inexplicably evolved into having an ability to speak her mind. "First, I'm not going to consent to wide-spectrum antibiotics without evidence of an actual infection. Second, isn't Percocet an addictive narcotic?"

The doctor does his glasses maneuver again. "If abused, it does have addictive properties. However, taken under careful medical supervision, it is an effective pain reliever, which—trust me—you'll want."

"With all due respect, sir, the number of addicts who began—"

"Dani." Stepping up to me, Sky takes my hand, her voice soothing. "No one is going to force pills down your throat. Take the doc's prescription. If you don't need it, so much the better, okay?"

I rub my face, feeling my cheeks heat again. Of all the times to argue medical approaches, this is not it. Especially not if I want to get out of here any time soon. "Of course." I give her and the staff the best smile I can conjure. "Thank you."

Sky grins. "Oh, and I just talked to Cullen." She shakes the phone in her hand, indicating the conversation she's apparently had with her fiancé. "You can stay with us until you heal up a bit. We have plenty of room, and, to be honest, I *love* houseguests."

Do you like decapitated houseguests? Because that's what you'll have if Eli finds out. I force out another smile. "Oh, no. That's really not necessary—"

"It is," she counters. "You can't go back to your hotel. There are stairs everywhere."

"I can take the elevator." I'm not taking the elevator, but Sky doesn't need to know my plans to hobble however many flights I need to.

"How are you even going to get to the Marriott?" Sky favors me with this look I can only qualify as a mix of concern, confusion, and trepidation. "You can't drive."

Shit. Fortunately, my clogged brain coughs up a solution. "I'll take an Uber. I'll be fine."

"Ms. Nelson." The doctor injects himself into the discussion, his tone turning impatient. "I'll compromise with you on antibiotics, and as your friend pointed out, no one will force you to take pain medication if you don't wish to do so. However, I won't discharge a concussion patient with an unstable ankle without an assurance that she'll be attended to. I simply won't take the risk of you falling a second time."

Damn it. One look at the doctor's face and I know I'll have a damn fight on my hands. But what exactly am I supposed to do? Whether I like him or not, Eli is a client and I won't jeopardize his well-being for my own.

"See, coming with me is your only choice," Sky confirms brightly.

"No, it isn't," comes a voice from beyond the curtain opening. A deep male voice with a British accent. Eli. "I'll take responsibility for Ms. Nelson, Doc. She won't be unattended."

Sky's eyes widen, a mischievous sparkle flickering over her face. "Eli. Oh. Okay, then, even better." She tosses Eli a quick look, but his features are as stoic as a brick wall.

"Excellent," the doctor says, unable to get out fast enough, and this time, I'm smart enough to hold my tongue until he and the other staff are out of hearing range.

"Listen," I say, spreading my attention between Eli and Sky. "I appreciate you all trying to look out for me, I really do. But it is truly unnecessary. I promise I can take care of myself."

Eli ignores me. "Sky, can you get one of the guys to cover for me until I get this squared away?"

"Sure," she says. "Take all the time you need."

Seriously?

"Um, hello?" I interject, and two pairs of eyes—Eli's included—finally focus on me. "Have I suddenly gone invisible?" I say, fully dropping the thank-you-so-much-you-are-too-kind act. "Can you hear me? I'm a perfectly responsible and capable grown-ass adult. I don't need a babysitter. I don't need to go anywhere but back to my hotel."

"If you were perfectly responsible, you wouldn't have been climbing the most dangerous and secluded area of the park alone," Eli growls out in a low tone. His brow is deeply furrowed, his jaw set, and his mouth is one thin hard line.

I open my mouth to reply, but Eli looks like he's about to start spitting nails, and damn it, I'm tired as hell. Bone tired. And out of all brilliant arguments to get myself out of the ER.

"Fine," I breathe, hopelessness and defeat settling around my shoulders.

And then Sky only makes everything worse.

"And here I thought you only did one-nighters," she says, jabbing Eli in the shoulder as the pair walks out of my cordoned-off space.

"Shut it, Sky. It's the right thing to do."

"Yes, it is. And doing that is something you excel at," she calls, her voice turning singsongy as it fades down the corridor. How in the world someone can be so happy after succeeding in making my life so completely miserable is beyond me.

10

DANI

*A*t least Michelle gave me some scrubs. Holding on to that piece of dignity, I settle into the same medical Suburban Eli brought me in and lean my head back against the seat. Having seen how the man handles gear, I'm not surprised to find his truck spotless, the scent of leather and cleanliness filling the cab. If this is how he leads his personal life, it's a miracle he doesn't mandate uniforms for accounts and saluting secretaries.

I cringe at my own thought. That's not fair. I'm supposed to be evaluating him as an employee, not leaching into his personal life. Which is exactly why this whole thing is a problem.

"There has to be another solution," I say as Eli pulls out onto the main road, the sun starting to melt toward the mountainous horizon.

"There isn't." His eyes stay on the road ahead, even as we come to a red light. "Sky has too big a heart for her own good. If she finds you aren't with me, she *will* ensure you're with her."

I rub my face. "You still think I befriended her on purpose?"

"What I think is irrelevant." Eli's hands tighten on the wheel, the ropey tendons in his forearms flexing as he drives. He's still in his tight-fitting uniform of black tee with black cargoes, and it adds insult to injury that anyone should be equally attractive in utility gear and a fancy business suit. Eli's attention stays on the road. "I do expect you to maintain your promise to stay out of my personal life, however. And to keep the reason for your *visit* discreet."

"Good grief, Eli." I shake my head and wave my hands up and down my body, which is pathetically awkward beside Eli's Greek-god-worthy frame. "I'm dressed in glorified pajamas, unable to walk, and apparently not allowed to even be home by myself. Do I really seem like a viable threat to you just now?"

Silence for the rest of the ride is all the answer I get. Wyrd. I wish I felt half as capable of great evil—or basic human function —as Eli imagines me to be. Forty minutes later, we pull up to the most expensive security gate I've ever seen—the kind that better fits into a secret-agent movie set than a Colorado town—and Eli opens his window to plug in a code. The motorized double-winged gate parts seamlessly, letting us onto a winding paved driveway. Dense green shrubbery and trees line the path, opening up at the last moment to reveal a rustic fairy-tale mansion.

The bottom story has been constructed out of burnished sandstone, the reddish-orange hue matching the upper story's cedarwood exterior. Two octagonal sections rise as turrets on either side of the house, reminding me of dual Victorian-era towers. To top it off, the center of the structure between the towers is an acutely peaked roof made of one vast sheet of glass that reflects the craggy peaks stationed like sentinels behind the residence.

"Wow." I let out a long breath. "This house is absolutely gorgeous, Eli."

A muscle at the corner of his jaw tightens, and I don't even want to know what kind of mental gymnastics he did to twist the sincere compliment into an insult.

"I'll pass your compliments to Madison's designer," he says

curtly, closing the vast garage behind us. "And don't call me Eli. We aren't—"

"Friends. Yes, I remember." I reach for my door handle, working out a safe way to get down to the ground. "Do we go around the house calling each other Mr. Mason and Ms. Nelson like Victorian-era aristocrats?"

His gaze cuts my way, reminding me how much easier this would all be if his gray eyes didn't hide so much intelligence and so many secrets behind too-long-for-fairness lashes. "Just *Mason* is fine."

"How very military of you." I reach around behind me to retrieve my crutches—I've never used them before, and the learning curve is unlikely to be fun—but before I get even halfway, Eli has extracted them, opened my door, and gestured for me to get out.

"Come on, then," he bites out, his rigid posture broadcasting his impatience.

Yet he steadies me as I bracket each stick of wood under my armpits, his touch gentle. This is something that bewilders me about him. Eli Mason may be a bastard and someone who, according to his own mother, must be unstable, yet no matter how angry he might appear toward me, or how nasty and closed-off he might behave, any physical contact he's ever offered me has been kind. It's sort of a mind fuck, if I'm honest.

Fortunately for my non-crutches-accustomed body, Eli leads me to a guest room that's just off from the large first floor space. "Bathroom is through there," he says, pointing to a door on the opposite wall from us. "The kitchen is on the other side of the living room. Self-service. Text me your hotel room number, and I'll have someone get your things."

"Good night to you too, Mason," I say quietly, but the door behind Eli has long since closed.

～

THE FOLLOWING MORNING, I wake regretting mouthing off about painkillers. Not because I've any intention of swallowing narcotics, but because asking about a place to get natural remedies would have been a better use of my time and energy. Eli turns out to be good for his word about my belongings, which have appeared in the corner of my room, my phone already plugged in and charging. I glance at the time—6:00 a.m.

I hobble to the bathroom to wash up, then grab my crutches and quietly make my way to the kitchen in hopes of finding coffee before Eli wakes up. Like the exterior, everything in the house is composed of wood, sandstone, and rich brown accents. The floor is of a plank design, light tans interchanged with darker cinnamon colors to create a simple yet gorgeous pattern. Whoever designed the humongous living room, with its fireplace and L-shaped leather sectional, clearly didn't need to use crutches to traverse it, though.

The mansion has obviously been created to show off its opulence, yet it has an almost museum quality that emits an aura like it hasn't been lived in. Either Eli spends no time at home, or he has one hell of an anal housekeeper.

I'm panting embarrassingly by the time I make it to the kitchen, which is equipped with everything my inner chef has ever wanted—with one notable exception: Eli Mason sitting at the granite-top island, a laptop and protein shake at his elbow.

Against the rising sun streaming in through the open bay window, Eli's silhouette is the most masculine thing I've ever seen, with a gray workout T-shirt clinging to tight muscles, a line of sweat running down his spine. A pair of shorts hints at a muscular ass, and there is no guessing about the state of his thick, corded thighs. Wyrd. Eli Mason is a cosmic injustice.

"I didn't expect you awake this early," I say, acutely aware that I'm still wearing the scrubs I'd left the hospital in yesterday.

He frowns at his Rolex. "It's six a.m."

Right. "How long have you been up?"

"Since four." Eli goes back into his emails, not offering to direct me toward anything. Ah yes. *Self-service.*

Not that self-servicing myself in a kitchen like this is any hardship, the whole crutches situation notwithstanding. The state-of-the-art stainless steel appliances and wide chef's oven and range gleam like quick lightning in the sunlight. I could lose myself here for three days straight if I didn't have life to deal with. Spotting the coffee machine, I get it going, then hobble to the fridge in search of milk.

It's there. Skim. Five gallons' worth. I can see that clearly because there is nothing *else* in the fridge, bar eggs, beef, and an ungodly amount of cherry yogurt. It's the kind of refrigerator a fourteen-year-old boy who'd been left alone in the house might put together, and I can't help the indignation bubbling up inside me. "E—Mason. Do you know what a vegetable is?"

He clicks to his next email. "Like a tomato?"

"That's a fruit, technically, but yes. When was the last time you ate one?"

Eli frowns in thought, taking a sip of a chalky-looking shake that probably claims to be rich chocolate smoothness on paper. "There was something red on my burger a week or two ago."

I think he's joking with me, but no. He's back at work, apparently not having heard anything odd about his own words.

"I'll give you my Amazon log-in," he says, his attention still on the screen. "Order what you need."

I stare at his wide back. "An Amazon log-in?" I clarify, clearing my throat tentatively. "So I can order *tomatoes* from Amazon?"

"It's the most efficient, in my experience." Getting up off his stool, Eli returns to his blender, dumping globs of powder, peanut butter, and skim milk into the container to make himself another concoction. The man has a chef's kitchen, and I'm getting the feeling the pantry is stocked with MREs.

Finishing our separate breakfasts—I settle on an egg omelet

made with the sad remains of a lone onion from what was probably a burger platter—we regroup again an hour later to head to the office. The sweaty Eli from the kitchen is gone behind a tailored suit and polished shoes, his unruly hair the only thing fully matching his eyes. Without asking, Eli takes my laptop bag off my shoulder and opens the car door for me.

As we pull into the garage at Mason Pharmaceuticals, I feel the weight of my business suit pressing down on my shoulders. At Eli's home, I'm his injured houseguest. Here… Here, I'm his evaluator. And while there's nothing about Eli's schooled face to mark any acknowledgment of the change, I feel it acutely.

Just as acutely as the nausea climbing up my throat as we approach the elevator, my laptop bag still hanging on Eli's shoulder. Shit. There's no way I can climb fourteen sets of steps with my crutches, and the only thing worse than being trapped in a small moving box is being trapped in there with a man who can snap me in two without breaking a sweat.

My heart stutters at the *ding* of the opening doors, my pulse hammering against my ribs. I can do this. I'm Danielle Nelson, executive evaluator, rape survivor, self-made educated professional. I can ride a damn elevator without turning into a puddle of goop.

"Look at me, Nelson." Eli says—no, orders—as we step inside. I've not heard this voice from him before, a confident military command that knows it will be obeyed.

My eyes slide to his of their own accord, and Eli gives me a nearly imperceptible nod, his slate-gray eyes consuming me. Over my racing pulse, I can hear the elevator doors whisper close, feel the slight bump of motion, but it's all secondary to that intense gaze that's a lifeline and a harness and security hold all in one. Eli is close enough that I can smell his fresh-grass scent, his broad muscular shoulders blocking out the world. I've never felt like this with another human being, not even when trusting a partner to hold my life on a belay line as I challenge a mountain.

Ding.

The elevator doors slide open, my attention finally ripping from Eli's gaze to the number fourteen blinking above us. We're here. I hobble out, Eli brushing past me and to his office without a backward glance.

Zana the intern, who'd destroyed my schedule yesterday, isn't here. A helpful coworker informs me that the girl rarely shows her face before nine thirty. Sitting down behind Zana's desk, I write a note asking that she email me the interview schedule as soon as she gets in and manage to find an empty conference room to set up my notes and review the file. The next item of the list has me talking to Eli again.

I almost feel bad for the man, but to be fair, had Zana done her job yesterday, I'd be meeting with Eli today anyway. *Sorry, Mason. Business is business.* Powering up my email, I shoot out a meeting invitation. Fifteen minutes later, I'm summoned to the boss's office.

"All right, let's get this over with for the day," Eli says, motioning me to a chair on the opposite side of his desk. I sit, feeling Eli regard me with the same alert caution a soldier would give an enemy force. Unlike in the kitchen this morning, his body is tight, his hand coiled snugly around a pen that I know he's seconds away from clicking.

There's something Eli Mason is trying to hide from me. I've seen enough clients to know the signs. I also know that sooner or later, I'll peel away enough layers to know what it is. I just hope I can leave the man in better shape than I found him. Because that's the downside of my job—I'm paid to identify problems, to bring festering wounds into the light. There's a long road between that and healing.

"So, I looked up the SERE course you mentioned last time." I run my hand over the lined pad of paper before me, as if the pressed sheets need straightening. This is my time, I remind myself. My domain. And no matter how fancy a desk Eli Mason is sitting behind, and how honed a body is hiding beneath his expensive suit, he's my evaluee. Not the other way around. "I'd like to talk about it."

He stares at me expectantly.

I count to ten in my head.

Nothing.

I sigh into the silence. "Mr. Mason?"

"You're the one who wanted to talk about it," Eli answers. "I'm waiting for you to start."

"All right. I imagine I should be grateful you're at least using full sentences this time around." I offer a small, disarming smile. "After what you had me read, I had an image of a name, rank, and serial number being repeated over and over."

"Would you like to know my rank and number?" Eli asks. "You already have my name."

Fine. I do a mental about-face and budget my questions more efficiently. SERE itself little matters to me, but given that it was one of the few specifics Eli volunteered, it's a good injection point to discuss his values and outlook. A backdrop against which I might get a glimpse into how he handles his company and employees. Plus, it might give me insight for how he'll handle the stress test—but that will come later. "Survival, evasion, resistance, escape. Which of the four did you find most challenging to teach? Which was most rewarding?"

"Instructing resistance was most difficult. Escape most rewarding."

"What made the resistance portion challenging for you to instruct?" I ask.

Eli leans forward, his muscular forearms braced on the edge of the desk as he stares at me. "I was the bad guy in interrogation and torture scenarios, Ms. Nelson. What does your background in psychology suggest about why someone might find the role *challenging*?"

I open my hands. "From my understanding, you were an

instructor and role player. It was your responsibility to create a scenario where people *felt* threatened while actually doing all you possibly could to protect them. Your ultimate mission was to build your students' resilience and mental self-defenses, not to destroy them. It sounds like a noble endeavor."

"You *have* done your homework." Eli snorts, and for the first time, I see the corner of his mouth quirk up. One, nothing. My point. He leans back in his chair. "Your description is correct. In fact, one might say I was doing the opposite of your job."

"How so?"

"Like you said, I make people feel threatened for the purpose of protecting them. You make people feel safe for the purpose of destroying them."

Not altogether incorrect. Point Eli. One, one. "What makes you think I'm not writing up a glowing endorsement of your actions and personality?" I hate to admit it, but the exchange is fun.

"The fact that you still have a job."

"You still think I'm a ringer hired to dig up dirt?"

Eli flicks a hand at my notepad. "Go ahead and send some preliminary findings saying that everything at the Denton Valley affiliate of Mason Pharmaceuticals seems peachy. See what happens."

"Interesting suggestion." Or would be if every single one of my clients wasn't one hundred percent confident that someone at corporate was out to destroy them. "Is there a way to test your theory without creating fraudulent paperwork?"

"What deficiencies have you found thus far?" Eli asks.

"Found?" I raise a brow at him. "Mr. Mason, the amount of energy you've put in to make sure it takes me hours to learn the smallest morsel of information about you could probably power a small schoolhouse. I can only conclude that you enjoy my company so much that you would like to prolong the experience."

"Tell you what." Eli reaches into a desk drawer and pulls out a thick manila envelope that he slides across the desk to me. "Since the staff here believe you're a guest from corporate, why don't you take charge of administering the employee surveys? Talk to every single person in the building, if you'd like. What better way to know how I run the company than to go to the source?"

Well, that's a first. Wait. I finger the packet, my forehead narrowing. "Wait a moment. Did you just find a way to have me talk to everyone here…except you?"

"Correct," says Eli, that heart-stopping, mischievous smile finally touching lips and eyes. "Better get started, Ms. Nelson. It's a large company."

Score: one, two. And the round goes to Eli Mason.

11

ELI

$\mathscr{E}$li stared at the boxes of groceries dropped off at his front gate. They weren't from Amazon, but from some farmer's market delivery service he'd not known existed in Denton Valley, much less had an app for. The smell of freshness drifted from the crates as he loaded them into the trunk, snagging a peach for himself before getting back into the front seat.

"Don't you dare put that in your mouth." Sitting in the passenger side, Dani grabbed his wrist in indignation. "First, it's a dinner ingredient, and second, they may use pesticides at this place. Protein powder may not need to be washed before consumption, but produce does."

Eli looked down at where she gripped him, and Dani let go as quickly as if jerking back from a hot stove. They'd hardly seen each other since he sent the woman off to deal with the employee surveys yesterday morning, and then they both worked late into the night. Well, at least he worked. He didn't know what Dani was doing on her laptop, but she didn't complain about needing to go home, which was good enough.

"You're cooking dinner?" he asked, letting her have the fruit, the lingering pressure from her cool fingers still tingling against his wrist. Not altogether unpleasant.

"I am." She cleared her throat, color rising to her cheeks. "I mean, if it's all right to use your kitchen. I shouldn't have presumed."

"Knock yourself out." He parked his Jeep Gladiator Rubicon in the garage.

"Why have a chef's dream kitchen if you don't like to cook?" Dani asked.

Eli ignored the question. He didn't have a kitchen because *he* wanted a kitchen, he had it because Madison wanted the head of Denton's Mason Pharmaceuticals presenting a certain image to guests. The whole damn house was set up the same way, and Eli hated every plank of it. Most especially because he wasn't allowed to change it. Madison had actually twisted the board's collective arm into writing it into the contract.

Appearances were important to her. It all came down to appearances. At any bloody cost.

Eli carried the plant life into the kitchen for Dani and disappeared into his bedroom to clear his head alone. With the concussion concerns, he'd slept on the couch outside Dani's room for the past two nights—the knowledge she might be dressing or undressing at any given moment mercilessly teased him rock-hard. It was ridiculous.

He had women all the time, for fuck's sake. And they'd done a great deal more than *undress* in another room. Maybe that was it. On the occasion Eli brought his hookups home, he kept the action to the living room. Never farther than that. Not that it ever mattered to them. All one-night stands, all more concerned with either their pending orgasms or his wealth to care why they never made it past the leather sectional. Having Dani in the house was nothing like that.

Plus, Eli was accustomed to being in the house alone. When he threw get-togethers, people came to enjoy the yard and pool, drank, ate, generally had a good time, and then *left*. They didn't shuffle his pantry to make room for spices, audit his fridge, or hang dish towels on chairbacks. Most of all, they didn't bring the house to life the way Dani did.

Stripping off his business suit, Eli took a quick shower and pulled on some soft blue jeans and a casual polo shirt before heading toward the clattering downstairs.

Dani had taken over his kitchen. There was no other way to describe it. Plates, bowls, a frying pan, and even a wooden cutting board he hadn't known he owned had been strewn across nearly every surface. Predictably, food accompanied it—though how all this managed to fit in the boxes he'd brought in, Eli had no idea.

A stack of flour tortillas sat off to the side of his stove top, whole onions and bell peppers lounging haphazardly next to the double sink. Water ran wild as Dani washed something red—one of her infamous tomatoes, no doubt—under the faucet. Behind her, something sizzled in the frying pan, a white-and-brown substance he hoped was chicken, because despite the abundance of objects being tortured, nothing else looked like protein.

Over the noise of the sizzling possibly chicken and the pouring water, Dani's clear soprano filled the kitchen. With her crutches off to the side and EarPods in, Red seemed like she was in another world. One where she was fully content.

In contrast to the day's business suit, she wore capris that hugged her gorgeous backside and a loose-fitting crop tee showing off a climber's taut belly. Coppery-red hair was up in a ponytail tonight, exposing a creamy neck. Eli's cock grew heavy behind his zipper, which pissed him off.

His body's reaction notwithstanding, he wanted nothing to do with Danielle Nelson, not even for nothing more than a mindless hour or two of passion. Eli might be open-minded when it came to casual hookups, but there was a line. And Red was firmly on the wrong side of it.

His stomach growled. With the sheer amount of food being

prepared, he had a notion that he was going to be invited to dinner, but it remained unclear what he could actually consume. Bloody hell, he couldn't even get to the refrigerator for some hot dogs without navigational assistance. The only saving grace was the fact that whatever meat she'd been cooking had started to fill the room with its slightly earthy aroma.

Still oblivious to his presence—though Eli was getting a sense the woman had so little situational awareness, she'd have missed the invasion of Normandy—Dani picked up a butcher knife and decapitated a pineapple.

"*Listen to me honey dear,*
Something's wrong with you I fear," she sang, pushing the blade back through the fruit.

"*It's getting harder to please you,*
Harder and harder each year."

Eli chuckled. He knew the song. Irving Berlin. And the next words fit his thoughts exactly.
I don't want to make you blue,
But you need a talking to
Opening up his voice, Eli added his own baritone to the mix:
"*Like a lot of people I know*
Here's what's wrong with you."

Dani spun around with a shriek, her eyes wide, the knife in her hand held like a spear. There was a desperation to her terror, the kind that made her breathing ragged, and it took several heartbeats of Eli standing very, very still before it dissipated.

"Mason," she gasped, her breath heaving in and out of her before she swallowed, color slowly creeping back into her face. "I...I thought you were— I mean, you startled me. Do you like portabella mushroom fajitas?"

"Right…" Eli frowned before deciding it was safe to move again. "Should I be worried you intend to eviscerate me like you did that helpless pineapple?"

Dani's pallor turned a delicious shade of pink. "Sorry. Now, portabella?"

Fine. She didn't owe him an explanation. He shouldn't even want one. "Just chicken, please."

Dani gave him a strange look, and Eli pointed to the skillet where the white-and-brown substance still sizzled enticingly.

"Those are the mushrooms, Mason. I'm vegetarian."

He stared. She had to be kidding. The one thing he thought was edible just turned out to be a fucking fungus. "Lovely. I'm not. You eat." He waved his hand over the farmer's market in his kitchen. "I'll grab some hot dogs from the—"

"Oh no, you don't," she interrupted him, actually hobbling into his path. "No offense, but your dietary habits are shit, Mason. You need to eat some vegetables."

"If you're desperate to feed carrots to someone, get a rabbit."

She put her hands on her hips, which was utterly unjust given her low rise waistline and high crop top. "Survival, evasion, resistance, escape. Seems someone who is supposed to be a SERE instructor should be a little less picky about what he puts into his mouth." Spinning over to the skillet, Dani skewered a mushroom with a fork and held it out to him. "Eat it."

"It's a fungus," said Eli. "Some of those things will kill you."

"Coward."

"Bloody hell." Swiping the fork from Dani's hand, Eli popped the piece into his mouth. It was a bit crunchy on the outside with a chewy inside that made the most of the spices. Damn. The fungus was good. He wanted more. Not that he was about to say so.

"So, then," Dani said, turning back to the tomatoes, onions, and bell peppers she was slicing into long skinny french fry-looking things. "Will you be joining me for dinner, or shall we fetch one of the MREs I saw in the garage for you?"

Eli's stomach chose that moment to let its feelings known, making Dani laugh. Red did have a nice laugh. The kind that made Eli's blood fume with desire to wring the neck of whoever gave her reason to jump out of her skin at the slightest provocation.

Taking thick slivers of mushroom, all the different vegetables, and the pineapple she'd gone through the trouble of cubing, Dani placed it all in the center of a tortilla, crowning the creation with a spoon of sour cream. Yeah. Eli was definitely hungry.

"You cook, I'll clean," he said, heading into the battlefield to rescue all four kitchen towels and disarrayed countertops.

"You don't have to do that," Dani called after him.

Turning off the still-running faucet, Eli looked over his shoulder without bothering to hide his incredulity. "Oh yes, I do."

12

ELI

"Mother fucking hell." Eli put his Rubicon into Park and trudged back into his house, his face and shoulder throbbing in equal measure. He'd risen at his usual predawn time and gone over to Liam's gym for some quality training and maybe—just *maybe*—he and Cullen had let themselves get a bit carried away with the full contact. In his defense, the blows hadn't felt quite so potent at the time.

Well, he sure as hell felt them now. With any luck, Cullen was in no better state.

He lumbered quietly through the house in an effort to avoid waking Dani. He hurt and was in no mood to spar with anyone else right now, not even verbally. A hot shower and a protein shake would set him to rights quickly, but at that particular second, he needed to be alone.

Which, of course, meant he wasn't.

He heard Dani laying waste to the kitchen before he laid eyes on her, and apparently, she heard him too.

"Good morning," she called out, her back to him. Even with her limp, she moved so sensually that Eli would have wagered she did it on purpose if he hadn't seen just yesterday how deeply into her own world cooking put her. Still, an amazing ass and delicious silhouette that her yoga pants and open shoulder top did nothing to hide were hard to ignore.

Maybe he'd change the temperature of that shower.

"Would you—" She emitted a sharp gasp and jerked around toward him, batter dripping from the wooden spoon in her hand to the countertop. "Mason. Were you mugged?"

"What? Of course not," he snapped despite himself. See? This was why he wanted to go off on his own for a bit. He wasn't currently fit for human interactions.

"You have a giant bruise on your cheek, a split lip, and an arm that seems reluctant to move." Tossing the spoon into the sink, Dani put her fists on her hips. "Add in the delightful attitude and you look like a thirteen-year-old sent to the principal's office after a schoolyard brawl."

Eli startled, a laugh he hadn't been expecting bubbling up inside his belly. He tried to keep it in, but the fierce look on Dani's face made it impossible to control. Once the first chuckle broke through his defenses, there was no stopping the tide.

"Not altogether inaccurate," he said finally, holding on to bruised ribs. From murderous brooding to full-out laughter in ninety seconds. Damn. Had anyone but Dani ever managed to do that for him before? "Training. With Liam, Cullen, and Kyan. We do it regularly. It's half tactical training and half workout. Today was heavy on—"

"Let me guess, hand-to-hand combat?" Dani said dryly.

"Your powers of observation astound me, Nelson." Eli gave her a mock salute. Fine. This was enjoyable.

"You know, I've always been curious—what carries a greater chance of brain injury? Accidentally slipping on a rock, or letting a lethally trained two-hundred-pound SEAL pound your head with his fists? Oh, wait, this is the place where you look me in the eye and tell me you wore headgear and a mouthpiece." Dani fluttered her lashes innocently.

"Low blow," Eli informed her, his lips pressing together to stop from laughing.

Dani shook her head, pointing to a stool at the kitchen island. "Sit."

Limping to the freezer, Dani filled a hand towel with crushed ice from the front door panel and brought it over to where Eli had obediently planted himself. Bracing a hand on the back of Eli's head, Dani pressed the ice gently against his lip and cheek.

Eli snorted softly but let her do it. It wasn't necessary, really. There was nothing life-threatening about a bit of bruising and blood. And maybe that was also why it was so confusing. There was nothing in this for her, and Eli didn't quite understand why she bothered with him. Certainly no one else ever had. The guys' idea of comfort was to chuck a bottle of ibuprofen full force into each other's chests, and other than the Tridents, no one would even notice.

Madison notwithstanding. If makeup and long sleeves couldn't correct appearances, an appropriate story would do. A rugby accident; that was acceptable. A fall from a polo pony would do in a pinch. Certainly not a fistfight. And nothing that happened at home. Ever.

Dani's fingers ran softly over his skin. She stood so close that her lavender scent filled his lungs. And—maybe because her busted ankle was hurting—Dani had shifted to place herself between his knees for balance. The coldness felt wonderful, but the position… that was dicey.

If she slipped any nearer, she'd feel exactly how much he was appreciating her touch.

Bringing his hand over hers, Eli lowered the pack. "Thank you."

Dani nodded, leaning in to examine his face, her balance shifting precariously. Eli braced her hips, his hands just at the crests of her pelvis, where the smooth curve to her belly started. She was staring at his lips, her jade-green eyes so close, he could make out the pretty starbursts within them. And suddenly, he was staring back at *her* lips, plump and soft and—

"Would you like a protein shake?" Eli asked, pulling himself together and away from Dani's tempting face. "I have chocolate and vanilla."

"I made pancakes." She looked back at the kitchen, regaining enough balance that Eli let go of her and pulled away. "I figure if I feed you, you might offer to clean the kitchen again."

"Safe bet whether you feed me or not."

Dani rolled her eyes, putting up with the teasing. It was nice. Certainly nicer than having her jump every time he clicked a pen too loudly, or swaying in the direction women who entered his house usually took—one that would give any appraiser a run for his money.

Taking the plate of pancakes out of her hands—and assuring Dani the gesture was out of concern for the food, not her—Eli set the table for two, the fork, knife, and spoon the only parallel objects currently in the kitchen.

"Chocolate chips?" he asked hopefully, forking a fluffy piece with dark little spots onto his plate. He was going to go change out of his sweaty tee first, but with smells like this, there was no way he was leaving the kitchen.

"Oh, wyrd. You *are* thirteen."

"No one made me chocolate chip pancakes when I was thirteen," Eli muttered, holding a forkful up before his face for inspection. "You didn't put mushrooms in these too, did you?"

"Just eat it, SEAL."

Pulling a forkful of pancake into his mouth, Eli chewed carefully. Ahh. Blueberries. Ripe and juicy. "Very nice."

"No mushrooms, as you can probably tell."

"Good." He filled his mouth with a second, larger bite.

"They are gluten-free, though."

Eli choked, and coughed out a laugh. It was an admittedly strange turn to have a houseguest. And not altogether unpleasant. Sitting on the other side of him, Dani indulged in her own breakfast, taking each bite with the attentive bliss actors on mindfulness commercials did. It was like watching someone from another world.

Finishing her coffee, Dani cleared their plates and Eli got up to load the dishwasher, wincing slightly.

"Oh!" Dani leaned on the countertop for balance. "I almost forgot about your shoulder." She waved a hand back to a chair. "Take off your shirt and shrink a little so I can take a look at what other training merit badges you brought home."

Eli's jaw tightened. "No," he said, the word sounding rougher than he'd intended. There were more than bruises from a friendly tussle beneath the sweaty cotton. "Thank you, but no."

"But—"

"I better shower off and get into something dry." He waved his hand over his workout gear. "Plus, I don't need to be making your kitchen smell like Liam's gym." Pushing away from the counter, Eli headed for the stairs before Dani could ask anything more. "Leave the dishes," he called over his shoulder.

Five minutes later, he leaned his forehead against the shower tiles, letting the frigid water pound his shoulders. For a moment there, with Dani between his knees and her lavender scent washing over him, he'd nearly lost his mind. She was different from any woman he'd met, infuriating and compassionate and confusing all in equal measure. And dangerous. Maybe that was why Eli couldn't get her out of his head. Being near her was as exhilarating as walking too close to a cliff.

Not that it mattered in the long run, of course. Eli enjoyed women, but he didn't do relationships. Never would. As for Dani, she'd be gone soon either way, leaving him with one hell of a mess to clean up with the board.

Finishing his shower, Eli tore off the dry-cleaning covering from the first suit he saw and slipped into his clothing. He was still adjusting the French cuff links when he came downstairs to find Dani laying out a spread of cosmetics on the cleared part of the breakfast island.

"Something wrong with the bathroom light?" Eli asked, turning toward the guest bedroom to check.

"No. These are for you." She scrutinized Eli, placing a thoughtful finger to the lips he'd nearly snogged. "It wouldn't be perfect, but—"

"If I knew it was that kind of party, I'd have worn my evening dress."

"Very funny." Dani pointed to a chair. Bloody hell, the woman was serious.

"I give up," Eli confessed, stopping his fidgeting to look at Dani patiently. "What in the world are you getting at?"

"The bruised face." She waved her slim fingers at him. "I mean, a CEO can't go into the office looking like he's just gone through a bar brawl."

Eli's jaw flexed, an uncomfortable sensation he'd not quite been prepared for slithering through him. Reality. Yes, that's what that feeling was called. And it did everything the cold shower had failed to. "I wasn't in a brawl," he said, all humor gone. "I was training."

"Unless you are going to pin a sign onto your back with an explanation, everyone who gets a glimpse of your appearance will get the wrong idea." She flicked a cosmetics brush. "It will only take a minute to cover up a bit. No trouble."

No, no trouble at all. There was never trouble covering things up.

"Family matters do well to stay within the family, Elijah," Madison had always been fond of saying as she called a new doctor or had their driver take them to a farther-away ER. But the simplest solution to cover up the latest beating had always been new clothes. *"Don't mind Eli,"* she'd say. *"The shirt was a present from*

London, and I couldn't talk him out of wearing it, long sleeves and all in this weather. It's a phase."

"You were hired to observe my company," Eli said, pulling his French cuffs straight, "not craft an image campaign." He didn't wait to see her reaction before heading toward the garage to start the truck. It wasn't Dani's fault she'd hit on just the wrong note, but it was a sharp reminder of who was behind her whole reason for being here. A reminder of why he'd long ago crossed *relationship* off his life plan. Women didn't want him, they wanted whatever image of a Mason Pharmaceuticals CEO they had in their heads. For many, it was money. For Dani, it was propriety. Somehow, that seemed even worse just now.

"Stay in your lane, Nelson," Eli called over his shoulder, pressing the remote startup on his key fob. "I'll do as much."

13

DANI

*A*s we head to the office, Eli is so focused on the road that you'd think we were driving over an Afghani minefield, all my attempts at conversation eliciting monosyllabic answers.

My mind spins, my professional and personal sides colliding to try to figure out what triggered the abrupt slam of the wall between us. Could Eli have misconstrued my offer of help as judgement on his competence as either an executive or a sparring partner? Had he suddenly remembered that he's supposed to hate me? Did the makeup offend his sense of masculinity despite him making apparent jests?

All my psychology training screams at me to dig deeper, to peel away the fascinating layers that make up Eli Mason until I can see the truth. Damn. If this incident had happened in the office, I'd be doing just that. When I agreed to make Eli's home off-limits, I thought I was agreeing to overlook hookers, not left hooks.

Well, once the staff start asking questions about why their boss looks like a thug, Eli's replies will be fair game. I shouldn't feel vindicated about that, but I do.

"I'm going to work on those surveys for you," I tell Eli as we get out of the truck, the security guards and reception we walk past giving him respectful greetings. That none are batting an eye at their boss's appearance suggests this is a regular enough occurrence to raise little new anxiety in the staff. "I'll be up in a few hours."

"Very good." Nodding coolly to me, Eli turns on his heel and heads into the elevator, the air around me feeling easier to breathe the moment he's gone. Wyrd. Whatever else, the man has presence.

As planned, I spend the morning strolling about the halls with climate surveys in hand, asking similar questions of whomever I lay eyes on. A few outliers aside, the answers come in a stable pattern.

Yes, Mason Pharmaceuticals is a good place to work. Job assignments are clear, hard work is rewarded, creativity is applauded—but only when it's in the position's description. Mr. Mason likes everything to follow protocol. Words to describe the company CEO? Confident. Decisive. Distant. Generous. Demanding. Always around, but not someone you'd start a conversation with.

"He's the kind of guy who'll remember that your kid is graduating high school, but you know better than to ask him about his," a researcher on the second floor tells me.

"How many kids does he have?" I ask, keeping my face to mild curiosity.

The woman leans forward conspiratorially. "I've no idea. But men like that don't stay single, do they?"

I smile noncommittally and move on.

"When my wife got sick, Mr. Mason didn't send a condolence card or anything," the repairman on four confides. "But he doubled my sick leave without me asking. I don't even know how he found out."

Three hours later, and I'm certain none of Eli's subordinates have ever heard him laugh or can even imagine him staring with a mix of hunger and apprehension at a spiced mushroom. To them, he's a general. Wise but untouchable.

"What about how he came to work today?" I finally ask, since no one is daring to mention the black eye.

"Oh, he's a Trident God," the lady at reception tells me, and I remember what Sky said about Eli and his three buddies being longtime friends and doing rescue work together. Apparently, that extends to beating the shit out of each other as well, and the whole town seems to know all about it. "They have their own things they do."

IT'S ALMOST lunchtime when I make it to the fourteenth floor, which for once means it's late enough in the day that Zana is actually at her workstation.

"Good morning." I stop at the intern's desk, my eyes unable to keep from flickering to the four social media streams up on her screen at once. "So, three times a charm? Did you have those three interviews set up for me?"

"I'll be getting to it this afternoon."

I stare at her, at a loss for words. We'd had this conversation at least four times, and my patience is long past exhausted. As I squint up at the navy-blue DNA strand painted on the wall, I dig my fingernails into my right palm until I feel four little bites of pain. "I think I'm a little confused," I say, bracing my left hand on the edge of her desk. "I'm certain I made it clear that the appointments needed to be scheduled *for* today, and not just being put into motion now. In fact, you told me you were almost finished last night."

"I'll do it ASAP, Ms. Nelson."

"That's what you said two days ago! This isn't acceptable!" I draw a breath, my heart pounding. I talked to Zana in person. I sent her follow-up emails. I even left a damn reminder note on her desk. "Were you lying yesterday when you said everything was on track?"

Zana swallows, looking at me with large doe eyes. "Your tone is making me uncomfortable, Ms. Nelson. I told you I'm working on it and will have it done ASAP. I don't know what else you want me to do."

"Your damn job, Zana!" The words fly out of me with the last vestiges of patience, two women in lab coats meandering down the pristine corridor suddenly picking up the pace. Apparently, my voice carries—but at this point, I don't care.

"I want you to turn off TikTok, Twitter, Snapchat, and whatever the hell else you're doing instead of your job, open my schedule, and start making calls. From what I can see, you certainly don't have any problems using a phone to find flipping cat videos, so using it for the actual job you're being paid to do shouldn't be a stretch." Leaning over, I turn her screen toward me, the YouTube window with a pirated movie still playing. "Wyrd. This movie is still out in theaters. What do you think will happen when security logs show you streaming illegally pirated media?"

Zana's face reddens, her already wide eyes brimming with tears that spill over her cheeks. Within a heartbeat, the girl is full-on sobbing.

"High school juniors show more responsibility than—"

"Ms. Nelson." Eli's cold voice hits me between the shoulder blades. Turning, I find the thunderous-looking man standing behind me, his bruised cheek doing nothing to soften his appearance. "A moment of your time. My office."

My jaw tightens, my pulse still pounding in my ears. Turning, I grab my crutches and hobble down the hall, setting them just outside Eli's office door before walking in. I only need them for longer distances now, and for some reason, I don't want to take them inside.

Closing the thick six-panel door behind me, Eli strides to his massive desk, the very air around him humming with leashed fury. Eli sits in his black leather office chair, his eyes on the grandfather clock in the corner rather than me.

I reach for my own chair.

"Stay standing." He doesn't raise his voice, yet the steel behind the words fills the room.

My chin jerks up. *Stay standing?* What am I, a military recruit? I open my mouth to demand as much, but Eli beats me to it.

"Precisely what is it you think you're doing?" he asks.

"I'm attempting to do my job," I fire back. "Which isn't easy when your intern seems either incapable or unwilling to do hers."

"Is there anything in your contract, job description, or even a bloody handwritten note from some board member that gives you any jurisdiction to reprimand my people?" Eli slaps his palms on the dark mahogany surface, making me jump. "What *my* intern does or doesn't do is *my* concern, not yours. You do not publicly lay into Zana or anyone else here under any circumstance."

"Really? That's what bothered you most about my exchange with Zana?" I say, enunciating every word as my pulse hammers in my ears. "Not her lying, or failing to perform any work, not even her illegal media streaming—but that I had the audacity to call her out on it?"

"Has the board placed you at the head of Mason Pharmaceuticals sometime when I wasn't watching?" Eli demands.

"What?"

"Answer the question."

"No." I meet him glare for glare. The gray eyes I'm used to seeing hold hints of impish humor stare back at me with a sheet of ice, Eli's beautiful chiseled features like a stone wall. It feels like I'm talking to a different person altogether, and I've no notion of which Eli is the real one. "The board has done nothing of the sort."

"And have you received any new decrees from the board that you haven't seen fit to make me privy to?" Eli presses. "Anything that expands your scope of practice beyond judging my suitability to run this organization?"

He isn't swearing, isn't even raising his voice beyond that level that manages to fill the room without shouting. And yet every new degrading shard he throws at me *hurts*.

I swallow. "I haven't received any new decrees."

"Then let me be clear. Zana Crusoe is *my* employee. If I discipline her as her boss, that's my prerogative, and if I fire her under those same auspices, that's up to me. You, however, are not her superior in any way, shape, or form. You're not even the superior of the guy scrubbing toilets in the basement. You have not been granted any sort of leeway to challenge, reprimand, or otherwise discipline anyone here. All you do, Ms. Nelson, is write a report. Are we clear?"

"Crystal," I bite out, fury, hurt, and humiliation battering me in equal measure.

"Good." Eli turns to his computer, his fingers moving over the keyboard as if he's on to a new matter entirely. "You may go."

I say nothing as I pivot and walk out of the room, making all the haste I can with my aching ankle. The moment I'm in the hallway, it feels like every set of eyes in the whole building is boring into me. I don't even look at Zana as I stride past her, grab my bag, and keep on hobbling toward the most remote bathroom I can find. Washing my face with cold water, I—just barely—manage to push back against the sting in my eyes.

I stay well away from the CEO suite for the next few hours, going through the employee directory one by one to set up all the appointments myself. This way of working will add a week to my assignment, but I'm not about to go to Zana or any other of *Eli Mason's* people to ask for anything again. By the end of the entire eight-hour workday, I'm only able to secure one hour of time with one of the lab techs and am starting to wonder whether this whole thing isn't to sabotage my ability to do my job.

I don't think it is, though. If it were, it would somehow not bother me so much.

Wanting neither to ride home with Eli nor face the elevator by myself, I take me and my crutches to the stairway. Fourteen stories isn't fun, but it's not impossible. Pausing before the final door to catch my breath, I call an Uber.

I'm standing outside waiting for the promised gray Toyota Corolla driven by Sunny of a 4.72-star rating when the very man I'm trying to not cross paths with strides by with a sharp "You're with me, Nelson."

I'm decidedly *not* with him. It's bad enough we have to share a place of residence right now, I'm not sharing a vehicle too. Not today.

Ignoring Eli, I wave to the fortuitously arriving gray Corolla and flash the driver a big *yes, I'm your fare, please let me in* smile.

The Corolla stops.

Cutting off my hobble to the vehicle, Eli goes right to the driver. There must be something about Eli's gait that screams "in charge," because poor Sunny pops up straight and all but salutes as he rolls down the window.

"Danielle Nelson won't be needing the ride," Eli says, handing over a fifty-dollar bill. "Our apologies for the cancellation."

"No problem, sir," Sunny says, not even looking at me anymore. "Whatever you need."

Before I can even protest, Sunny of the 4.72 stars is gone, and I'm still standing in front of Mason Pharmaceuticals.

"Precisely what is it that you think you're doing?" I ask Eli, throwing his words right back at him.

"Saving you from standing stranded at the entrance gate," he says. "I never gave you the security code."

My jaw tightens.

"So, you can either walk or get in my Rubicon. The choice is yours." He shrugs, his ginger hair ruffling messily in the breeze and, without pause, marches off to hop behind the steering wheel of his Jeep pickup. "If you choose the former, I'll be home in time to let you in."

For a second, I contemplate hiking my way to his house. I really do. But I can't escape the pure impracticality of it. Or the childish temper tantrum just calling another Uber would look like. Once this ankle heals, though, I'm out of here. ASAP. Stuffing down every last vestige of my pride, I follow Eli into the truck.

The ride home somehow manages to be even more tense than the morning ride into work. Having nothing to say to the man, I stare out the passenger window as if all the secrets to life are written there on the side of the road. I just succeed in getting lost in the scenery when the Rubicon's Bluetooth connection cues off a ring from Eli's phone.

"Aaron Nettles." Eli somehow sounds positively sociable. As if that person who managed to rip me apart with a few phrases never existed. "Shouldn't you be too busy in some law book to have time for calls—or, you know, breathing regularly?"

"I'm on break." A young man's voice replies over the Bluetooth speaker filling the car. "Not only on break, but about an hour drive from Denton Valley."

Eli rubs his eyes with the heels of his hand.

"… So if you wouldn't mind the pleasure of my company on Saturday," Aaron's voice continues.

"I guess I can put up with you for a few hours," Eli says. "I'll ask the Rescue to switch my shift around, then you pick a restaurant. Law students are always starving, and the more you eat, the less I have to listen to you talk."

Aaron lets out a deep laugh, clearly taking the insult as a sign of friendship. "Oh, no you don't. I already called the Rescue to deconflict—"

"Of course you did." Eli shakes his head, though I hear pride in his voice. Right until Aaron says the next bit, and Eli chokes on air.

"A lovely lady named Sky told me the here-for-one-night-only Eli Mason show has a live-in girlfriend."

Eli flinches.

I wonder if it's petty of me to enjoy that discomfort, then decide I don't care. I'm drinking in every moment of this.

"It's complicated, Aaron," Eli says, managing to sound nice despite the string of silent curses coming from his mouth. "I know they teach rhetoric in law school, but can you get to the bloody part where you pick a restaurant?"

"Chez Eli Mason," Aaron retorts. "If you think I'm missing this epic moment, you've got another think coming."

The line disconnects, and for a moment, I just sit there savoring Eli's predicament. Aaron is clearly an old friend, one whom even the formidable Eli Mason can't tell to pound sand, which leaves him dancing around this little ruse of ours.

Two breaths later, professionalism finally gets the better of me. Whatever else, creating problems for Eli's personal life is a line I won't cross.

"I'll say hello and claim a conference call with the East Coast," I say, speaking to Eli for the first time since the asshole coerced me into the vehicle. "Tell your buddy that I'm a temp from corporate staying with you due to the ankle injury and move on. It's the truth, after all."

Eli gives me a sidelong look, as if appraising a piece of jewelry. "Yes. Will work like a charm, no doubt."

Frankly, I don't see why it shouldn't.

The phone rings again. "Skylar Reynolds," Eli says in a resigned tone before the caller ID even flashes on the screen.

"Eli!" My once-a-friend's upbeat voice fills the Rubicon. "I heard your old intern is in town and invited himself to your house Saturday, no less."

"And how exactly did you hear that?" Eli asks dryly.

"A journalist never reveals her sources. Anyway, I thought a three-person thing might be a bit awkward. What do you say if Jaz and Cullen and I stop by? We'll bring dessert and—"

"And pump Dani for nonexistent information?" Eli holds up a hand, though obviously, Sky can't see the gesture. "You're on speakerphone, Sky. Whatever it is you were going to say, please don't."

"So, we'll see you Saturday?"

"Apparently." Eli cuts the line. "Still think that conference call will work out, Ms. Nelson?"

14

DANI

I'm in an interrogation room, Eli shouting questions into my face. His muscles are coiled, his beautiful gray eyes flashing with fury, each new demand lashing me like a whip. He isn't touching me, but somehow the words make me bleed anyway.

I step away, my heart pounding. Blood rushes so quickly through my veins that the room around me fizzles at the edges. I gasp as Eli steps closer, his features morphing into Brock Talbot's older face.

"You think you can destroy my life, bitch?" Brock roars so loudly that I clamp my hands over my ears to muffle the noise. I can't run away, though. We're in a closet, the same closet I was raped in back in school, and it's so tight in here. And Brock is between me and the door. This isn't what happened. Brock wasn't the one in that closet, but it doesn't matter, it's him now. He lunges toward me, one hand on my neck, the other unzipping himself. I—

I wake shrieking.

Scurrying across my bed so quickly that I nearly fall off the far side, I save myself by clasping one of the bedposts. Sweat drips down the sides of my face, my breath quick and ragged. I get to my feet. I can't stay in this bed. Can't stay in the room. There isn't enough air here. Hobbling as rapidly as my ankle will allow, I dash out into the living room, rushing by the giant bay window and L-shaped sectional to flip on every light I come across—the last one illuminating a large form flying down the steps, gun in hand.

Grabbing the first thing my hand lands on—which happens to be a table lamp—I swing it before me like a berserk banshee. I scream again as the metal base connects with something solid.

That something solid rips the lamp from me, an iron-hard hand scooping me around the waist. I keep swinging, my punches connecting with solid flesh over and over until I'm held tight against a chest of muscle, the scent of Eli's aftershave washing over me like a fresh wind.

Tossing his gun onto the side table, Eli brings his free hand to the back of my head. "Easy, Nelson," he says into my hair, his hold gentling with my slowing breath. "You're welcome to pound on me some more if it helps."

He isn't kidding.

Wyrd take me. Heat rushes to my face, and I pull away as quickly as I can from my host. "Sorry, I…"

"You either stopped a break-in or had a nightmare," Eli says, setting the lamp back to rights, the shade swiveling around the lightbulb like a bell. "My Spidey sense whispers it's the latter."

I back away until the backs of my knees hit the couch sectional, then sit, shaking my head at the patterned wood beneath my feet. "What the hell is wrong with you?" I whisper.

"With me?" Eli blinks. "I was under the impression it was actually you who just gave a supersonic jet a run for its money."

"You!" I point a finger at him, my heart still racing as words I hadn't realized were even forming slip from my mouth. "One moment you're normal and human, and then I blink an eye and you're shoving me away so hard, you'd think I was a child molester. And then you rip me to bloody shreds in your office. And then, just as I fully get the message, you insist on driving me home—only to *not* get upset when I assault you with…with your own priceless lamp. There is nothing—*nothing*—that makes sense about any of that." I stop to catch my breath, which is speeding to ragged pants all over again.

I drag my hand through my hair. I'm supposed to be the professional. The cognitive psychologist who figures things out. But with Eli Mason, it's one rotary after another with no warning or signposts. My head pounds. "Tell me you have multiple personality disorder. Or that you channel ghosts. Hell, I'll take alien possession just now if that's all you've got. Because the only other explanation is that I'm the one who's utterly lost her mind."

Eli settles slowly on the sectional beside me, his knees slightly open and forearms braced on muscled thighs. In a pair of boxers and an undershirt, the man looks like an underwear model. And the way this assignment is going, I'm not sure I'd even be surprised if I discovered he is one.

"You're not crazy, Dani," he says finally. "And no, I don't have multiple personalities or aliens—but I do have a past, and a personal code. Neither of which I chose to make you privy to. Did my behavior have anything to do with the nightmares?"

"No."

Eli cocks a questioning brow.

I rub my face. There's just no way to answer that without sounding stupid. I *was* out of line yelling at Zana, and the company CEO told me to cut it out. His words—the way he said them—hurt like hell, but they weren't unjustified. It wasn't what Brock did. It wasn't what happened in high school either. I don't even know how the whole mess ended up in my dream together.

"I could do with a lot less of the tone I heard from you earlier today," I say, carefully picking my words from the mess in my head. To keep from making eye contact, I focus on the decorative grate in front of the fireplace that dominates the room opposite us.

Eli lets out an audible breath. "I'm not going to apologize for what I said because it needed saying, but I'm sorry if it had anything to do with your sleep being disturbed. Did I frighten you, Nelson?"

"Can you please, just for right now, call me Dani? Would that kill you or something?" I don't know why I asked. Maybe I'm just too raw from facing those menacing images to employ my typical filters.

A corner of Eli's mouth twitches as if he finds my outburst amusing. "Dani."

Right. I pull myself together enough to at least sound reasonable. "Look, about today—I agree that I overstepped, but the way you went about expressing your displeasure didn't feel like a conversation between colleagues. It felt like punishment."

"It was."

So much for reasonable. "What?"

Eli shrugs a massive shoulder, his tone matter-of-fact. "My words hurt you because that was their intention. You were out of line. That was the reprimand. As far as I'm concerned, the matter is closed. I can promise you that none of the staff will bring it up—and neither will I." He opens his palms. "Look at the bright side: you asked how I handle discipline at the company, and now you have your answer. A win for your report."

I try and fail at even faking a smile. Not only are there too many unpredictable sides to this man, but his proximity somehow turns all my psychology training to mush. My finger worries the seam along the leather couch cushion. Everything might be over and done with for him, but it isn't for me.

Eli studies my face carefully, his serious slate-gray gaze penetrating too deep for comfort. Then he holds his arm out to me. "Come here."

"Why?" I ask, though I'm already moving, as unable to help myself as a mouse trapped in a snake's hypnotic stare.

Eli waits until I'm within reach, then pulls me against him, his wide palm between my shoulder blades breathtakingly comforting. "To soothe the sting," he says quietly, his body tight until I relax into the groove of his shoulder, then easing slightly. "Both ways. I didn't enjoy the events either."

We sit together for long minutes, Eli's heart beating strong and steady beneath my cheek. It's one of the most novel sensations, to be held in a man's arms and feel safe. Attractive as he is, Eli is exactly the kind of man I stay away from. Beautiful and powerful, with women's gazes following his every step. He probably could have a harem of women if he wanted to. Get any sexual pleasure he desired.

I flinch.

"Want to tell me that thought?" Eli asks.

"Not particularly," I mutter into his shirt, ordering my mind to focus on something other than how comfortable the man's arms feel. At twenty-six, I've had fewer relationships than most high school girls, and those never lasted. I couldn't satisfy the men sexually, and had zero interest in them even trying to satisfy me. The one or two who might have gone somewhere despite the sex, well, I fled. I told myself I was making career decisions. And I was. But that wasn't all I was doing.

I look around the room, the pristine appearance broken only by Eli's gun and a few photographs positioned in ruler-straight lines along his hearth. I recognize Sky's and Jaz's smiling faces at once, the other three men's names coming a few moments later. Sky's fiancé Cullen, Liam, and Kyan—the latter always wearing a hat. The same series of faces repeated again and again. The four men in uniform. The four of them in a gym. All six of them drinking beer by Eli's pool.

Then it occurs to me. Why aren't there pictures of anyone else? Shouldn't his family be in at least some of these? I flew into

Colorado for a few weeks, and I brought a family picture to keep in my hotel room. Eli *lives* here.

"Where did you learn to sing?" I ask. "It just seems an odd military track for a SEAL."

A chuckle rumbles through Eli's chest. When he isn't being an overbearing ass, the man is surprisingly easy to talk to. "Same place as I got the British accent. Madison had a very strict view of an appropriate education. By the time she declared me a lost cause and sent me off to military school, the damage was already done. I play the piano too. And dance."

"Why do you call your mother by her first name?"

Eli shifts uncomfortably. "Mutual preference. What about you? Are you going to tell me who attacked you?"

I jerk away—only to find Eli pulling me back against him. "Reputation aside, I'm not nearly as dumb as I look," he says with that strange mix of lightness and sincerity. "The nightmares, the claustrophobia. You nearly carved me up for coming up on you unawares the other day. Hell, I've had to rid my desk of clicky pens just so you don't accidentally startle yourself out the window." He wiggles his fingers. "Unfortunately, having such an object in reach and *not* clicking it is beyond my abilities. Should I keep the list going?"

"Please don't."

Pushing me away from him, Eli takes my chin between his thumb and forefinger. "Are you in any danger now?" he asks. "I won't pry into your past, but if there's someone who may try to hurt you while you're here, I need to know."

My stomach clenches, but at least I have enough wits about me not to ask a man with a loaded gun to be on the lookout for Brock Talbot's ghost. Taking another's paranoia as fact is how accidents happen. How people get hurt. Brock is back in Boston, nearly two thousand miles away. As far as you can get from here and still stay in the continental US.

"No one in Colorado is trying to hurt me," I say, biting my

106

lip. "But sometimes I'm scared all over again, no matter what my brain and common sense tell me. I know it doesn't make sense—"

"It does," Eli says with such quiet certainty that I can't help believing that he does understand. And isn't that the irony of the century?

15

ELI

$\mathcal{V}$egetables, Eli decided, were not an altogether terrible concept when someone cut them up for you and put them onto a platter. To be fair, the carrots, sweet peppers, and celery sticks Dani prepared weren't intended *directly* for him, but close enough. If Dani didn't like him demolishing her carrots, he could go back to clicking pens—but she'd probably like that even less.

"Why are your friends assuming you want to host a pool party if you dislike the notion so much?" Cringing at the decimated platter, Dani veered away from the kitchen island and headed to the fridge.

"I like parties," Eli called after her. "I just...—" He put down his carrot. He'd almost said, *I just never had a girlfriend with me before*. Except Dani wasn't his girlfriend; she was his executioner. The rest was a game. An illusion that was as creative as anything Madison had ever pulled—better, actually, because last night, with Dani in his arms, there was a second when Eli wanted it to be true. "How much longer until you complete your evaluation?"

Dani stopped, her hand on the fridge. She looked pretty, her simple rust-and-cream-striped T-backed sundress matching her cinnamon-colored locks. Swimsuit straps, tied with a loose bow at the neck, peeked from beneath the dress. What did she have on under there anyway? A one-piece? Something that showed off her taut stomach? Eli had no idea, but his cock fairly howled at him to find out.

"It depends on how much cooperation I get," she said cautiously.

"I fired Zana." Eli snapped a carrot in two. Right after he put Dani in her place, he'd cut the intern loose. He'd given the young woman all the chances he could, but firing her still felt wrong. "If you have additional problems getting things on the schedule, see me."

Dani bit her lip. "I see. And when I talk to you next, are we going to be back to monosyllabic answers?"

Eli sighed, reality rushing back to him. "I don't know," he said honestly. "I like you, Dani. But I don't want you in my head. It's what Liam would call a hard limit."

"Hard limit: a nonnegotiable position, often used in reference to a particular sexual activity that a participant absolutely refuses to engage in." A corner of Dani's mouth curled into an attempted smile. "In layman's terms, you don't like getting mind fucked."

"Not inaccurate."

The smile faltered. "Noted."

She didn't say she wouldn't do it, Eli noted. Maybe he should appreciate her candor. Hell, maybe he should just tell everyone who Dani was and why she was here. *That* would end the party before it ever started and probably get the woman escorted out under guard. But there would still be questions. Especially from Sky and Jaz. If Dani just disappeared after a week or two, however, well, she'd have been just another one-night stand that happened to last a bit longer than usual.

The buzzer sounded just as Eli was finishing his thought, and he rose to let in the guests who, by the looks of the surveillance camera on the outer gate, had arrived as a full invading force. Together with the brisket.

"I'll take that off your hands," Cullen was saying to the Pierce's delivery guy as Eli stepped outside, the large meat-filled box changing hands right there in the driveway. Pierce's Barbecue was a hole-in-the-wall place that barely qualified as a restaurant since all it had inside was one bench and a couple of barstools. Nevertheless, it delivered the best barbecue in all of Colorado.

Cullen inhaled the smoking brisket appreciatively, his face splitting into a massive grin. It was something he did much more frequently these days, ever since Sky came into his life. And speaking of Cullen's fiancée…

"Eli!" Jogging up to him, Sky rose on her toes to kiss his cheek, her strawberry-blonde locks flying around her face. "It's wonderful to see you. Where's your girlfriend?"

"Please don't."

Her smile became wicked, her voice taking a turn for innocence. "My mistake. Where is the gorgeous woman you insisted come live in your house so you could personally care for her scraped ankle?"

Fine. That was worse. "Dani is in the house conspiring a way to turn wolves vegetarian." Without giving Sky a chance to follow up on the comment—Eli knew when he was outmatched—Eli made a smooth turn to Aaron. The curly-haired young man was just relieving Cullen of the case of beer the man was trying to balance along with the brisket, and saluted Eli with a six-pack.

"Mr. Mason!" Aaron grinned. Despite the drastic change in their relationship, he'd never been able to break earlier habits and call Eli by his first name.

"Welcome home, mate. How's Seattle treating you?"

"I hear it's beautiful, but if you want a firsthand account, you'll need to ask someone who isn't spending his every waking moment inside a law text." Aaron sardonically tipped his head to the side. "So what's this I hear about a girlfriend?"

"Funny," Eli said dryly and turned on his heels. He didn't do girlfriends. He did sex. Mind-blowing, best-night-of-your life, no-commitment sex. And if the small sparkles of silent communication Sky and Cullen had gotten into the habit of exchanging did sometimes make Eli yearn for something more, he was enough of a realist to know his own limitations. Picking up the rest of the alcohol from Cullen's car—Sky liked the fruity stuff instead of normal beer—Eli led everyone to the back patio, where the kidney-shaped pool already had a volleyball net strung across it. Madison's landscapers had framed the pool with ferns and palm trees on one side and a wide, patterned cement area on the other, and even Eli had to admit they did a phenomenal job. The grill, wet bar, and firepit were Eli's personal additions—and the place where he truly enjoyed entertaining.

Usually.

Today would be more a trial than a pleasure. As if to underscore the sentiment, Dani chose that moment to limp out of the house with a checkerboard-designed platter of fruits and berries surrounding a bowl of yogurt. Eli hurried to take it off her hands. He appreciated the gesture and the food, but it made them appear even more, well, *domestic*. Which was exactly what he was trying to avoid. Bloody hell, but he hated playacting. Especially in front of the few people in the world whom he could usually be himself around. He'd even taken his shirt off around Sky once, after Cullen assured him his investigative journalist fiancée would not ask a single question about the scars.

"Is that Pierce's brisket I smell?" Jaz's musical voice preceded her entry into the yard, Kyan and Liam following behind her. Unlike Aaron, who'd gotten a ride with Cullen and Sky, Eli was quite certain those three didn't drive together. Kyan loved his sister, but he'd pulled back from his modeling family after a mortar round left him with burns on forty percent of his body and Jaz simply didn't have the notion of *space* in her vocabulary. As for Liam and Jaz, those two were oil and water. Which did have entertainment value. Jaz's face lit up when she saw the pool. "Ooo! So, boys-against-girls volleyball?"

"That would be five against three," said Liam. Judging by the man's harsh gait and granite face, he was in a mood. "I know gym teachers don't need to learn much, but I'd think they cover basic arithmetic."

Jaz stopped, a muscle ticking in her jaw as she turned to Liam. "First, my master's is in exercise physiology. And second" —her voice turned saccharine—"the teams are even by my count. Everyone without balls on one side"—she pointed to Dani, Sky, herself, and Liam—"and the men on the other."

Liam's return smile didn't reach his eyes. "I've a ball gag in the car. Since your mind seems to be there anyway, perhaps you'd like to try it."

Jaz's face darkened, the petite rock-climbing champion looking like she was truly considering taking the SEAL down. A few more words like that out of Liam's mouth, and she just might try.

Eli opened a beer and handed one to Cullen, lest the man interrupt what was promising to be a good show. Cullen snorted, leaning back against the bar as if to say *you don't need to worry about me.*

"Five bucks she tries to push him into the pool," Eli murmured.

Cullen squinted, weighing the situation. "You're on."

Jaz's nostril flared as she faced Liam. "You are—" Jaz started, clearly working her way up to the good insults when—

"So how are the wedding plans, Sky?" Dani said, sticking a margarita in Jaz's hand and steering her toward the bar where Eli and Cullen stood. Bollocks. "Have you decided on the venue?"

Cullen moved over to create space, covertly giving Eli a

triumphant glance. The bugger had accounted for Eli's other houseguests in betting.

"Not even close," Sky said, accepting a hard cider Eli opened for her. "My mother keeps asking if she can invite my stepfather's friends. I keep telling her no because if I do that, half of Manhattan's medical community will show up, and I want this ceremony simple," Sky said.

Eli swallowed a comment on the woman's fantasy thinking. Cullen Hunt ran the lion's share of Denton Valley's hospital facilities. There would be no stopping everyone and their mother from dropping by to wish the couple well. But that was what made Sky special. When she looked at Cullen, she truly saw *him*, not the CEO of Trident Medical Group with a bank account to put most small countries to shame.

Be careful what you wish for, Mason, Eli reminded himself. *If any woman truly sees you, she'll be on the first plane across the country.*

"What about you?" Sky asked Dani. "Is Eli being a tolerable, err, host?"

Lovely. Exactly the conversation Eli wanted to be privy to.

"He's been very accommodating," Dani said diplomatically. "He's allowed me to use his gorgeous chef's kitchen, so that's been a treat. I love cooking, and it's difficult to do that in a hotel."

"Wait, Mason." Cullen turned to Eli. "Let me get this straight. She cooks for you *and* thinks you're doing her a favor? That's a nice trick."

"Oh, I imagine he makes it up to her." Sky wiggled her brows.

Dani's cheeks colored, making the whole suggestion look even more guilty. Bloody hell. For once in his life, Eli hadn't taken a beautiful woman to bed—for all the good the truth was doing him just now.

"Hunt, will you please at least attempt to control your fiancée?" Eli asked.

Cullen let out a burst of derisive laughter. "If you ever work out how that's done, please enlighten me."

Unable to stop himself, Eli let his gaze drift over to Dani. The sun did wonders playing off her red hair to make it look woven with strands of fire. Perched on the edge of the barstool, she looked delicious enough to be taken in the way Eli's friends had all been certain he'd had her. Absurdly, however, Eli found himself drawn not to her breasts, but her eyes.

Which were larger than usual just now.

"Mason," Dani said with a quiet urgency, her attention split between a discarded pile of Liam's tee, socks, and shoes and the water's still surface. "How deep is your pool?"

"Twelve feet. Why?"

"Because one of your friends went underwater in the deep end about a minute ago...and he's not come up."

16

DANI

I wait for Eli to launch himself into the water, only to have him slide a shot of tequila across the bar top to me instead.

"I'm fairly confident Liam can swim," Eli says with a smirk, as if the thought of someone *not* being part fish was simply beyond the realm of logic. Never mind that his little pool was deeper than most anything commercial.

"The guys have an absurd little competition going on who can hold his breath the longest underwater," said Sky with a long-suffering sigh.

"I always win." Cullen toasts me with his beer.

Eli shoves him. Hard. "Except for the last three times when you lost to me, Commander."

"Asshole." Cullen glares.

"Takes one to know one," Sky croons before turning back to me. "The whole thing makes about as much sense as whacking each other on the head with clubs to test skull thickness, but I've got bigger battles to wage."

Liam emerges from the water and leans his elbows over the

edge of the pool, dripping all over the patterned cement. A few feet away, Kyan finishes his drink in a single gulp and hops into the water with his T-shirt still on. The psychologist in me notes the clothes and concealment. The normal-person Dani… she's just absurdly glad to have an excuse of an aching ankle. Because I suddenly really, *really* don't want Eli to discover that I can't swim.

Liam and Kyan holler from the water, Kyan rolling his eyes as Jaz joins Eli's and Cullen's walk to the pool. Lengthening his stride, Eli comes up behind the petite climber and pulls her small ponytail. I bite my lip. Jaz is the kind of woman Eli needs. Gorgeous and adventurous and so impishly positive that she brings Eli's boyish side to the surface without effort.

"They aren't into each other," Sky says, sliding closer to me, my face flushing at how plainly the woman had read my thoughts. "Plus, if any Trident even thought about getting into Jaz's pants, Kyan would rip his head off. He doesn't particularly like having his kid sister around, but he's also protective as all shit."

"That seems to be a theme." I frown as Eli tucks his shirt into his swimming trunks before diving splashlessly into the deep end. The thought of all that water sends a shiver through me. "Is swimming dressed a tradition around here?"

Sky gives me a tight smile but says nothing.

"May I join you?" Aaron hoists himself up to sit on the deck railing a few feet away from us, his face wet from the dip in the pool. "Those five are making me feel inadequate."

"Because holding your breath underwater is the height of intellectual pursuit?" Sky inquires, extending the young man a beer.

Aaron shakes his head. "I don't think I'll ever look at a beer when Mr. Mason is around and not twitch."

"Why's that?" I offer Aaron a Diet Coke instead, and the man pops the cold can open gratefully.

"When I interned at Mason Pharmaceuticals, I was...er... rather fond of my partying life and found the damn job a rather inconvenient buzzkill. So one day I show up managing to somehow be both hungover *and* drunk. I might have slipped below the radar too, except there was a too-pretty receptionist in my way and—well, so was Mason."

My chest tightens and I smile politely, acutely aware that we've now crossed directly into the work territory that I promised Eli will stay at work. On the far side of the pool, Eli is climbing out for another dive, the water running down the grooves of his chiseled muscles and dripping onto the ground. With the way his opaque shirt clings to his body, there is little left to the imagination. I can't help the way the lowest part of my pelvis begins to ache as I watch him in all his wet glory, and have to cross my legs to stifle the effect. What's worse, he shows no sign of returning to break up this conversation. Or at least witness it.

Aaron continues. "Anyway, Mason gets this dark look in his eye. And then next thing I know, he has me in this huge-ass file room, with a stack of some bullshit papers to slide into folders. Said I had to file everything before I went home if I wanted to keep my job."

"That doesn't sound like an unreasonable job for an intern," I offer brightly, quickly pivoting the discussion to safer ground. "Tell me about law school."

Aaron laughs. "Wait, you haven't heard the important part."

Yes, that was the point.

"So I look around the file room and think much as you did. Normal intern bullshit. It wasn't until about fifteen minutes later that I realized the bastard had turned on every single bright light in the place and killed the air conditioner. And those files I had to get to? Every single one of them was in a file cabinet that you needed a step stool to reach—and he'd replaced *that* sucker with a concrete block. Top it off with the blaring music he piped through the loudspeakers. Hell, I think I spent the next hour just whimpering on the floor as each note sent a jolt of agony through my hungover head. I'm pretty sure it would have hurt less if he'd put up one of those old-fashioned whipping posts and flogged me."

Shit. That's…that's one step away from torture. For a moment, I'm sure Aaron is joking with me. Eli—playful, laughing Eli currently tossing Jaz into the pool—is not capable of cruelty. Then I recall his transformations and know, deep in my gut, that Aaron is telling the truth. And I so, so wish he hadn't. "Eli is lucky you were a good sport and didn't sue him."

Aaron snorts. "Oh, I was going to do exactly that. See, my father's a lawyer, so I grew up with the whole sue 'em thing. Except Dad had cut me off for being a screwup—hence the internship—so I didn't have the money for an attorney. So once I could blink without wincing again, I spent the whole weekend researching labor laws and writing up a whole brief on it. I had nothing better to do since I couldn't look at a beer without gagging, and apparently, being sober increases productivity. Come Monday morning, I go into Mr. Mason's office and dump the stack on his desk."

"What happened next?" Sky asks, hanging on Aaron's every word.

"He read every word," Aaron tells us. "And then had his general council read it. Next thing I know, I'm sitting in a room with a whole bunch of lawyers and my papers."

I slide off my chair, looking for an escape before the kid tells me Eli had his legal department scare him off filing a whistleblower violation or something.

"They told me I needed to go to law school," Aaron says, his face turning serious. "Gave me my brief back with comments and a free ticket to an LSAT class. Eli said that if I scored well enough, there was a law school scholarship with my name on it." He raises his palms. "And, well, here I am. Finishing my second year of law school."

I pause, processing the pieces of the story uncomfortably. As much as I want to give Eli credit, it doesn't feel quite logical.

"You look like you don't believe me," Aaron says.

"It's more that I find your conclusions interesting," I say. "For example, why do you think it was Eli—your boss and tormentor—and not your father, who was actually a lawyer and exposed you to the profession in your formative years, that was the catalyst for your decision?"

Aaron snorts. "My father used his courtroom skills to prove beyond a reasonable doubt how worthless I was, while using his paycheck to bail me out from trouble—until he'd had enough, that is. I guess Mason did the opposite. There was no getting bailed out with him, but instead of telling me I'm an idiot, he let me prove to us both that I wasn't." Aaron scratches the back of his head and laughs. "That, and also the whole sober-weekend thing. That was a novelty at the time. Come on, Dani, haven't you ever had anyone give you a good kick in the ass to get you moving in the right direction?"

"No," I say truthfully. "I don't even remember my parents raising their voices at me growing up. Just the thought that I *might* disappoint them kept me on the straight and narrow."

Aaron puts down his coke, a shit-eating grin splitting his lightly freckled face. "Well, *Hermione*, you know what I think?— That we're at a pool party and you're entirely too dry."

Before I can process what's happening, Aaron lifts me into the air. I screech my protests to high heaven as he carries me toward the pool, where the others are already breaking into volleyball teams. My final "*Aaron, don't!*" is lost in a slew of laughter as the kid dumps me dress and all into the water.

I feel the impact first, then cold wetness rushing all around me as I flail. Water rushes up my nose, stinging the back of my throat. Panic rushes through me, twisting everything, making colors flash over my vision. Pain sears my lungs, the need to breathe like a liquid knife cutting into my throat. My heart pounds, my fingers clawing the water to get to the surface and losing losing losing.

I hit something solid. A ladder. A person. A tree. I don't know. I don't care as I try to climb it to the surface.

The thing before me shifts easily, moving to grip me from behind. An iron hold around my waist pulls me through the water, something else propping my head up until air nips at my skin. I gulp greedily, my legs still kicking for purchase as I alternate gasping and coughing.

"You can stand here, Dani," Eli's calm voice instructs in my ear. "Stop flailing and just put your feet down."

I follow Eli's instructions to discover the tiled pool floor is closer than I think. Hell, I probably was never more than a yard or two from shallow ground to begin with, something even a chihuahua could have handled, if she didn't panic. My face blazes as my weight settles onto solid ground, but the humiliation does nothing to slow either my racing pulse or the fit of reflexive coughing that gives away exactly what happened—just in case someone at the party had failed to notice.

"Dani, I'm so sorry," Aaron appears at the edge, his face white with contrition as he crouches beside where Eli still holds me. "I was just playing and I didn't realize—"

"If you're so keen on carrying things around, fetch us a couple of beers," Eli tells Aaron easily, sending the young man away. Shaking his head like a dog to get the water off his hair, Eli settles himself on a nearby submerged step—pulling me with him.

I inhale sharply as my backside settles onto Eli's lap, his arm holding me from floating away while the water laps our chests. On the other side of the pool, Cullen, Liam, and Kyan make a point of returning to the volleyball game, though I now compute that at least two of them are playing without being able to touch the bottom.

"I'm sorry," I whisper to Eli. "I'm—"

"In need of alcohol and swimming lessons," he finishes for me—a habit he seems to be getting into. "Yes. So I gather."

I try and fail to smile. I've always considered myself athletic and comfortable with nature. Water that went beyond wading in the occasional creek or hotel hot tub just never entered my repertoire. And now here I am, doing a panicked wet rat routine in front of four Navy SEALS, one of whom is my evaluee.

I blow a burst of air through my teeth. "All right. Can we get the making fun of me over with in one big shot now? I don't think I can go through the day waiting for when the other shoe will drop."

"My first jump in Airborne, I decided to change my mind at the last moment. The instructor shoved me out of the plane, but damn it, I grabbed on and fought every step of the way. There I am, all dressed, parachute on, Cullen and the other blokes staring at me as I'm clinging for dear life and begging to be let back into the lovely plane." Eli's voice tickles my wet ear. "If they didn't go after me for that as seventeen-year-old arseholes, they won't hunt you down either."

I twist toward Eli just as he accepts two conciliatory beer bottles from Aaron and hands one of them to me. "Let's not compare getting tossed from a plane to getting tossed into a backyard pool."

Eli cocks a brow, as if to say *why not?* And the funny thing is, I think he believes it. The professional in me would tell a patient that fear is fear no matter the cause, but I'm a psychologist, not a trained Navy SEAL.

A trained professional psychologist sitting on a Navy SEAL's muscular lap. In a pool. With beer. And damn it, but it feels good. Safe.

Reaching up, Eli brushes a strand of hair away from my face, his calloused thumb scraping against my skin. The light touch echoes along my nerves, waking everything to Eli's presence. The way I can feel his heart pounding in his chest. The slate-gray eyes that look so much older than his twenty-eight years. The full, quick-to-smile mouth. The strange mix of power and gentleness that might combust at any moment.

My breath hitches, my face leaning into his touch.

Only to yank back as a volleyball smacks Eli right in the ear. "Mason," Liam calls out, "if you don't tell which neighbor owns that drone that this is a no-fly zone, I'm getting paintball gear and declaring it open season."

Giving a strangled sort of sigh, Eli looks up to where the little mechanical toy is moving jerkily against the clouds' backdrop. "Shoot away, Rowan. Gear's under the porch."

17

ELI

*E*li glared at the chortling Tridents at the other end of the pool. Liam was set on a new task of making some fourteen-year-old's toy into target practice, but the others were being, well, less than discreet. The blokes wouldn't make light of Dani's fear, but the chance to give Eli a smack just as he was about to…whatever it was that he was about to do…was plainly too irresistible to let pass. Bloody hell. Eli didn't know whether he wanted to drown the bastards or thank them.

"I'm going to go get dry," Dani said, letting Eli steady her as she rose. The sun shining off the water made her already large eyes sparkle and sent peculiar ripples of light reflecting off the house windows in the background. Together with the wet dress hugging her hips and breasts, the scene had the appearance of a siren ready to sing her enchantment.

Right, mate. Just ask Homer how that ends.

And Dani did have a very nice soprano.

Aaron, Sky, and Cullen were the last to leave the party, Eli having pulled Cullen away to his granite-top kitchen island to get

ALEX LIDELL

a second opinion on the block of real estate Mason Pharmaceuticals intended to acquire. Most of the small business currently there, including the Petal Florist, Winnie Kids' Books, and Big Dog Hot Dog, were onboard with temporarily moving out in exchange for a lease reduction in a new complex, but the slumlord abusing most of the residential—Eli used the term loosely—properties put up one legal hurdle after another.

"Are those the blueprints for Mason Village?" Sky wrapped her arms around Cullen's waist as she leaned over on her barstool to join the conversation, Dani hovering in the background.

"Hey, no spies behind enemy lines," Eli hip bumped the petite reporter away. Sky worked primarily for the internal affairs of the local PD nowadays, but she freelanced special-interest articles to major papers all over the country. "When I want your grubby little hands to touch my stuff, I'll grab someone from media relations to use as a human shield."

Sky threw back her head and laughed. "He thinks if he keeps me away, I won't be able to get Mason Village to stick as the common name," she told Dani. "But he underestimates me."

Dani shifted her feet, looking everywhere but at Eli. Because the acquisition brushed too closely to the business decisions she was supposed to be evaluating or because of what happened in the pool? Bollocks. Realizing that, on top of everything, he'd just missed whatever Cullen had been saying, Eli rubbed his face—only to feel his phone vibrate in his pocket.

Madison.

Sending the call to voicemail, Eli turned back to Cullen. "Sorry, Commander. You were saying?"

"Never mind. I'll have my legal guys take a look."

Eli's phone buzzed again, putting a final nail in the end of a relaxing afternoon when Madison's name flashed *again*. The woman was nothing if not persistent.

Getting himself under control, Eli clicked the autosuggest text reply. *Busy. I'll call you later.*

"Can I give you some veggies to take with you?" Dani piped up a few feet away, already steering both Aaron and Sky toward the heap of leftover food. Eli hadn't even thought of the notion, but the woman was a perfect hostess, already pulling out Tupperware and waving away Aaron's polite protests. "Please. Take it. That one has the dietary habits of a toddler and has to be bribed to eat a mushroom."

"Bribed?" Cullen said very quietly, wagging his brows.

Eli punched him. Hard.

The phone commenced vibrating a third time. With a normal person Eli might assume an emergency, but when it came to Madison, the urgent business might be anything from appendicitis to the sun shining too brightly for her complexion. Unfortunately, Eli knew the script too well—when she got into one of these moods, she'd just keep calling until he answered. Giving the departing guests a wave off, Eli steeled himself and headed upstairs, accepting the call. "Yes, what is it, Mother?"

"Watch your tone, Elijah. My assistant informs me she hasn't received your travel arrangement for next week. You know it will take time to arrange an airport pickup with my schedule, and I expect a little more consideration from you."

Next week. Right. Eli paused with his hand on the doorframe, letting his fingers squeeze the wood. "There's no need to pick me up, Mother—"

"Nonsense," Madison snapped on the other end, her voice curt and final. "How would it look if I didn't personally pick up my son when he comes to visit his sister's grave?"

"—because I won't be coming."

"You would miss the anniversary of your own twin's death? What in the world is possibly more important, Elijah? Tell me that."

Once, when Eli was seven, he'd had the audacity to point out that since the twin was stillborn, the anniversary of Ella's death also happened to be *his* birthday. Which seemed an important and worthy event on its own. He remembered the whipping from the resulting conversation on selfish behavior each time he took off his shirt.

"I'll mourn Ella in my own way," Eli said, gritting his teeth against the guilt raking through his body no matter how prepared for it he thought he was. How the woman could still manage to get under his skin with every word was beyond him. He wasn't seven anymore. Wasn't even fourteen. It was like some sort of witchcraft. "You don't need my company."

"Your *father* is coming," Madison retorted to underscore the importance of the occasion. Now that Eli was grown and his parents had the excuse of running different affiliates of a major corporation, they got away with only having to spend a few days a year in each other's presence. For a couple who loathed each other as much as Mr. and Mrs. Mason did, however, they were incredibly photogenic together.

"Then he can help you carry the bloody teddy bears to the cemetery." Eli hung up the phone and, after a second's pause, turned it off completely—but not before looking at the date again. It hadn't changed. He didn't know how he'd managed to forget about it earlier. He should have expected the call. Been braced for it. It was, after all, one of Madison's great annual shows of family values and pious grief.

Maybe that was what hurt the most. The tears Madison shed for Ella were real. Her perfect little girl who took only three breaths. All because of Eli. Because Eli had killed Ella, had been the twin to take everything even in the womb. The space, the nutrients, the whatever it was that made one baby thrive while the other withered.

"Mason?" Dani's voice brushed Eli's shoulders. "Are you— what's wrong?"

Eli pushed away from the doorframe, belatedly realizing that he never actually entered his bedroom and still stood in the hallway in his bare feet. His toes dug into the plush carpeting, leaving distinctive imprints behind, the tension in his body gripping him from stem to stern. Still, this was the second floor. *His* floor. One that Dani had no business being on.

"Why are you up here?" he demanded, turning around.

"Your voice carried down the stairs…"

He'd been that loud? Bloody hell.

"So you decided that called for prying?" Eli didn't bother checking his tone. Dani wasn't an innocent bystander. She'd knowingly positioned herself in the line of fire. Eli's private life in this house was just that. *Private.* Dani sure as hell knew that.

Standing at the top of the stairs, the woman braced her hand on the grand sweep of the walnut banister. "In this case, yes."

"Then you made a bloody bad decision." Eli lowered his voice an octave, giving it that flavor of reprimand he knew Dani hated. Madison had pressed all the right buttons, and he didn't need Dani up here pressing more. He didn't need anyone up here.

Instead of skittering away, the woman strode up to him and placed a hand on his shoulder.

Eli flinched at the contact. He didn't want to be touched right now. He just…didn't. Yanking out of her grasp, Eli headed back briskly toward the stairs.

Dani caught up to him, awkward gait and all. "Are you going to run down the steps now?" she asked impertinently. "Up down, up down. Good exercise."

Eli stopped. Turned. Glared. "Get out of my way, Nelson. Now. And never try to get into my head again."

"Well, somebody needs to." The woman made a noncommittal noise, blocking his path downstairs. "You know, there's a misconception many people have about my profession. They think we're all about handing out hugs and leading sob circles. But what we really do is give people what they need. And you know what you need right now, Eli Mason? A slap upside the head."

Or a lash across the shoulder blades. Eli felt his pulse racing out of his control, his emotions beating against hard-won calluses. He knew what he needed. A good fuck or a damn good fight. A merciless brawl that would leave him cut up and bloody and too damn throbbing to feel.

Dani gripped both his elbows with a ferocity he didn't expect. Which was a stupid thing for her to do. A dangerous thing.

"Listen, damn you," he snarled. "The board sent you to spy on me at work, not here."

"Exactly," Dani shot back, her chest rising and falling in harsh breaths. She stepped closer, invading what was left of his personal space. "Consider this payback for pulling me out of the pool today."

Eli glared, unable to understand why Dani was still here. Why she'd not fled. This close, his every breath drew in her scent of lavender mixed with hints of chlorine, her jade-green eyes piercing too deep into his soul. The fingers she had pressed against his elbows sent currents of energy through him, his muscles contracting and pumping with a tension that needed somewhere to go. His cock stiffened, his gaze grazing the curve of her hips and neck and lips.

"Back away," Eli whispered softly, his words no longer a plea but a warning. His cock pulsed mercilessly, his heart hammering against his ribs. All the tension inside him compressed like a spring, ready to explode. It was potent enough to make his head swim. "Not... interested...in talking."

The words came in rasps.

She drew a small gasping breath, her lips parted, and she leaned toward him. Leaned into his erection. "I know."

Eli pressed his mouth on Dani's, the rosebud softness of her lips yielding to him generously. The intensity of the connection ricocheted through him, his hand coming up to tangle in her long red hair, the other gripping along the tantalizing line of her jaw. With her hair still wet and cool from the pool, the contrast to the heat inside Dani's mouth made all of Eli tighten with need.

A soft moan escaped Dani's lips, Eli swallowing the delicious sound as she pressed into the kiss. Into *him*.

18

DANI

$\mathcal{M}$y heart pumps so wildly, I can feel it *everywhere*. The heat of Eli's tongue claiming my mouth. The tiny prickles along my scalp where Eli's hand tangles in my hair. The firm controlling hold along my jaw. Wyrd. The sensations alone are enough to make me feel drunk, more so because everything inside my brain tells me to be terrified—and yet I'm not.

Instead of spurring me to run, the dominating intensity of Eli's kiss feeds my anxiety just enough to meld it to panty-soaking arousal, the resulting cocktail echoing right to my sex.

Releasing my hair, Eli's hand slides expertly down my back to cup my ass just above the thighs, the motion lifting me. I have a heartbeat to gasp against his mouth before my limbs rebel against my brain, and my legs wrap snugly around the man's waist.

Eli inhales sharply, his already rock-hard erection giving a hearty jerk. His other arm wraps around me, pressing me against his solid chest, his muscles so chiseled that I can feel them move beneath my thighs as he carries me easily through the hall. Kicks a door open with his foot. Breaks the kiss only when my back is up against one of the carved wooden posts of his bed.

My lips tingle from the sheer potency of it. My tongue flits out between my lips to taste any remnants of him that may have been left behind.

Eli's gray eyes darken to the color of a storm cloud. Leaning toward me, Eli nips my earlobe, the brush of pain morphing into a bolt of lust that zips all the way to my core. His mouth moves to my neck, cranking my need another notch, the deliciousness of his full cock reaching me even through clothes.

My back arches, my sex pressing into him as I rake my fingers along the cotton shirt on his back.

Eli exhales against the curve of my neck and shoulder, then drops me onto the edge of his too-high mattress, the linens made with five-star-hotel precision. With the click of a switch, his bedroom is illuminated, but I'm too enraptured to register much outside of a chocolate-brown color scheme and the massive California King surrounding me.

Wyrd.

Returning to stand before me, Eli whips my sundress up past my hips, along my torso, and over my head. Cool air brushes my exposed skin, the wet stain along my panties no doubt visible. My heart skips, beating a fluttering, anxious pulse.

Eli pauses, standing perfectly still at the foot of his mattress as his gaze brushes along me. That same intense look I saw earlier is back, but dialed to an eleven—though, damn it, he still looks like he's about to ravish me, to devour me whole.

The craziest thing about this is that I want him to. I'm *dying* for him to. Even if anxiety grips my chest. The inside of my thighs. My belly.

My hands curl around the bedspread. I want this. I want to want this. *Don't let some high school jerk from a decade past deprive you of more than he has already,* I tell myself, as I always do before sex, though the self-talk is getting harder and harder to believe. I'm not good in bed. Too skittish. Too shy. Too scared to do, well, most anything. And sooner or later, the men I'm with, no matter how gentle and patient, figure it out.

"You look scared, Red," Eli purrs.

I swallow. "Just losing my mind over how long you're taking." My words come out naturally breathless, which fits the situation perfectly. Especially since my sex pulses in the same maddening rhythms as my heart.

Running the tip of his tongue over his front teeth, Eli moves in and takes my face in both his hands, making it impossible to look away from his piercing eyes. "You look aroused too. Which is it more?"

When I don't answer, Eli slides his hand along my belly and dips it right into my lace panties, his smile growing content as his fingers slip in my moisture. "What do you enjoy?"

Heat rushes to my face, which I don't turn away only by virtue of Eli still holding my jaw. There's a predatory aura about him, the force of his attention blocking out the world.

I can't talk. Can't even bring myself to answer. In my defense, it wasn't like I expected any man to ask. My breath hitches, the truth leaching all the joy from my spirit. "I… I don't."

"You don't enjoy sex?" Eli cocks a brow, his hand still in my panties, moving teasingly around my sex. Pulling the hand out, Eli displays the glistening evidence of my arousal before sucking his fingers clean. "Delicious."

"Not…not with a man, okay?" The words stumble out.

"You prefer women?" Eli watches my face. "Or are you a virgin?"

At least those are easy to answer. No. To either. Which doesn't leave a great many possibilities as far as how else I might find my pleasure now, does it? Wyrd. "I've had plenty of sex," I say quickly, which only makes the whole situation worse. "I'm just one of those women who is…err… I have a broken libido."

Eli snorts softly. "Then challenge accepted," he says, tugging me slightly sideways to first undo the decorative bra tie at my neck, then the one beneath my shoulder blades. Black fabric slips down to expose my breasts, and Eli's mouth somehow encompasses my left nipple before he's even done pulling off the top.

Maybe it's because my skin is still chilled, but his mouth around my nipple feels more than hot, it feels molten, each suckle searing its way right to my aching sex. Which isn't something that happens to me. Not ever.

"Lie back," Eli orders, holding my gaze captive until I comply, anxiety and arousal rushing around each other, making every shift along the great bed so much more naughty. Needy.

As my shoulder blade touches the bedspread, Eli's tongue circles my right nipple, his hand lowering to the curve of my hip. I close my eyes, as if that might mask the fact that I'm lying open before the most gorgeous, powerful, chiseled man in the universe. I'm so focused on the feel of his mouth on my breast, I don't register what else he's doing until my panties are halfway down my thighs and my sex is open to the air.

A rush of anxiety races through me, my breath quickening. We're actually doing this. Having sex. At least starting to. Which means that in about fifteen point five seconds, the bedroom god and playboy that is Eli Mason will discover that I'm a dud of a dead fish.

"Wait." I grip his shoulder, only to realize I don't know what to say next. So I go with the truth. "I'm not very good at this."

Eli gets on his elbow, leaning over my body as he drags a finger down my cheek and across my bottom lip. "Good thing I am." His eyes flash with predatory desire. "And I *really* like leading the show."

I'm about to ask what he means by that when the gleam in his eyes advises me to be quiet.

"Open up for me, Red." Eli taps the insides of my knees. "And stay very, very still."

Once I nod, he slides my bottom all the way down while maintaining eye contact. My feet are hanging off the end of the bed with him standing between them still clothed. When Eli trails his fingertips upwards from my ankles, along my shins, past my knees to my inner thighs, I shiver.

Using the pads of his fingers, he moves closer to my core, my anticipation growing until I'm vibrating with it.

"Open up further," Eli commands, the steel in his voice somehow feeding my arousal. "I want to see you."

I move my legs apart a few inches.

"Wider," Eli says. He could obviously adjust my legs to his liking himself, but there's something about ordering *me* to do it that gives the whole thing a fresh erotic twist. "Wider, Red. Mmmm. Excellent."

Easy for him to say. He isn't the one splayed open on the bed.

Eli stares unabashedly at my core for a few moments, then drags his fingers along the inside of my legs to my sex, caressing between the folds. His pupils widen, his nostrils flaring delicately as if taking in my scent. "So drenching wet," he mutters, his fingers sliding up and down through my slick folds, my sex clenching with glowing need at each teasing caress.

I moan, raising my hips to meet Eli's touch.

"Don't move," he warns.

Shit. I force my body still, which only makes my desire to reach up to him worse. How the hell did he just do that?

With a knowing smile, Eli flicks his finger over my clit, and this time, I have to press my hands into the mattress to keep from writhing.

Eli's touch disappears, and I can see him moving toward the side of the bed, where a tall walnut dresser is situated. Although I can't see what exactly he's doing there. I glance up to the heavy beams crossing the ceiling and am amazed at how eager I feel for him to return. So far, this is the best sexual experience I've ever had, and I hope it stays that way.

19

ELI

*E*li retrieved the condom packet and the miniature back massager out of his drawer and made his next requirement of Dani.

"Close your eyes."

After blinking over at him with her pale, guileless eyes, she did it. So much lust coursed into his bloodstream and down to his cock that it was a miracle he could stay on his feet. Typically, his escapades were more of the wham-bam-thank-you-ma'am variety. He'd meet a woman, find out she was good to go, fuck her senseless, and either leave her wherever they'd been—like that one time at the Vault he'd never tell Liam about—or shoo her out of his home. It'd always been a case of one and done.

Yet, with Dani, it was different. Not that he minded at the moment.

The woman lay before him like a buffet, offering herself up as a delectable treat, and he didn't plan to be finished until he'd gotten his fill. He'd follow through on his promise first, though. He'd meant what he said about making her feel brilliant. Eli took the massager—it was the palm-sized kind with four little feet—

and placed it carefully over her clit. He used one hand to work a finger gradually inside her, then he flipped the massager on with the other, barely touching her with it.

Her eyes flew open as her body stiffened.

"Shhh," he soothed her, then showed her the massager. "Just offering you a little assistance in getting there. Lie back down and close your eyes again."

She concentrated on it, then nodded. He enjoyed how she surrendered to him, especially considering how antsy she'd been. Dani kept resisting before giving in, over and over. It'd become this peculiar rhythm with her. But convincing her to fall under his spell each time felt like a victory. The buildup to what was on their horizon was both destroying him and making him want to beg for more. Drawing things out like this was excruciating, but he craved seeing Dani come more than he craved his next breath.

Once she'd relaxed somewhat, he trained one of the little feet on the tip of her clit. She moaned faintly, and he smiled. She'd been so silent up till then, and he didn't want her to be. His cock had become as rigid as a crowbar. It was a good thing he wore swim trunks instead of jeans or the zipper might've done him physical harm by now. Inserting a second finger and twisting them into a beckoning motion, he felt for that special patch of skin that designated her G-spot. Once found, he stroked it with confidence, resting the massager against her clit at the exact same time.

She gasped, and her walls began to kick around his fingers as he gave her a new demand. "Look at me, Dani." After she did, her face a fucking picture of ecstasy, he said, "Now let me hear you. Nice and loud."

As if she couldn't do anything else, three heartbeats later, her body pulsed around the two fingers he'd sunk into her. She moaned, then shrieked, pushing up onto her elbows. Holding her gaze as if their lives depended on it, he repeated his motions as she rode out her orgasm, memorizing everything about her. The way her cinnamon hair flew about her bare shoulders. The dewiness of her ivory complexion. The pure pleasure as she inclined her head backward, opened her mouth, and screamed through it. He yearned to keep this image of her in his brain forever.

As she quieted and calmed back down, he turned the massager off and pushed it to the side of his mattress. Dropping trou, he glanced down to see the visual evidence of his arousal. He'd been leaking precum ever since removing her dress, and holding out this long had been an exercise in restraint. He was glad to sheathe his cock in a condom and know relief was near. For some reason, holding back felt so much more difficult. He didn't know if it was because of just how gorgeous Dani looked when she came or because he'd allowed her into the bubble he and his friends occupied, but he was barely hanging on. Unlike the sex he had with other women, this sex didn't feel like business as usual.

Climbing up onto the bed, he levered himself beside her. God, she was gorgeous, lying there all warm and sated. Her skin smelled of lavender and sex, and he couldn't think of any scent that might be more appealing. Too appealing, really. If she kept looking like that, not exploding the instant he pushed into her would be a bloody miracle. He needed a fresh strategy.

"Turn over for me. Ass in the air."

Her eyelids had been at half-mast, but this made them fly all the way open. "What?"

"I'm going to take you from behind." He tapped her on her hip the same way he'd tapped her on the knee earlier. "Come on now."

"You mean like…anal?" She looked horrified, and he realized his error.

"No, love. No," he reassured her. The endearment slipped out of him beyond his volition, but he hoped if he didn't draw attention to it, she wouldn't notice. "Nothing like that. Come on, up on your knees."

This time, she didn't hop to all at once. Instead, she sat up and ran a hand over his T-shirt-clad chest before sneaking her hand underneath. "Aren't you going to take this off?"

"No." This time, he spoke more harshly. Nothing on heaven or earth could make him take his shirt off in front of Dani or anybody else. She went a bit rigid at his tone, but then ran a thumb across the evening scruff growing on his chin and cheek.

"All right. But I'd rather see your face." She licked the seam of his lips, and he welcomed her in. Everything about her was so glorious, and he wanted her. All of her. Right fucking now. Luckily, he wasn't so crass as to say it like that.

"A compromise it is, then."

Instead of taking her in the traditional doggie-style pose, he came up beside her. He pushed in close to her on his side, moving one of her legs over his thigh. Arranging her limbs so they didn't block his way, he held his head up with one hand and braced his other on her waist, his chest partially cushioning her back. Keeping his eyes on hers, he pushed the head of his cock into her entrance. She inhaled sharply, eyes enormous.

"All right?" he asked her, lowering the hand on her waist to brush against her clit again.

She moaned and relaxed, letting him slide in another inch. Revving her up further, he managed to get himself all the way inside her, but it was the tightest fit he'd ever experienced. *By far.* The next shaky breath came from him. Her silky wet heat felt beyond incredible. If heaven was a real place, Eli was pretty fucking sure he'd just found it.

Fully seated, he wrapped his arms around her from behind, cupping her ample breasts in his hands. With her silky wet heat surrounding him and her nipples beading against his palms, he couldn't keep from moving. He rocked against her, into her, around her, and the friction nigh on drove him around the bend.

It'd been easy to maintain eye contact while he'd been concentrating on her before, but it was more difficult now with his own pleasure about to spike.

He edged higher and higher toward the summit, but her moans were becoming noisier and noisier. She was close, and he wanted to watch and listen as she came again. And this time, he was going to come with her.

He thrust into her, his balls tightening as her interior walls gripped his length. She clutched at his enveloping arms until her fingernails dug into his flesh, and shouted out her ecstasy. It was all over for Eli too, as he rode out his own euphoria with a helpless grunt, emptying himself into the condom.

Afterward, they rested there together, catching their mutual breaths. His biceps were up against her chest so that he could feel her heartbeat racing. It felt like hers was in tune with his. Pressing a brief peck to her temple, he released her. She turned her bare body around to face him more directly, bracketing her elbows beneath her.

"Hi," she said, appearing ironically shy. It was kind of cute.

"Hi."

"I uh… I should probably go."

And for the first time in his whole life, Eli almost said no. Almost. Instead, he said, "Okay. See you in the morning."

Turning her back on him, she removed herself from his bed and limped around, gathering her clothing. Then, with an awkward wave and a grin that resembled more of a grimace, she left.

20

DANI

*M*y head buzzes as I sit behind Eli's breakfast bar, staring dumbly at my computer. It is just past five thirty in the morning, which means Eli is busy with the other Tridents as the four try to kill each other in the name of training and I have the house to myself. The house and the reality.

I slept with the man I'm supposed to be evaluating. The ethical implications of that are enough to make my head spin, and not just because it can cost me this contract and my license. No matter which way I approach the problem, I can't see a way out. Can't even put my thoughts in order enough to try. All I know is that I have to do something before everything I've worked for disappears from under me like a crumbling sandcastle.

Biting my lip, I say a mental thank-you to the time zone differential and pull up my calling app. A few clicks and my mother's smiling face fills the screen. Wyrd. Even though I'm the one who made the call, I suddenly want to hang up.

"Dani, sweetheart!" Mom's warm voice fills me even through

the screen's distance. "I'm so glad you called. How are you feeling? How's the ankle?"

"It's a lot better," I assure her, though my words do little to wipe the worry off her face. It's actually nice to be talking about something as simple as an ankle injury for a moment. A normal-person thing for a mother to be concerned with. An easy point for a daughter to soothe. Unlike trying to explain what possessed me to break every single rule of psychology. I lean toward the screen. "Mother, I promise I'm telling the truth. I haven't used crutches in days. Want to see me walk?" I do a little demonstrative circle for her peace of mind, ending the show with a curtsy.

"Then it's your head?" she presses. "Tom, come here. Your daughter's concussion is still lingering."

"What?" I raise my hands. "No, no, it isn't. How did you even come to that conclusion?"

"What's wrong with your head, Dani?" My dad leans over Mom's shoulder. "Dizziness? Double vision?"

"No." I wave my palms before the screen. "I've been telling Mom there's actually nothing wrong. She just won't believe me for some reason."

My mother frowns, exchanging a look with my father, who frowns as well. "Of course we believe you, sweetheart," Dad says. "It's just that it appears you're still in…that house. Wasn't it just a medical arrangement?"

"Yes, of course it is. Was." I stop myself from cringing just in the nick of time. My parents have a point. No matter how I twist and turn things in my head, I can't justify living at my evaluee's house now that I can plainly navigate on my own. The fact that I've come to enjoy spending time with the man—and that he's a god in the bedroom—is no justification. Hell, it's a reason to leave as fast as my feet will carry me. I clear my throat. "I mean, you're catching me on my last day. I'm moving back into the hotel shortly. Tonight, actually. So I'll start my work week from there tomorrow. It was just working out better that way logistically." The plan spills out from me, surprising me as much as anyone, though for once, my parents seem fooled. Or maybe they're just too pleased to care.

"That's great news," my father puts in, nodding with approval. "Men like Elijah Mason are toxic, and not just because of the crap they manufacture to put into people's bodies."

"You don't actually know Eli, Dad."

My father scoffs. "I know what type of human it takes to run a conglomerate like Mason Pharmaceuticals. You don't get to that level without being willing to bulldoze a few villages of regular folks just trying to survive. It's been the same throughout all of history. Do you imagine the great pyramids were built with any respect to human dignity?"

The sound of keys jangling by the front door makes me jump. Quickly saying my goodbyes, I turn to find Eli standing there, his shoes already off and stowed neatly on the rack as he takes care to hang up his unusually noisy keys. As if he'd made the extra sounds on purpose.

My face heats—both at the thought of last night and the possibility that he'd heard any part of the conversation with my parents. The very, very likely possibility. "You're back early," I say with more hesitation than I wish was in my voice.

"I need to get to the office and catch up on work." There's restrained gruffness in Eli's voice. "You're up early. Big day, though. I hear you're moving out."

I quickly rewind the conversation with my parents. If Eli heard my departure plans, he'd also heard my dad's assessment of him. Shit. I finger the granite countertop, the kitchen suddenly uncomfortably warm with discomfort. "Eli—"

"Mason."

Right. Back to that. I straighten my spine, forcing my eyes to meet his, only to discover an impenetrable wall behind the slate gaze. Fine. "Mason. Please don't take my father's words to heart.

He lost his apothecary practice to a major corporation and likes painting everyone in the same light."

Eli shrugs one shoulder. "I run an international conglomerate. The number of people I've never met who *know all about me* is probably in the thousands."

"The joys of being a celebrity," I try and fail for humor before readying myself to roll straight to the heart of the real issue. It's probably not the best of moments, but I'll work myself into a panic attack if I put it off. Drawing a fortifying breath, I raise my chin. "Listen. Last night... It was the best sex of my life. It was also the most unprofessional thing I've ever done. If you would like to reach out to the board of directors to—"

"I don't."

"—void this evaluation, we can do that now."

Eli shakes his head once, the sweat-soaked curls swaying. "So that they can send someone else out and I can enjoy the mental enema all over again? Not bloody likely." Eli strides to the kitchen and mixes his protein shake with military precision. "I've no intention of discussing last night with anyone."

Relief so potent that I nearly lose my balance washes over me, but I tamp it down. "I need you to know my report will be impartial no matter what," I add, though I know I may be snatching defeat from the jaws of victory. "Whether you decide to go to the board or not, it won't have any bearing on the result. I can't—"

"You think I'd *blackmail* you?" Eli spins on his heels, his eyes flashing.

"I didn't say that. I just wanted to lay my cards out in the open in case... Just in case."

"Noted," Eli snaps and turns his back to me, the muscles of his back rippling under his sweaty T-shirt as he shakes his drink. "Stop making a quick fuck into something it wasn't, Nelson. It doesn't hit my radar enough to bother discussing with anyone."

21

ELI

*T*he morning of his birthday, Eli stared at a mushroom. A leftover relic from three days ago, when Dani was still trying vegetarianism at a barbeque. Strangely, he missed her intrusion into his ordered kitchen and meat-eating lifestyle even more than he missed the sex. Granted, that had been bloody euphoric. Watching Dani climax was like reliving every pleasure anew again. But there was a different, quieter contentment in sharing breakfast, in the way she tried to hide her cringe each time he came back from training with a new bruise to show for the fun, in being able to calm her with his touch when a nightmare—or a near drowning—had her unsettled.

Eli rubbed his face. Despite a good workout last night, he'd again slept poorly. A three-day pattern. At first, he thought the problem came from Dani's scent clinging to his sheets. An easy fix—he'd torn them off and thrown them in the wash. But then it was the *absence* of her lavender fragrance, mixed tantalizingly with sex, that got under his skin.

No one to blame but yourself, mate. He'd known from the start that Dani wasn't for him. And if the fact that she was a shrink for hire who'd literally come to Denton Valley for the sole purpose of digging through his head wasn't a tip-off, then hearing her father talk about men like Eli certainly put everything back into perspective. A perspective that he should never have lost.

Actions had consequences. He'd let himself get attached to an illusion and walked face-first into a brick wall. That was before even considering the impossible professional position he'd put Dani in because he couldn't keep his damn fly up.

Sweeping the mushroom off the breakfast counter into the trash, Eli pulled out the plans for demolition/reconstruction back on the counter. Cullen had sent over an opinion from his legal team. If Garibaldi put as much effort into maintaining his buildings as he did into fighting for them, Eli would never have had to start the project. He was in the pharmaceutical business, not a real estate one—but one glimpse of live wires and kids living without heat in the winter was enough.

He glowered at his own reflection in the bay window. It was still early enough that the sun hadn't fully risen, but he wanted to get the plans reviewed and underway sooner than later. And no, it wasn't because he might run into Dani. She was busy finishing up her project, and Eli had made it a point to *not* check her schedule the past few days. He didn't need to know. Didn't *want* to know. If she needed him, she knew where he was.

Realizing that his phone was vibrating and skipping along the granite countertop toward a possible demise, Eli shook himself and snatched up the call without looking. "Mason."

"Mr. Mason, this is Stephanie Ann, your mother's assistant."

Eli raised a brow. Whatever he could say about Madison, she wasn't in the habit of having her assistants call him on her behalf. That was more his father's tactic.

"Yes?" he prompted, ignoring a small tightness along his neck. It was another antic. It always was with his mother.

"I'm sorry to interrupt your day, sir, but Mrs. Mason is on her way to the Mass General ER. She started having chest and left arm pains early this morning, and by the time she'd let me call an ambulance, she was having shortness of breath as well. I'll—"

Bloody hell. "You'll call her cardiologist and have her come in," Eli snapped into the phone. "Then get through to cardiology and tell them that the woman who is paying all their salaries is on her way in. They should have a cath lab prepped."

"Yes, sir," Stephanie Ann—who was clearly no Zana and caught on quickly—said into the receiver. "Should I set you up with a pilot?"

Eli hesitated for a moment. That would probably be the wise course of action, but he wanted to be in control just now. "I'll fly myself."

"Very good, sir. If you get me your flight plan, I'll ensure it's filed and will alert the tower to expect you. Please reach out if there's anything you need—otherwise, a car will be waiting for you by the airstrip."

"Thank you," Eli said, and meant it. Walking toward the door, he tried and failed to ignore the shiver running down his spine.

LANDING SMOOTHLY at the private airstrip, Eli quickly buttoned down the plane and headed toward the limo he could already see waiting for him. In the distance, Boston's skyline rose against a graying day. With its finicky weather, weaving streets, and family roots, Eli hated Boston. And it little liked him in return. But today wasn't about that.

Nodding his thanks to the limo driver holding open the car door, Eli growled softly at his phone as he climbed inside. For all her efficiency, Stephanie Ann seemed unable to either tell him what room Mass General had finally settled Madison in or provide any useful medical update. Giving up on text messages, he was about to call and shout at the woman when his gaze registered the limo's other passenger.

Madison Mason herself, in full healthy glory and a black Donna Karan dress.

The heart attack had all been a bloody show.

"Good afternoon, dear. How was your flight?" Madison asked primly.

Eli's heart hammered its fury against his ribs as he stared at his mother. He'd been manipulated. Played. Worse, for several hours there, he'd been bloody terrified. How was it even possible to utterly hate someone and be utterly afraid of losing her at the same time? His jaw tight, Eli reached for the door handle, swallowing a curse when he found the limo locked.

Madison pursed her lips. "I don't appreciate that look on your face, Elijah."

"The look on my face?" Eli's brows rose. "You outright lied to me."

"Don't be so dramatic." Madison smoothed her dress along her thighs. "For heaven's sake, would you have *preferred* to see your mother in the morgue?"

"I would have preferred the truth."

"I tried that last week." Madison threw her hands up into the air. "Or do you not remember telling me you planned not to come to your own sister's memorial? Quite frankly, that I must concoct an elaborate ruse just to get an adult child to fulfill his family obligations is beyond ridiculous. Unless the next words out of your mouth are an apology, I want to hear nothing more on the matter."

Breathing out a long, slow stream of air, Eli blanked out his expression. Anything he said or did now would only be twisted against him. Even if it was an admission of relief, no matter how thickly it was covered with fury. Maybe he should have seen this coming. Madison had never taken no for an answer, so why would she have started now? Maybe it was his own fault for thinking some line shouldn't be crossed just because it hit him too deeply.

"Here." Madison thrust a garment bag onto his lap. "We're heading straight to the cemetery, and that gray pinstripe simply won't do."

For a moment, Eli considered tossing the clothes on the floor, but decided there was no point. He was in Boston, and he wouldn't be leaving until late evening at the earliest—just long enough for the Masons to attend the memorial ceremony and endure a small family dinner the world would expect them to indulge in. A family strewn across the continent by circumstance, snatching a few precious moments to grieve together. A bloody lie from start to finish.

The only genuine fiber in all of it was the tears already glistening in Madison's eyes. How different Eli's childhood would have been if the woman offered him a quarter of the love she bestowed on Eli's stillborn twin.

As they approached the cemetery, Eli saw a large group of sympathizers already waiting beside the pastor in the graying afternoon. Getting out of the limo after him, Madison gripped Eli's elbow—a favorite move that allowed her to steer Eli around while appearing to follow his lead. For a woman in her fifties, she was as strong as an ox.

As they approached infant Ella's headstone, Eli saw another familiar figure already there. Standing stalwart and tall by his daughter's grave, Eldridge Mason struck a formidable pose. Eli had inherited his height and all his features, except his gray eyes and curly hair, from his father, but that was where the similarity ended.

If Madison's tears for Ella were real, his father's were all for show. In fact, as Eli peered around, he caught sight of a black-clad photographer who had joined their ranks. Leave it to Eldridge to twist his dead daughter's memorial service into a fucking photo op. Even the way he held his arm out to Madison was staged. Maybe that was what it had taken to build the Mason empire from nothing, but Eli had met rocks in Afghanistan that had more of a soul.

For the next thirty minutes, Eli did what was expected of him. He held his weeping mother. Bowed his head. Dropped the single white rose over her sister's resting place while wondering what would have happened if he'd been the one who'd died, either at birth or in Afghanistan. Would Madison cry for him, then? Was that what it would take ?

By the time the Masons returned to Madison's Beacon Hill estate—another façade since they hadn't resided in the same house for more than a decade—Eli was spent, with dinner and his subsequent departure the only beacons of light keeping him moving. The food promised to be good, at least. It was one of the few things Eli and his father could agree on: if the three of them were to be stuck together for a few hours, they might as well eat well.

Walking into the formal dining room, Eli saw that Madison's staff outdid themselves. The set-for-three table already held plates of sizzling lamb chops, bacon-wrapped filet mignon and grilled lobster tails, the mouthwatering aroma filling the room. Pulling out Madison's chair, Eli seated his mother before taking his own place, his gaze surveying the dishes with odd disappointment. Dani would have laid a platter of colorful sauteed peppers in the middle of the spread—and then insisted on Eli eating them.

"Is there something you wanted?" Madison asked, following Eli's gaze.

"Do you know if there are any mushrooms?" Eli asked despite himself.

Madison frowned but started toward the intercom on the wall. "Let me check. I didn't know you'd developed a taste for them."

Neither had he. But suddenly, that was all he wanted on his plate.

"So, Elijah…" Eldridge helped himself to the filet mignon while the kitchen staff apologized for the lack of Eli's requested fungus. "Have you given any more thought to another active duty tour?"

"Not a bad idea," Madison said, returning to her seat. "Stock values soared the last time. That heroic bollocks makes for solid PR."

Eli shook his head, not bothering to argue the sanity of viewing a SEAL team deployment as a publicity tactic—or to reveal that his life with the other Tridents was the only thing keeping him sane nowadays. He just needed to get through dinner and leave. "I have responsibilities in Denton Valley. But I do have another project that will play well for PR."

"Make sure finance runs the return-on-investment projections," Eldridge pointed a fork at him. "The last time you tried—"

"PR *and* revenue producing," Eli assured him wearily. "There's a city block in Denton—"

"Can we not talk about money for one bloody moment?" Madison's usually controlled voice rose together with her, cutting Eli off. "It's time for the candle lighting." Striding over to the intercom on the wall, she pressed the small button. "Rosalee, bring the candelabras to the dining room, if you please."

Bloody hell. Eli had forgotten about this part. Inevitably, his mother would insist on the three of them lighting a candle for each year Ella had been gone. And childish as it was, Eli always felt like it was *his* birthday candles that were being given away. What kind of man thought like that? Maybe Madison had a point about him.

He'd just braced himself for the ritual when Eldridge grunted his disapproval. "Not now," Eldridge snapped. "Elijah and I are talking business."

Madison's eyes glistened, her fleeting glare cutting into Eli with condemnation. As if this was *his* bloody fault.

"Just let her do it," Eli said, holding up his palm toward his father.

Shoving his chair back, Eldridge stalked to the intercom. "Never mind, Rosalee," he said, a vein starting to pulse along his temple. "Return to your quarters."

"Eldridge, this is important," Madison protested.

"Enough is enough," Eldridge snapped, his face darkening in a way that made Eli's stomach clench on instinct. "No amount of burned wax is bringing that stillborn to life, and I've wasted enough time on your charade for the day. As I told you, I was discussing business with—"

"Her name was Ella." Madison rounded on the man, her voice rising. "She was our daughter. And we will honor—"

It happened so fast, Eli didn't have time to intervene. One moment, Eldridge's hand was still hovering by the intercom button, the next it was sailing through the air. The sound of a backhand hitting flesh filled Eli's ears, followed by a soft gasp as Madison stumbled backward from the strike, a drop of blood snaking from her lip.

Eli's pulse pounded in his ears as he vaulted over the table, somehow clearing the crystal goblets before wrapping his hands in his father's shirt. A small buck of the hip sent the older man sailing into the oak china cabinet, the dishes inside rattling from the impact.

"Don't *ever* touch her again." Eli's words came in a snarl, his breath puffing. Good fucking God. How long had *this* been happening under his very nose? How long had Eli, who'd set up shell accounts to keep his support of domestic violence shelters from reaching Eldridge's finance people, been blind to what happened beneath his own roof?

Eldridge wiped his hand across his face, snorting at the blood. Then he pushed himself upright, his face turning from angry red to a cold, deadly kind of fury. The kind the younger version of Eli had learned to fear.

Stepping away from the cabinet, Eldridge removed his black suit jacket, hanging it with too great a care on the back of a chair. "You're a naïve child," he said, sparing Eli a glance before unbuckling his belt. "Even now."

"You want to whip me?" For a moment, Eli could only blink at the absurdity of the scene. At another time, he might have found his father's delusion comical, but tonight, tonight it was just dark. "What do you imagine you're going to do with that?" Eli's voice was low. "I've been stronger than you for several years now."

"Have you now?" Eldridge asked with a nonchalance that sent an uncomfortable shiver down Eli's spine. "I beg to differ."

Eli let the man have a few seconds, working out how he was going to put a stop to everything if Eldridge was stupid enough to attack. How this bloody mess of a day had come to this, Eli had no idea, but it was probably his fault. It usually was.

"Your problem, Elijah," Eldridge continued, looping the belt around his palm, "is that you're still under the illusion that muscle has anything to do with power. Case in point, it's come to my attention that you've been engaging in certain extracurricular activities outside of Mason Pharmaceuticals." Reaching into his pocket with a free hand, Eldridge pulled out his phone and scrolled down the screen. "Denton Valley Battered Women's Shelter. Hannah House for Displaced Mothers with Children. Safe Harbor. Samaritan House, Inc. Any of those ring a bell?"

Eli went motionless. He had no clue how his father had traced down those particular donation accounts, but how little mattered just now. His mind spun. "I'd check with your people again," he said, hoping like hell he was right. Those shelters needed the money. Badly. "The donation chains are so integrated with other transactions, you'll lose more on forensic accountants than anything."

Eldridge snorted. "Oh, this isn't about the funding—though with the money they've been getting, you'd think they'd have invested a bit in cybersecurity." He flipped his phone, displaying lines of text. "These are the names and addresses of every resident inside those walls. Guess how easy it would be to make that information public? I dare you."

Eli felt his eyes widen as he absorbed his father's threat with a throat that had gone utterly dry. *Either you obey, or those women's attackers will be given all they need to locate their victims.*

"So who will it be Elijah?" Eldridge asked, looping the lash around his palm one final time before looking up. "You or them?"

The world stopped. Then started again as Eli slowly, deliberately removed his suit jacket. Once Eli walked out of this room, he would have Liam's hackers scramble the database, but until then...until then, his father had won the damn round. Doing his damnedest not to think about what he was doing, Eli started to unbutton his shirt.

2 2

DANI

*O*n my third day of avoiding Eli Mason, I finally admit failure. Not in the physical sense—Mason Pharmaceuticals is big enough that we could probably spend six months in the building without crossing paths—but in every other way. No matter what I do as I sit in the empty conference room to finish my report, I can't get thoughts of the man out of my mind. Or my other parts.

Yes, sex with Eli was…world shattering. Just thinking about it makes my sex tingle, my thighs pressing reflexively into the ergonomic chair. It is fascinating—and extremely satisfying—to know that such extraordinary levels of pleasure and bliss are even possible for me.

Yet for every pang of arousal the memory of Eli's touch brings me, there are two memories of a different sort that I miss no less than physical pleasure. The devastated look on his face when presented with tofu instead of chicken, followed by boyish surprise upon tasting the dish. The strength of his arms wrapping around me protectively, shielding me from my nightmares. The wonderful, homey feeling of his friends treating us as the couple we pretended to be at the barbeque.

Most of all, though, I miss Eli's sharp, intelligent mind that's always on, even while his demeanor somehow shifts between that of an overgrown teenager and a deadly special forces commando. I miss the puzzle that is Eli Mason. I miss *him*.

And that's…well, that's not good. Very not good.

Eli does one-night stands. And I do my work, not men. Work that a single night of wanton pleasure nearly destroyed. Flipping open my calendar, I look at the dates. Truth to tell, I'm almost done with my evaluation. Eli's giving me carte blanche access to his staff, and they'd actually filled in the gaps his reluctance to speak to me directly created. Another day or two, and my preliminary report can go to the board for comments and inquiries.

Then I go home to Boston.

Eli stays in Denton Valley.

The end.

I close my laptop with a sigh. I lived in his house. Cooked in his kitchen. Held ice to his bruises and clung to his chest when demons chased me in the middle of the night. We talked and we argued. Though he'd no doubt denied it if asked, we *had* become friends. And then I turned on my heel and walked out because he'd given me a mind-blowing orgasm and because I hadn't known what to say to my parents. Whatever else, I owe him an apology over how that went down.

Walking up the stairs to the CEO's suite, I make a beeline for Zana's old desk, where a pretty woman in her thirties smiles her welcome.

"Ms. Nelson, isn't it?" she asks, pushing back her shiny raven hair. "I'm Louise. Please bear with me—I'm new to the position and still learning the faces. Can I help you?" Already, the woman is light-years ahead of Zana.

Yet Eli had given the young intern every chance possible,

though he surely knew that someone like Louise of the raven-hair clan would make his life run smoother.

I clear my throat. "Yes. Is Mr. Mason in?"

"Unfortunately, no. He left to visit his family and will be out of town for a few days. Would you like to leave a message for him?"

"No, thank you." I swallow my disappointment, both at finding him gone and at having lost the inside track to Eli's life. Then again, maybe this is fate trying to push me back from the ledge.

By the time I return to the Marriott in the late evening, my neck is stiff from typing furiously for the whole day—though I have a nearly finished report to show for it. Waving to the receptionist, I grab the delivery menu from the stack near the front desk and trudge to my room. Second floor. No elevator needed. Which is fortunate because my key card won't work and I have to take another trip to reception and back before the Marriott's smart locks let me into the room.

Menu in hand, I unlock my phone to call in the delivery order when a new email pops into my box.

Stay safe, girly.

There's no signature, and the email is a no-return address of sales@protect69.com, but I can hear Brock Talbot in every word. The way he's called me *girly* in that chainsaw-like voice of his from day one. My blood chills, the phone falling from my hands onto the bed.

I order myself to breathe deeply, letting the air flow low into my belly. In and out. In and out. There's something about these hotels that makes me jump at shadows. Probably because I'd stayed at another Marriott when doing Talbot's fateful eval. But Talbot isn't here. Never was. And the email? Even if it's from him, it means little. The message went to Danielle.Nelson@Exec-utiveEvaluations.com, which anyone can find on the internet, not my personal account.

I pick up the menu again, getting ready to order a white broccoli-and-cheddar pizza, but find myself texting Sky instead.

Your friend with a security company, do you have his number?

Liam. Sharing contact. What's wrong???

I cringe. Hesitate. Then evade. *Was hoping to ask him about computer security programs. Think that's all right?*

Go for it. Talking security gives him a hard-on.

I snort despite myself and shake my head at the screen before accepting the contact share and calling.

"Rowen." The military staccato of the voice sounds so like Eli's when he's upset that it takes me a moment to find my breath. To remember that this is a casual call.

"Liam, good evening. This is Dani, Eli's friend." I hate the way my voice goes up at the end of that, but I forge on. "A quick question for you. Is there any reason why I might get more spam when I'm in a hotel than I did at Eli's, or would it just be coincidence?"

Liam pauses. "Assuming you're using the same devices, there's no reason for a spam filter to function differently, but a hotel's public Wi-Fi system isn't secure like Mason's is. It's vulnerable to malicious code. I wouldn't log in to your bank account from there. Why? Are you seeing suspicious transactions?"

Do phantom emails with veiled threats to feed my imagination count? "No." I hesitate. "I just don't want to be seeing any. So crossing *check account balance* off my list for today."

"All right." Liam's voice hardens. "But if you're worried about something specific, you call me back, got it?"

What is it with these military types? "Yes, sir." I make a mock salute in the air even though Liam can't see me and hang up as he's chuckling. Malicious code sounds like the exact opposite of Talbot's MO. The man could barely check email without help. No use making a mountain of a molehill.

I ARRIVE at work the next morning with fatigue bags under my eyes and a finished report sitting in my laptop. Having given up on sleep, I stayed up all night finishing the thing, and the narrative is now ready for a few figures from my notes and the Send button. Truth to tell, I'm rather proud of how I established Eli's executive blueprint through staff interviews. At least that aspect of what I've done with him has been thoroughly professional. As will our goodbye.

In the time it takes for me to walk from the busy reception area to my usual work spot, the scuttlebutt in the corridors informs me that Mason Pharmaceuticals' lord and master has returned. Chest suddenly tight, I change course for Eli's office and mentally rehearse my speech, trying to polish the peppiness I should be feeling.

Mason, welcome back. Some good news for you. My report is done. No more interrogations. As soon as it's accepted by the board, I'll be out of your hair. How was your trip?

Or something to that effect. Followed by an apology. Or maybe I should just leave it there. Maybe I shouldn't ask about his trip at all. Family is a personal matter for him, and we—

"Ms. Nelson, hello." Louise greets me, her voice tight as if she's expecting me to yell. "I'm very sorry, but Mr. Mason isn't in."

I stop short. "The whole building seems to think he is."

Louise flinches.

I cringe, backpedaling as quickly as I can. "I'm so sorry, Louise. I didn't mean to imply I don't believe you."

Her shoulders fall in obvious relief. "Oh, he's back in Denton Valley—the airport registered his Gulfstream's tail number, and this town has far too many busybodies—just not in the office. And I have twenty-five people who are mad about it."

The Gulfstream's tail number. Apparently, when Eli flew out, he actually flew. Like he *flew* himself. Wyrd.

"If he just flew in, I imagine he wants some food and a shower," I tell the receptionist. "Don't let the twenty-five jerks get to you."

"That's what I told them too, but I guess it's not like him not to come in. If you..." She hesitates, wringing her hands over her keyboard. "It's my first week, Ms. Nelson. I *need* to get this right. I'm a single parent and...I hear you and Mr. Mason talk regularly. If you might find out when he's planning to return, it would be a lifesaver."

"Let me see what I can do," I tell the petrified woman. "I'm certain Eli isn't going to fire you for not reading his mind, though."

Louise's nervous smile at my use of Eli's first name reminds me of the distance he keeps between himself and others here. Which makes the intimacy we shared that much more special. Unusual. Taking out my phone, I dial his number—frowning when it goes directly to voicemail. Giving Louise's hopeful face one last look, I call myself an Uber and hope Eli hasn't changed the gate codes since I moved out.

He hasn't. Walking through the silently opening gates toward his immaculate cedar-and-glass abode, I feel my breathing quicken inside my chest. By all rights, I shouldn't be here. In Eli's home. Uninvited. But for every argument against taking the next step, another one sweeps into place. Louise is worried. I'm worried. And then the biggest, most impossible one of them all: I *want* to see him too desperately not to take this chance.

"Mason?" I call, knocking on the outside of the front door before testing the handle, which is under my hand. "Mason, it's Dani. The door is open. Can I come in?"

Silence.

My heart stutters. "Mason?" I call his name a third time, knowing that he's in there. That he never leaves the door open otherwise. When silence greets me again, I take a breath and let myself inside, the familiar sight of the sunlit living room with its leather sectional and bay window greeting me at once. Sweeping my gaze over the expanse of the open first floor, I'm about to call Eli again, when I finally see him.

23

DANI

Sitting slouched on a stool at the breakfast bar, Eli looks like something off the set of a bad karate flick, right at the part where the hero loses against the forces of evil. Pale skin. Split lip. Black eye. Rips and cuts and dirt all over his clothes and knuckles. One arm wrapped gingerly around his ribs. But that's not all. Along with a bottle of Grey Goose vodka and a half-empty glass atop the breakfast counter, the rest of the granite space is covered nearly with…papers.

Ones that Eli appears to be reading and sorting meticulously into neat piles.

Though obviously aware of my presence, he hasn't looked up to so much as acknowledge the intrusion into his space. Even now, as I move closer, his attention remains on his reading, the smell of alcohol reeking from his clothes. What in the ever-loving hell…?

"Whatcha doing there, Mason?" I ask, my tone carefully nonjudgmental.

"Working."

No eye contact, but the verbal response is clear, appropriate, and slur-free. I breathe out a small sigh of relief and look closer at the papers, bracing myself for anything from a manifesto to the words *Redrum Redrum* written over and over on the white pages.

Regular Mason Pharmaceuticals reports look back at me. The kind Eli often brings home to catch up on in the evenings. "Why don't you do that in the office?" I ask.

Raising his head, he waves a hand across his disheveled self. His black eye is accompanied by a two-inch cut along the same cheekbone, the cut flowing into a split, blood-oozing lip. Dirt smudges his chin, and debris—including what appears to be broken glass—is littered in the reddish curls of his hair. The knuckles of his right hand, which is holding an expensive fountain pen, are busted open and filthy, and the silken tie he tends to wear with all his suits is nowhere in sight. "Not professional."

Well, yes. I rub my hands over my face and throw all my psychology and crisis intervention training out the window. "What the hell happened, Mason?" I demand, putting my hand over the report he's reading. "I heard you went to Boston. Did you get into a street fight on the way back?"

"No."

Not good enough. I keep my hand right where it is, covering his report.

"It wasn't a street fight—it was a bar fight," he says, trying to pull the paper free. "Here in Denton Valley. I started it last night."

"Why on earth would you do that?"

He shrugs stiffly, the motion cautious. Too cautious. And as unlike him as the fact that he's still not attempted to throw me out.

The man just told you he was in a brawl, I tell myself. *What do you expect?*

Not this. Nothing about this is right. Including the fact that

Eli isn't acting like some cocky bastard who started a brawl. In fact, there's something familiar about it all, something I can't quite put my finger on, until it hits me straight in the face. He's acting the way I had when someone hurt me. Camouflaging the pain, guarding against more.

I reach for his shoulder, my throat tightening when he flinches. "Come on, soldier. Let's get you cleaned up."

I'm more than a little relieved when Eli obeys, letting me lead him from the kitchen to the guest bathroom that was once mine, the familiar grand shower stall gleaming with brown tile. Eli's feet are already bare, and I toe off my own shoes before walking us both inside the stall, clothes and all, and turning on the spray.

"I do have a washer for laundry," Eli informs me as the water drops on us like a fierce rainstorm from the extra-wide showerhead. "A rather good one."

"Yes, well, you're too tall to be stuffed into one." I pull a washcloth and bodywash from a shelf. "Actually, you're too tall period. Sit."

Eli lowers himself to the tiled floor, the water now fully soaking Eli's once-pristine black business suit and the ivory sheath dress I shouldn't have chosen for today. Working the bodywash into a lather on the small towel, I lower myself beside him, deliberating my next move. Something that wouldn't be a bridge too far in the tentative trust between us.

Taking his hand onto my lap, I run the washcloth over busted-up knuckles. "So, why did you start a bar fight?"

He winces. "Easier to pick than a street fight."

Not exactly what I was asking, but Eli knows that. I nod for now, going along with the diversion for the sake of keeping him talking. "True. The North Vault?"

"Funny. No. Liam would murder me." Another tiny wince as the soap gets into the cut. "My goal was just diversion, not bloody suicide."

Could have fooled me. I tug on his suit jacket, cuing him to take it off. Its fine fabric, likely a tightly woven expensive wool, is torn, with dirt and blood caked over the shoulder blades. With the shower nozzle raining down on us now, it looks more like mud. One sleeve's seam is ripped open from wrist to elbow, the other showing a horizontal gash with blood seeping from within. Between the clothing mess and the carefulness of Eli's movements, I feel the next logical question bubble up inside me —though I'm not the one who's a medic.

"Hey, Mason? Let me see your pupils."

Eli's head stays down. He hasn't met my gaze once. "I'm not concussed, if that's what you're getting at. Everything is…" He pauses for a beat. "Superficial."

"All right, I'll trust you on that. But I do need the jacket off." Maybe he agrees with my unassailable logic, or maybe the word "trust" triggers something within him, but Eli tilts to the side and shifts one arm. I grab the end of his sleeve to help him, but his motions stutter midway as he takes a sharp inhale. For the briefest of moments, I catch the tightness around his eyes as he regains his breath, the quiet curse under his breath that betrays just how much *superficial* pain the man is in.

Taking his left lapel, I edge the jacket off Eli's shoulders and stand up to hang it on the shower door.

"Just toss it into the rubbish," he says. "There's no salvaging it."

Raising my eyebrows, I do as he says. Considering the tattered nature of the garment, he's probably right. Either that or he doesn't want a reminder of whatever happened.

With the jacket gone, the tang of vodka dissipates, leaving behind the faint fresh-grass smell I always associate with Eli. He's scooted out from under the spray and is more or less facing me, but as I resituate myself next to him, I catch a glimpse of his back.

And nearly choke on air.

Long swaths of burgundy stripe what used to be a pristine

white button-down, the cloth somehow intact despite the blood soaking it now. As if Eli put the shirt on *after* being sliced open. Which makes not an ounce of sense. Or maybe it makes all the sense in the world.

"This isn't bar-fight damage." I only realize that I've spoken aloud when Eli's jaw tightens. I half expect him to yell at me that this is none of my business, but he doesn't. He says nothing. Doesn't even move.

I touch his hair, which is only misty due to the angle of the showerhead, dislodging a few fat droplets of water from the curls. But when I run my fingers through it, he leans into my palm, the rare show of vulnerability gripping my heart.

Someone had hurt Eli. Someone against whom he couldn't— or wouldn't—fight back, not even to defend himself. And so Eli turned around the moment he could and picked a brawl. A fight he *could* pour his strength and ability into. One whose injuries he'd hoped would mask the pain he couldn't bear feeling. The bar fight was an attempt to reclaim himself. And I'm willing to bet money this isn't his first go-round with the cycle.

I wait for Eli to unbutton his shirt. Though his hands are stationed at the top button, he merely curves his fingers around the fabric, not actually unfastening it. In fact, Eli is clinging to the collar, keeping it closed.

"Hey…" I kneel before him to make myself eye level. "Let me help with those?"

With the slightest nod—one so subtle I can't be sure he truly gave me permission—Eli drops his hands, settling them on the tile on either side of him. On my knees, I bend forward and brush the back of my hand along his cheek. Even tight with pain, Eli's face holds the kind of gorgeous beauty photographers travel the world to seek out, the mist of water on his lashes making them look even longer and fuller than they are.

Eli's posture is rigid as a board, but he makes no move to stop me as I methodically release each button until a broad swath of

Eli's muscular chest is exposed before me. With a start, I realize this is the first time I've seen it bare—he'd kept his T-shirt on at the pool party, had even kept it on when we had sex.

Now, however, I can see the full expanse of lean, carved muscles, the defined line between his pectorals pointing to a chiseled six-pack that glistens in the shower's dampness. There's a bruise along his ribs, right over the area of his heart, and it's a grayish purple in coloration. Running my hands over his smooth chest, I feel the coiled power beneath Eli's taut skin vibrating through my own body. Despite everything, my sex clenches, my core heating in aching response.

Sliding my hands along Eli's clavicle, I pause with my thumbs hooked inside the fabric, Eli's shoulders shifting tightly beneath my touch. "Ready?" I whisper.

Eli nods.

I ease the shirt off him, sliding around back to peel the wet fabric from where it sticks to the wounds beneath. A mess of lash marks glistens back at me, the skin welted and split where cuts cross. But the fresh cuts aren't the frightening part—the scars beneath them are. A myriad of pale lines, some thin and angry as if made with a rope or electrical cord, others deeper and thicker, crisscross muscled flesh from the tops of the shoulders all the way down to where the skin disappears beneath Eli's elastic waistband. It's the kind of thing they show in lectures on child abuse and shows about Scottish Highlanders.

My heart quickens, nausea rising up my throat. Eli has been beaten for decades, hasn't he? The perfect all-powerful CEO of Mason Pharmaceuticals, the envy of men. The one who knows all the important events in his employees' lives but never lets them in on his own.

My eyes sting, and I bite my lip to keep my emotions in check. Taking the body wash and washcloth back off the shelf where I'd left them, I work the soap into a thick lather. Eli's head is down, his chin on his chest, so I start with his nape, letting him get used to the touch against healthy flesh before gently dabbing the cuts.

He holds so very still that I'd think he's lost feeling in his back if not for him curling his hands into fists, trembling at his sides. Bracing one of my palms against his rigid abdomen, I wash away the caked blood until the water running down the drain is no longer pink. Until I've surreptitiously wiped away the tears I couldn't keep in check, though he has kept his.

"How badly do you hurt?" I ask.

"I'll live. I always do," he says, soft enough that I can hardly hear him over the shower.

I sweep down his arms—other than one long thin cut along his forearm, the rest of the mess is mostly bruises and abrasions, the torn-up knuckles notwithstanding. Taking one of those hands in mine, I wait until Eli's slate-gray gaze meets mine.

"What the hell happened in Boston, Mason?"

He snorts without humor. "Just my birthday party."

"I didn't realize it was your birthday," I say on reflex, cringing at myself for picking on that particular aspect of the current situation. "And is that…" I wave toward his back, at a loss for words. For a trained psychologist, I'm an utter failure at keeping composure.

"It's not a satanic ritual, Red." Eli raises a brow, some of his usual spring back in his voice. "I got on the wrong side of my father." Eli sighs, taking the washcloth from my hand to scrape at his knuckles. "The worst part wasn't the lashing, though. It was that he caught me utterly off guard. I thought I had the upper hand on him for once, and, well, I didn't. You look like a wet rat, by the way."

"What?" I look down at myself. My thoroughly drenched ivory dress is now transparent, the outlines of my panties and bra as evident as the nipples poking up against the wet linen. My face heats, my hands rising to cover my chest.

Eli chuckles, catching my wrists gently. "A very attractive wet rat," he says, his voice growing stronger now that it's me—not himself—he's trying to bring back into balance. "Will it help if I'm more undressed than you are?"

The hint of a mischievous gleam in Eli's eye as he rises, undoes his belt buckle and steps out smoothly from his combined underwear and slacks is unmistakable. And, that quickly, I don't know what in the world to do with my eyes. Is it better if I acknowledge his muscled thighs and cock so large that I don't know how it ever fit inside me, or do I pretend *not* to see the big velvety elephant in the shower booth, even if it makes my mouth water?

Eli reaches for the shampoo and leisurely lathers his hair.

"Stinker." I glower at him, the heat spreading through my whole body—right until my gaze hits his now-bare ass and the lash scars that extend across it.

My eyes sting all over again, and I quickly duck under the spray. My parents never raised a hand to me. The mere thought of pain coming from the people who matter most to me in the world twists my gut. To think that I'm taking direction from one of them for the job. Wyrd. If Eli ever learned of my meeting with Madison—

"Dani."

I realize that it's not the first time Eli has spoken my name and turned toward me just as the man brushes my wet hair away from my face.

"Don't worry about the scars. I don't."

I shake my head. *If you didn't, you'd take your shirt off during sex.*

"Some days, there's pain," Eli clarifies. "Like yesterday. And it's unpleasant. But most days, there isn't. There are plenty of people who were much worse off than me growing up." Eli traces his thumb along my cheekbone, his scent filling my lungs. "Yes, my father likes things his way. And Madison, she has her reasons for disliking me. But all in all…I've always had food, clothes, and a roof. The best education. It's more than most people can hope for. Just because there was some darkness behind my gilded white picket fence is no reason to feel sorry for me."

"Who's feeling sorry?" I ask primly, knowing better than to challenge his hard-won control over himself just now. There's a great deal more pain inside Eli's soul than he's willing to admit, but I don't dare slice those wounds open now. Wrapping my arms around Eli, I pull him toward me. "I just think that the pain in the ass who made me ruin my dress owes me a vegetarian dinner."

Eli's embrace is tight and desperate, his breath tickling the top of my head for a few heartbeats as he presses me against him. Then he takes another full breath and separates us, his nonchalant mask back in place as he tosses a whole handful of water right into my face.

"When it comes to my pain-in-the-ass tendencies, you've not even scratched the surface," he assures me.

2 4

E LI

*E*li stared at Dani through the shower's mist, his heart pounding harder than in any battle. He couldn't fathom how he'd gotten here, smiling and thinking straight after a night of spiraling darkness. Couldn't fathom why the hell she was still here and not running for the hills.

His whole body ached, the stinging cuts on his back competing with a deeper ache of cracked ribs and darkening bruises. Yet the pain was distant, a backdrop to the much more immediate longing for Dani's touch. And for once, he didn't mean her lush mouth around his cock—not that he'd mind that either—but just the touch of her fingertips against his cheek.

His body tightened at the closeness of her mouth, the moist heat of the shower that wrapped them together. A small dip of his head and he'd be able to taste her, the way he'd been tasting her in his memories. But he owed her too much to try that. Fuck. He'd already scared her off once—already nearly cost her her job and her license. He wouldn't risk it again.

"Vegetarian dinner?" he repeated Dani's request, hooking on

to the words to draw himself back into the now. "What am I, a squirrel?"

She lifted her chin, clearly oblivious to how irresistible she looked with that now-sheer dress clinging to her skin. "I don't know. But if my arithmetic is correct, you flew a plane back from Boston last night in the kind of emotional state where you shouldn't have been trusted with a ballpoint pen and shoelaces. So, squirrel...potato... You know."

Eli glowered at her, though beneath the easy tone, he knew she was right. Hell, in all objectivity, he deserved the lashes on his back just for getting into that cockpit. "I'll get us some clothes," he muttered. "And white broccoli pizza."

"With peppers and mushrooms and garlic," said Dani. "Oh, and fresh tomatoes too. The cherry kind."

"And extra cheese," Eli shot back before she made even pizza healthy, and quickly stepped out of the shower before Dani could offer a return volley.

Drying off, then pulling on a pair of sweatpants, Eli brought a pair of his shorts and a tee for Dani to dress in after the shower. If it were any other woman, he'd have steered the evening toward nudity instead, but this was different. Dani was different.

Eli yearned for her to stay as long as possible. He couldn't explain it either, other than not wanting to be alone. Deep down, he knew she hadn't come over to his house for more than a few minutes—she certainly hadn't come to take care of him—but he didn't want to think about that. He didn't want to think about anything that had transpired in Boston. Fortunately, he was already on his way to blotting the past twenty-four hours from memory.

"Hey, Mason." Walking out of the guest bedroom, Dani swam in Eli's clothing as she dried her hair with a fluffy white towel. Damn. He missed her living here. Missed coming back from morning training to find her at the breakfast bar complaining about his protein shakes. Dani ran her fingers through her hair, untangling the wet strands. "I found some Neosporin, but with those cuts from the bar, don't you need a tetanus shot or something?"

"Possibly," Eli hedged.

"Assuming that you aren't going to a hospital, do you want to call one of your Tridents?" she frowned. "Wait, is that the kind of thing you guys have on hand?"

"Kyan has everything on hand." Eli stretched and immediately regretted it. He was bare to the waist, the first time he'd been so when not alone for as long as he could remember. It was oddly liberating. "But we aren't calling him."

Dani motioned Eli to a chair, which he obediently straddled to let her apply the triple antibiotic to the cuts. "Why not?"

Eli looked at her over his shoulder. "Because I don't like needles."

"I'm serious."

"So am I," said Eli.

"But…" Dani sputtered, her hand pausing on the top of his shoulder. She was quite adorable when flustered. "But you're a Navy SEAL."

"I am," Eli agreed companionably.

"What about the self-inflicted torment, and SERE training, and general misery you all embrace?"

"What about it?"

"I mean, all that's worse than a needle prick." Dani ran her hand along the tight muscles of Eli's back, her soft fingertips finding a path across healthy flesh. Her voice lowered, sucking the humor from the conversation. "So is all this."

Eli rose off the chair, turning to face Dani. With his legs braced far apart, it felt like he was straddling her even though their bodies didn't touch. "I didn't say I was afraid of pain, Red," he said, savoring the way her scent washed over him. Despite sharing his shower, she still smelled of lavender. She always did. He didn't even know how she managed it. Without her bra,

Dani's full breasts fell naturally beneath Eli's shirt, her nipples as bunched and hard as his cock was getting. A corner of his mouth twitched toward a hint of a smile. "I said I was afraid of that particular type. It's not all that strange. I happen to know someone who dislikes the sound of clicking pens."

Dani's cheeks darkened, and Eli put his arms around her to keep the woman from stepping away. Because he wanted her next to him. And because he wanted her safe—both to be *and* to feel safe. Protected. "I just mean to say that maybe it's all right if we know something about each other."

Dani swallowed, the creamy skin along her neck moving smoothly. "Yes," she whispered into the mere inches of air between their lips. "Maybe it is."

Ding dong dong

Eli closed his eyes as the doorbell chose that moment to echo through the living room, the sound repeating itself with growing insistence.

Ding dong dong.

With a sigh, he walked over to the intercom on the wall, pressing the button to allow the most ill-timed pizza delivery person in the world through the gate.

Fifteen minutes later, Eli broke his own rule of habit and settled right there in the living room with pizza spread open on the coffee table beside the sectional. Having won the coin toss, Dani had pulled up *Battlestar Galactica* on Netflix, the opening credits of which already rolled through the sound system. Calm and easy and downright homey—the opposite of dinner at the Masons' mansion in Boston.

Eli opened a beer for himself and a hard cider for Dani before sliding a slice of pizza onto his plate, the mozzarella stretching deliciously from the main pie. He'd not eaten since last night, Eli realized, and his mouth watered in anticipation that made even the vegetables look scrumptious.

Once he bit into the slice, however, the food turned to ash

in his mouth. Bloody hell. Forcing himself to chew and swallow, Eli choked down the slice anyway, chasing it down with a can of beer while unwanted images played in his mind on a nauseating loop. On screen, spaceships fired their thrusters, launching themselves into the darkness. Though Eli's eyes had stayed on the screen, he realized he had no idea where they were rushing off to or why they bothered. He'd taken in none of the show.

"Hey, you." Dani's voice brushed Eli's consciousness, bringing him back to the now as she ran her fingers through his hair. Still wet from the shower, Eli's curls had managed to drip down onto her thigh, the droplets pearly against her skin. "Have you heard of towels?"

Eli shook his head like a dog, sending more water over Dani, who let out a squeal. Having longer-than-regulation hair was one of the few things Eli savored about civilian life, but he'd never gotten into the habit of drying it off. He ended with his head resting against Dani's shoulder and soaking her shirt.

Just as Eli was bringing himself to pull away, Dani's fingers drifted through his hair, massaging his scalp. It felt good. Soothing. The bar fight had done its job of sanding the edges off the Boston trip, but the memories were still there. Lying in wait.

Eli's eyes drifted from the television to the decorative finery that surrounded him. He'd chosen precisely none of it. Not one piece. This place was a shrine to Madison, to keep up the appearance that his family was successful and normal and happy. People others could look up to. What a load of bollocks.

"I hate this house," he muttered, barely cognizant of speaking out loud. "It's such a bloody farce."

Dani's fingers continued their movement. "What do you mean?"

"It's not mine, not really. Madison commissioned it to be built to her exact specifications from the ground up, including all the furnishings and decorative touches. I had no say in the matter.

And I'm not allowed to change it even though I'm the one who lives here."

"I don't understand."

Eli snorted. "Mason Enterprises is a large brand, and my family is at the center of it. As CEO, my house is an ambassadorial residence of sorts, so it has to match. It's sort of like running an Apple store—you can't just decide that your location will be done up in Victorian-era decor instead of clean white. Except in our case, it's family image and reputation. We're supposed to be this loving, upstanding, larger-than-life, perfect family. Pillars of our communities. The embodiment of the Mason values and image. Every public appearance is calibrated to reinforce that. Like yesterday."

He went silent, not certain why he'd said as much as he did. Maybe it was simply that he couldn't contain it anymore.

"Your birthday party?"

Eli made a noise in the back of his throat. "My twin sister Ella's memorial. I killed her twenty-nine years ago yesterday."

Dani jerked. "Wait, what?" Her hands stilled, but Eli could still feel her moving. Shaking her head. "Wait, didn't *you* just turn twenty-nine? Unless you were some kind of herculean baby—"

"In the womb. I took more than my fair share of nutrients. Didn't leave enough for her to survive."

Dani drew a breath, and he immediately regretted saying anything. He knew better and couldn't for the life of him fathom what had made him speak now.

"That, Eli, is total bullshit," Dani said, her tone fierce. "It is literally impossible that you killed your twin. You had no control whatsoever. I know you know that."

He did. He wasn't suffering from lunacy. Cerebrally, he knew Madison's grief had warped her common sense on this one, and the condemning words he'd grown up hearing over and over were neither true nor rational—even if they were *technically* accurate. But when it came to parents, rationality didn't always help. Maybe it was the years of growing up with the proverbial scarlet letter stitched on him. Or maybe it was something else. "Growing up, I kept thinking how if Madison had so much love inside her, how unfair it was that Ella should get all of it. But then that just sounded like me trying to take more for myself."

"What about now?" Dani sat up, her cool hand on Eli's cheeks as her brilliant eyes met his. Her tone was soft, but there was steel behind it too. Like she was ready to support him, but would also give no quarter. "You aren't a child anymore. The only way those lashes happened was with your cooperation. Why?"

Eli laughed without humor. "I was of the same mind. But my father sharply reminded me that there's more power in information than in muscle." Outlining the basic ultimatum, Eli reached for another slice of pizza. It tasted better now. Like something Dani might make instead of ash. "If I had to do it over again, I'd still have made the same choice. Well, I'd hide my bloody accounts better, but you know what I mean."

For a long heartbeat, Dani just studied him. Then she rose onto her knees and brushed her lips over his, pressing her mouth gently on the opposite side from Eli's split lip.

"What was that for?" Eli asked.

"For being a good man."

Eli stared back at her, his chest tightening. That… That was not what he'd expected to hear from a woman who'd walked in this morning to find him a disheveled mess. From the one who'd spent the past weeks digging up every bit of psychological dirt she could. Bloody hell.

Eli's mind spun, the heat from Dani's body and eyes utterly intoxicating. Tomorrow, tomorrow, Eli was sure he'd awake with a hangover and dull dread as he remembered everything he'd just told her. More than he'd shared even with the Tridents. The men were loyal to a fault, and Eli knew they had the means to retaliate against Eli's parents, which he didn't want. But today…today the only thing that mattered was that he'd laid his soul bare at her feet and she'd found it worthwhile. Found *him* worthwhile.

Catching the back of Dani's head before she could pull away more than a few inches, Eli pressed his mouth over hers.

Dani's lips parted in invitation, her mouth opening generously to him. Heat and need rushed through his core as he enveloped the woman in his arms, taking the inside of her mouth with deep claiming strokes that felt too intensely desperate to be real.

25

DANI

$\mathcal{M}$y mouth opens to Eli's, the feel of him in my mouth spreading warmth through my entire core before my brain even registers what we are doing. And by then, I can't bring myself to care, not with every one of my nerves firing with sensation that somehow rushes right to my sex.

Eli's fingers thread through my hair, the sureness of his hold making my breath hitch with excitement. My pulse quickens, blood rushing faster through my veins. Wyrd. I don't know how the man does it, how he manages to consume my mouth and my body the way no one ever has.

Eli's hands slip from my hair and go downward, his fingers skimming my beaded nipples over the cotton of his own shirt. I gasp into his mouth as his skilled fingers tease the peaks until they're throbbing, aching for more of his touch.

My hands rise, longing to grip his hard muscle—stopping just in time, a millimeter away from his chest. A rush of panic washes through me, the fear of hurting him, of ruining *this*, of giving so much less than he deserves.

Me being rooted to the spot apparently captures Eli's

attention. Breaking the kiss, he pulls back, his eyes alight as he studies me. Alight and damn aroused, as if catching sight of me frozen in place, my hands stationed over his torso like a perp being arrested, is the sexiest thing he's ever seen.

"Bloody hell, Red, you're going to be the end of me," he whispers, his lips parted slightly as his breath quickens. A wicked spark flashing in his eyes, he seizes one of my hands and places it right over the hard bulge pushing against his sweatpants.

Stroking the sizable length and girth of him, I savor the memory of all that inside me—which even now is intimidating and exciting in equal parts. I stroke him again, dipping inside his sweats to savor that velvety cock against my fingers, to imagine what it would feel like filling my mouth.

Eli groans, his gorgeous face morphing to guarded bliss as he tilts his head back, his good eye closing. "You're amazing, Red," he whispers, the praise sending as much gratifying pleasure through me as the purr that escapes his lips.

Unable to resist Eli's exposed neck, I lean toward it to find a patch of flawless skin and suckle there, Eli's pulse tickling my lips in a deliciously rapid *tap tap tap*. With one hand on Eli's cock and my mouth on his neck, I'm leaning over him now, his warmth and grassy scent wrapping around me in contrast to the cool leather beneath my shins. Somewhere outside a stray woodpecker chooses this moment to knock against the tree, the sound a perfect harmony to my own heart.

"You're delicious," I mumble without thinking.

"Is that right?" Eli's palms plunge under my shirt and along my back, his hands creating sizzling paths up and down the tiny bumps of my spine.

"It is." I nip his pulse point before shifting my teeth to his Adam's apple. Down his throat. To his right nipple.

"You're a little minx, Red," Eli says, his thighs tight, his cock pulsing helplessly under my stroking hand.

"When the occasion calls for it." I switch to the other nipple, only to jump as Eli hisses slightly. I lift my face up to study his, the mischievous glint in his gaze battling the tightness of lingering pain, and stop, reality hitting me square in the face. What the hell am I doing? What the hell are *we* doing?

Eli's hands drop to my cheeks, his gaze searching mine intently despite the swelling around his left eye. "Talk to me," he says quietly. "Am I hurting you?"

"Hurting *me*?" I put my hand on his wrists. "Mason—Eli— it's not me being hurt I'm worried about."

"I can literally lift you off me with one hand, Red. If any part of me needs guarding, I'll adjust for it." From another man, the words might sound arrogant, but Eli's matter-of-fact conclusion is somehow comforting instead. He shifts his body, leaning closer to me, his eyes glowing with reined-in desire. "But the last time we danced to this tune, you couldn't leave the house fast enough."

My breath hitches, that morning rushing back to me. The jeopardy I'd put my work in. The conversation he'd overheard. The words he'd said. I try to avert my gaze, but Eli's hands on my face won't let me escape. As if there's nothing at all more important to him than to know what I'll say next.

Except I don't know it myself. My report is done. But it isn't terribly professional to sleep with an evaluee at this point either.

Eli blows out a long breath. "We've already had sex. No amount of abstinence now will undo that naughtiness." Despite the tension, his British accent makes the last word sound delicious, his bruised eye as intent on my lips as every other part of his being. "As to where we go now, the choice is yours. Not to rush you, but please make it before my balls explode."

I stare at him, my channel clenching over my mind's turmoil, his readiness to withdraw both comforting and tantalizing. A breath later, my body sidelines my thoughts, making the decision for me. Reaching for the elastic waist of Eli's sweatpants, I tug them downward, releasing him into the open.

Wyrd take me, he's large. Long and flushed, with velvety skin strung tight with hardness along the head, Eli's cock makes my mouth water. I feel myself aching low in my pelvis and flush at the thought of how damp and slick I'm making the shorts he loaned me. Glancing up, I latch on to Eli's gaze and tilt forward decidedly to lick off the tiny bead of white liquid at his tip.

"Bloody fucking hell," Eli grinds out, his voice strained as his hips jerk toward me, his nails digging into the expensive sectional.

After our last time together, the sight of this Eli, so desperately on the edge of control, is deviously delicious. Bracing my palms on Eli's biceps, I reach up to trace my tongue slightly down his centerline, over his sternum, and work my way across the ridges of each formed abdominal until I'm right back at his waistline, the V of his muscles pointing to a pulsing cock.

Giving him no warning, I slip off the couch and drop my mouth over him, taking him in as far as I can. I don't quite manage to deep throat him—his vastness means I literally can't—but I do my best. I vacillate between sucking on his head and dragging the flat of my tongue along the underside of him from root to tip. Upping the ante, on my next suck, I bring my hand to his balls, cupping them gently but making sure he feels me.

"Oh, fuck. Fuck, fuck, *fuck!*" Eli growls, throwing his head back as his voice breaks. "You have to stop, or I'm going to come."

Excitement rushes through me at the thought. The twin promises of tasting Eli and watching this Navy SEAL and CEO come undone beneath my mouth is more than my body can resist. Straining and bucking beneath me, Eli jerks a final time inside my mouth before his wonderful warmth fills my throat.

"Dani!" The sound of my name on Eli's lips as he finds release echoes through the whole house, his powerful body shuddering again and again.

Sitting back on my heels, I grin up at him like a Cheshire cat and admire the view.

Which is when Eli pounces.

26

ELI

*E*li's hands wrapped around Dani's tight ass, her strong, luscious cheeks made even more taut by how she crouched. Her surprised shriek as he hoisted her onto his hips was a bloody wonderful sound, as arousing as the endorphins coursing through him, masking his pain to a distant, irrelevant sound.

Pain was easy. Anyone who went through SEAL training learned to befriend it, to let it remind you that you were still alive and fighting. Eli could take blows that came from hand-to-hand combat, march on feet fractured from strain, swim despite lungs knifed with lack of air. But there were a few sensations he couldn't bear. He didn't like needles. And even now, at twenty-nine, the sting of a whipping still sent him tumbling into a thorn-filled dark pit from which he never climbed out with his soul intact.

Advil didn't help. Alcohol didn't help. Not even the bar fight, the bruised ribs and black eye that he'd hoped would overpower the shouting of his back, helped.

But Dani? *Bloody hell.* The woman was salvation and

temptation all mixed together in a sinful package that turned Eli's world on its head. And damn it, if he was going for the kind of crazy spinning high that only endorphin overload could produce, he was taking the little minx with him.

"You're going to pay for that mouth," Eli murmured into Dani's ear, savoring the way his threat made her shudder even as she gripped him tighter. Trusting him.

Lowering Dani's back onto the leather sectional, Eli pulled his sweatpants all the way off before unhooking Dani's legs from around his waist and sliding her shorts off as well. Dani's breath caught as cool air brushed her sex, her face blushing beautifully at Eli's pushing her legs wide apart to expose her pinkness. With the oversized shirt having ridden up, Dani's nipples now hardened into dark tempting peaks.

Eli brushed his hands down Dani's supple skin, tracing his fingers over her breasts, her nipples, her hips, his gaze drinking in her face. Her wide pupils. The quickening speed of her breathing as he stroked his fingers firmly along her slit, back and forth, back and forth, until she clenched with need. Stopping with his finger directly over Dani's clit—and his own cock already hard and pulsing—Eli tapped the delicate bud lightly.

Dani gasped, wriggling against his hold, her sex seeking the pressure of the fingers he now held still.

"Mmm. Vengeance." Eli smiled.

Dani whimpered.

Sliding his fingers through her slick, slick folds, Eli circled her opening, feeling it clench with desire, before sliding his finger inside her. One. Two. Three. Dani's hips arched toward him, her channel clenching around the digits. Hell take him, before meeting Dani, Eli would have sworn up and down he preferred more experienced partners, but nothing compared to the exciting possibility of watching this woman discover just how damn sexy she was. How utterly good she deserved to feel.

With his free hand, Eli brushed against her other opening,

drinking in the savory mix of Dani's sudden anxiety and the fierce embarrassed arousal suddenly flushing her cheeks. More arousal slicked around the fingers he held inside her. Yes, he'd have to explore anal with this woman one day. Teach her to embrace her own body's wondrous responses.

"You wouldn't," Dani breathed.

Eli stroked a lubricated finger around the tight muscles of her opening before pulling back. "Oh, I would. But since you're so opinionated, I can be flexible," he said, withdrawing his hands. "Touch yourself for me."

She looked startled, her eyes popping wide. "What?"

Taking one of Dani's hands, Eli placed it on her breast. "Touch yourself," he repeated. "Show me what you like."

Breath hitching, Dani rolled the nipple between her thumb and forefinger, the areola darkening.

"You're doing beautifully, Red," Eli told her with sincere admiration.

"I've never done this," she whispered.

"You've never pleasured yourself?"

"Never in front of someone."

"Then let me help." Eli closed the distance and sucked the breast she wasn't kneading into his mouth, flicking it with his tongue. She tasted clean and fresh, the smell of lavender as tantalizing as ever.

Taking her free hand, Eli moved it between Dani's legs. "Here next," he whispered. "Go on, then. Show me."

Shutting her eyes, Dani stroked herself tentatively, her motions growing surer and more confident when Eli added his own fingers to hers. Slowly, steadily, the pair of them increased the vigor of strokes until Eli could hear the wet noises coming from her drenched folds.

Growling in satisfaction, Eli pressed his lips to hers, sucking her tongue into his mouth just as she started to moan in earnest against the rhythmic motions.

As Dani's moans grew to elongated and needy whimpers, Eli brought his lips to her ear. "You're the most stunning woman I've ever seen, Dani. Outside and in. Especially when you come."

That did it. Her frame seizing, she came, crying out as she did.

Giving her a moment to regain her breath, Eli caressed her cheek before opening a hidden compartment in the armrest of the sectional, pulling out a condom.

Dani gasped lightly at the sound of the tearing foil, her hips rising to meet the throbbing head of his cock as he positioned himself at her entrance. Hoisting Dani's legs onto his shoulders, Eli inserted himself slowly inside her, letting her tight, hot channel adjust to him before moving on. Moving faster.

Thrust. Thrust. Thrust. The quickening plunges sent shocks of need through Eli's core, the wet slaps echoing through him. *Thrust. Thrust. Thrust.* Reaching down, Eli stroked Dani's clit again, his shoulders tightening to fend off his need. How long had it been since he'd made love to a woman face-to-face? Hell. He wasn't sure he'd ever *made love* to any woman before. Not like this.

Moving together, they undulated as one, her body engulfing him in flames that rose higher and higher with each stroke. He felt her trembling, then shaking, then pulsating as she came again, this time calling out his name.

"*Eli!*"

The raspy sound toppled him over the edge, his own release shooting so powerfully from him that pain and pleasure mixed together into a molten heat that shook his entire core.

It took several breaths for them to recover, and another several minutes before Eli could bring himself to pull away from where he lay sprawled over Dani, their limbs tangled together.

"Hey there," he said, rising on one elbow to look down at her. She made an exquisite picture, cinnamon hair spread out and glowing in the golden light of the lamps.

Dani bit her lip. "Hi."

Eli's throat tightened, the words hovering on the tip of his tongue more frightening than a firefight. "Come to bed with me," he whispered, not letting himself back away.

Dani's brows pulled together. "Didn't we just—"

"I mean sleep," Eli clarified, his heart pounding. "Stay the night. With me. In my bed."

For a moment, he was sure Dani would laugh and walk away. Had braced himself for it. But she threaded her fingers through his hair instead and leaned forward to brush a kiss over his cheek. "Only if you have an extra toothbrush somewhere."

An hour later, Dani slid in beside him between the crisp chocolate sheets, Eli snaking his arms around her back. With her pert breasts against his chest, her smooth legs tangled with his, their bodies fit together like puzzle pieces—his cock naturally falling into place at her crotch. Said cock rose, out of either instinct or habit, but Eli didn't thrust it against her. For the first time in his life, what he wanted most was to hold a woman against him all night long.

27

BROCK

*B*rock Talbot glared at the minicam feed he'd set up outside his Marriott hotel room and seethed at the empty hallway. He'd been so careful, followed the bitch's movements so closely, but here he was waiting for her, and she hadn't shown up. After days of being as reliable as clockwork, returning to her room by six thirty every evening, she went and fucked up the schedule.

Danielle Nelson had fucked up a great many things. Sashaying into his office with those perky breasts and full lips, she'd done everything to make her desires clear. Brock couldn't blame her for that. He had all the things women wanted. Money. Good looks. Expensive cars, boats, and houses. He even had a helicopter, for fuck's sake. He would rain down diamond trinkets without a dent to his bank account.

That women had been falling at his feet all his life was a simple matter of evolutionary advantage. Women were hardwired to want protectors and providers, to admire strength and reject weakness. Since the beginning of time, the women who'd been able to recognize such traits in men survived to bear offspring; the ones who didn't died from attacks, starvation, or both. The modern world was no different.

Men—real men—were hardwired too. They grew their strength, they took instead of asking, they looked at a woman and instinctively knew whether she was the right one to carry their lineage. And Brock Alford Talbot III was a real man. He came from old money. His great-great grandfather had been an oil tycoon, and each male Talbot in the line had then branched out to become successful one by one in various other ventures. Brock's game was insurance, and he was goddamn good at it. Why? Because he never fucking took no for an answer. He played hardball in every negotiation and didn't stop until he got exactly what he wanted. The deal he wanted. The numbers he wanted. The employees he wanted.

The woman he wanted. No, the woman he deserved. Earned.

Four months ago, Danielle Nelson had walked into his office and handed him an order from the board of directors that Talbot was to…*talk*…to her. Intimately. So he did. For hours, for days on end, he'd discussed his thoughts and his work, giving freely of himself to the pretty little psychologist. He'd fed her expensive dinners, had taken her on personal tours of the office. He'd even flown her about on that helicopter, showing the vastness of his empire. Women needed to know who they were dealing with. It was only fair.

And after all that, all that he'd done for her on credit, Danielle Nelson decided it wasn't enough for her. The evening it happened was never far from his thoughts, Danielle's audacity forever emblazoned in his brain.

"I came to say my goodbyes, Mr. Talbot," Nelson said, her hands fingering a white pencil skirt. She'd worn a high-necked pink blouse, the color clearly designed to draw Brock's attention to what other pink parts the woman possessed. "The board of directors notified me this afternoon that they've accepted my report, so there's no need for me to impose on your time any longer."

"Very nice," he complimented her, something he did rarely and hoped she appreciated. Looking her up and down, Brock let his eyes linger on the woman's hips and breasts. Wide and full. Good for bearing healthy children. "You do good work, sweetheart."

"As I've said previously, I prefer Dani or Ms. Nelson."

He smirked at her. "You also said that our business together was concluded," he countered. Surely a woman as smart as Danielle had understood the rules of the game. She was the stripper inside the birthday cake, and eventually, it would be time to come out. Everything that she'd done, that he'd allowed her to do, was at his pleasure. She'd no more right to call the shots, to decide whether their business was concluded or not, than Talbot's secretary did. "You seem uncomfortable, sweetheart. Come sit on my lap, and we can make it better."

"I'm leaving now, Mr. Talbot. I don't wish to interact with you again." Twisting on that little heel of hers, the woman actually stomped for the exit.

It took Talbot a full heartbeat to realize that the flirt was baiting him. That she wanted to see Talbot in action, a show of physical strength to complement the financial. So he'd obliged. He did what the bitch was asking for.

Standing, Talbot pushed the rolling chair into her path, using her moment of hesitation to grab her by the hair. Seizing her breast, he hissed in her ear, "When I say come do something, sweetheart, that means I expect it. Now."

Talbot pushed his chair away from the monitor and paced across the room, picking up and examining the photographs he'd been collecting. They were printed on paper the old-school way. Some he'd even developed himself, though what he got off the drone was annoyingly digital. Digital was another word for glitchy—like the trojan malware he'd sent to tap into Nelson's laptop camera and GPS , which worked one of every three times at best. Utterly unreliable—just like the woman herself.

He appreciated ferocity as much as anyone. But there was a limit. And the bitch had crossed it when she sank her fucking teeth into his hand so hard, he needed stitches. He even got rabies shots, just in case. Then, adding insult to injury, she went and fucked up the report she claimed to have submitted. That was the only explanation for the "leave of absence" the board had insisted he take to "manage his stress."

Leave of absence, his ass. Danielle Nelson had a reckoning coming. No one toyed with Brock Alford Talbot III and got away with it. Certainly not some trollop with a made-up profession.

28

DANI

I wake bit by bit, registering the luxurious mattress and million-thread-count sheets beneath me as I inhale Eli's fresh-grass scent. The sensation of being not alone in the bed is disorienting at first, then morphs into calm pleasure as I blink my way to full wakefulness to catch sight of a mass of reddish-brown hair pressed into the pillow beside my head.

Eli Mason. *Asleep.*

It occurs to me that in all the time I lived with Eli, he has always been the first to rise. Always. No matter how early I set my alarm. Heck, he usually not just woke up earlier, he managed to get a solid workout in before I found the coffee. Yet, here I am, holding the advantage.

Eli lies on his belly, the blankets kicked away, his shoulders rising and falling with deep even breaths. In the dappled sunrays sneaking in through his curtained windows, his muscled body is sculpted with lights and shadows that make even the savage stripes across his back look beautiful. When I run my hand over his mussed hair, Eli presses into me like a cat—all without waking.

"A kitty cat, you're not," I tell him quietly. "Maybe a panther. Or a tiger. Probably a tiger, given that set of stripes." My fingers move to his back, gently caressing the rock-hard muscles. Whatever else, I'm certain I've never met anyone as complicated as Eli Mason before now. Wyrd. Everything about this man is some kind of cosmic contradiction, isn't it?

Leaving the overgrown feline to sleep in the sun, I slip out of bed and plod toward the door in the same shirt I slept in—one of Eli's tees that hangs halfway down my thigh.

"There are chocolate chips if you're in a cooking mood," Eli mutters.

"And here I thought you were still asleep."

"I am."

I snort softly, turning back toward him. "And what exactly do you expect me to do with chocolate chips?"

"You'll figure something out." Grabbing the edge of the blanket, Eli pulls it over his head to block out both further discussion and the sunlight.

My noble intentions of a healthy breakfast fall apart when I explore Eli's kitchen a few minutes later, realizing that his food inventory had reverted to protein shakes and packaged meals while I was gone. Fortunately, eggs and flour are still in place. Combining the scant ingredients with the promised chocolate chips, I end up with decent pancakes which finish sizzling just as Eli appears in the kitchen with impeccable timing.

"Are those what I hope they are?" Eli stretches in the doorway, his gaze on the filling plate. Dressed in flannel pants, he's left off socks and his T-shirt—a sign of trust that warms me despite the cringeworthy mess of cuts and bruises. And it's not just the lash marks that draw attention—the black eye he managed to get in the fight he himself picked looks significantly worse than it did last night.

"You look like Rocky Balboa after he went a few rounds with Clubber Lang," I inform him, sliding over the plate. "Whatever you pay your employees to pretend not to notice, you should double it."

Eli curses.

"Sorry," I backpedal quickly. Now that I know more about Eli than I thought possible, I'm even less sure of what to say. "Poorly chosen joke. You look…well, your shirt will cover the back scars, and it's not like you haven't shown up at Mason Pharmaceuticals with a shiner and skinned knuckles before."

"It's not that." Taking a barstool, Eli frowns at his hand before separating two pancakes from the serving platter and pulling the entire remaining heap toward himself. "The Mason Pharmaceuticals staff, I'm not worried about. The domestic violence fundraiser I'm supposed to speak at tonight is a slightly more delicate matter."

"Oh." I bite my lip.

"Right."

Absurd laughter bubbles inside me, and I gulp a mouthful of coffee to keep the chuckle to myself, though Eli's morbid gaze tells me he sees through the act.

"You may laugh now"—Eli points a pancake-filled fork at me —"but karma will come and bite your arse, Red."

I hold up my hands. "All right. On a scale of one to ten, how flexible are you willing to be to get that looking better?"

"Nine point two five." Eli cocks his brow suspiciously. "Why?"

Here goes nothing. Going to the purse I left on his sectional, I retrieve my phone and call my dad on FaceTime. Tom Nelson might hate everything Eli stands for, but he's never turned a patient away in his life, and I'm sure he won't start this morning. I just hope he keeps the more caustic thoughts to himself.

"Dani, sweetheart, so good to see you." My father's smiling face fills the phone screen, the slight rasp in his voice reminding me of home. He frowns. "You have that look. Is everything all right? How can I help?"

I shake my head with a smile. I don't know how my dad does

it, but he always knows when something is on my mind. I still don't know how I managed to keep the rape in high school from him, except that sometimes some things are too hard to admit. I clear my throat. "My friend has an…inconvenient black eye that needs to look better in about twelve hours. Any ideas?"

My dad cocks a brow. "And would your friend be Eli Mason?"

"Does it matter who it is, Daddy? Is there anything that can be done?"

My father opens his palms. "It would help if I could see the problem. Unless, of course, someone of Mr. Mason's stature would not condescend to speak to a mere apothecary directly," he continues, my stomach sinking with every word. "With a whole pharmaceutical industry at his fingertips—"

"I'm right here, sir." Stepping into the camera shot beside me, Eli nods respectfully to my father. I notice he's obtained a T-shirt somewhere. "If there's anything in your expertise that might help, I'd be grateful."

My father blinks a couple of times, plainly regaining his balance while Eli waits patiently. When Dad speaks however, his tone takes on a blissfully professional note. From the tightness around his eyes I see that he's still not thrilled about helping anyone running Mason Pharmaceuticals, but the clinician in him is winning over, as I knew it would. "All right, young man. Let's take a look. Move the camera around so I can see."

Eli follows the instructions with unquestioning obedience, including unflinchingly informing my father that he earned the shiner courtesy of a fight. Just when I'm starting to wonder whether I've wasted everyone's time and patience for the morning, my dad taps the table in a telltale sign that he's come to some sort of conclusion. I pull the phone back toward me.

"Any ideas?" I ask hopefully.

"Only time will get rid of it completely, but we can certainly speed up the process. The first part is easy—steep and chill two bags of tea to use as a compress. The cold and caffeine will help reduce some of the inflammation."

"And the second part?"

"Leeches."

"What?" I rub the heel of my hand over my nose. "Daddy, please. Can we joke another time?"

"It's not a joke," Eli—*Eli*—says behind me, his voice heavy with resignation. "It's accurate. Just not what I wanted to hear."

My dad's brows pull together. "I didn't realize Mason Pharmaceuticals invested in alternative medicine education," he says into the camera, trying to get a look over my shoulder at where Eli is sitting on the couch, his corded forearms braced on his thighs.

"We don't." He glares at the camera. "The US military's medical corps, on the other hand, is rather keen on people surviving even out of Amazon Prime's delivery area. I'll choose antibiotics over garlic any day of the week, but running into a pharmacy isn't an option in some places."

A corner of my father's mouth actually twitches toward a smile at Eli's sulky tone. It's hard for him to dislike someone who appreciates his craft, and Eli's words make up for in respect what they lack in enthusiasm. "So what's the problem, then?" he asks.

"Leeches," Eli answers.

"You dislike slimy things?" Dad asks.

"I dislike things sticking sharp little teeth into my bruises," Eli replies with a shudder.

I see Dad get his clinician face on again as he tells me to give Eli the phone. Handing over the device, I hear my father's voice explaining the process and decide to give Eli his privacy while I check my email—the message from Madison Mason promptly dropping my mood.

Carrying my laptop over to my old bedroom, I close and lock the door before pulling a jacket over Eli's T-shirt, donning headphones and opening the video conference line, half hoping that the woman won't answer. But she does. All perfect hair and clothes and smiles.

"Mrs. Mason." I smile politely. Compartmentalizing information about clients is a skill I've learned over the years, but after last night, it still takes every ounce of willpower to maintain my professionalism.

"It's just Madison." She returns my smile warmly. "Thank you for making the time to speak with me."

We both know I'd be an idiot to not make time to speak with my client, but the overture is calculated to make me think well of her. Just like the invitation to use her first name. If Eli does what he can to build walls, Madison works just as hard at creating the illusion of connectedness. An illusion I fell for right along with the rest of the world. "What can I do for you?" I ask.

"I wanted to follow up on your progress. I see the preliminary notes in the portal, of course, but there's nothing like a human touch to put things into context."

"Actually, my draft report is—"

"I see that even in your short time with Elijah, you've already confirmed some of the board's most pressing concerns about him," Madison continued as if I hadn't spoken.

My brow twitches. "I wouldn't say that, no. Perhaps—"

"Well, I see here you note at least one incident of bullying behavior that you've observed personally." Madison interrupts me again, setting us back on her path. The screen splits, a copy of my raw notes flashing to life. "If I'm reading this correctly, September ninth, the Mason Pharmaceuticals CEO ordered a young intern into his office and remorselessly reduced her to tears?"

"Mrs. Mason—Madison—like you said, these are raw notes. While your statement is technically correct, it lacks context. In this case, Mr. Mason was attempting to correct inappropriate behavior."

Madison's smile is ice-cold. "Undoubtedly. However, our

company policy instructs such corrections to be administered through counselling, performance appraisals, and written performance improvement plans provided both to the employee and to the human resources department. Company policy additionally instructs managers to provide training and remedial support to underperforming employees. Tell me, did you observe additional training or remediation be extended to this individual?"

"Not to my knowledge, no," I acknowledge. "But again, to be fair to the context, I believe those options had been exhausted previously."

"Strange." Madison frowns. "There's no documentation in the intern's personal file to this effect."

Eli and his damn paperwork. You'd think a man who hangs photos with a ruler could be bothered to keep his files in any kind of reasonable order. Then again, who am I kidding? Eli deals with reality, not paper.

"Perhaps that was an isolated incident," Madison continues on the screen. "Have you personally witnessed similar behavior during your time at Mason Pharmaceuticals? Directed against you, perhaps?"

An uncomfortable shiver runs down my spine. "I'm not sure I understand the question."

Madison purses her lips. "I'm asking about your personal firsthand experience, Ms. Nelson. Was Elijah, in his capacity as the CEO of Mason Pharmaceuticals, ever verbally abusive toward you?"

"No."

"So he didn't order you into his office on September seventeenth and proceed with a tirade that didn't end until you yourself, a trained professional cognitive psychologist, were reduced to tears?"

My stomach tightens. I hadn't documented that incident in my notes, and I'm sure as hell Eli didn't call his mother to discuss it. Yet Madison knew. Either she has her people embedded in the CEO's suite or…or she has Zana. A spoiled, vindictive, upset-over-being-fired Zana.

Madison turns a page over in the manila folder on the desk. "And later that day," she continues, "did Mr. Mason not prevent you from getting into a vehicle you hired, despite your protests, forcing you instead to get into *his* personal car?"

Wyrd. I walked into a cobra's den, and now I don't even know what to say. I swallow. Choose my words. Madison beats me to it.

"As I said, Ms. Nelson, I appreciate your sharing your preliminary notes with Mason Enterprises and look forward to the actually completed report." She closes the folder, her eyes piercing into me right through the screen. "Please don't misinterpret my politeness for weakness again, Ms. Nelson. When I hired you to write a report, I expected a full account of Elijah's behavior not a cherry-picked version that his pretty face and more might have inspired. Try to play me for a fool again, and I'll have your license." She stops. Smiles. Reaches for her keyboard and halts. "And Dani—do straighten that Monet landscape behind you. I hate to see my son's place in such disarray."

29

ELI

*G*ame plan in place, Eli hopped into the shower and changed for work while Dani finished up with her emails. He didn't remember the last time he'd slept in, but there was nothing normal about any of the last twenty-four hours, nothing remotely common about the highs and lows that had swept through his soul.

Demands of reality aside, all Eli wanted to do today was lounge in bed, having sex with the little red firecracker in every position possible. He wanted to watch her come while beneath him, on top of him, beside him. To see her face filled with blushed satisfaction, her body rag-doll limp from pleasure. His cock twitched so hard at the thought that Eli had to stop to press his forehead against the wall until the pressure eased.

Finally returning downstairs, he paused for one more moment to just watch the way Dani sat at the breakfast bar, her delectable bottom lip between her teeth.

Dani was...different. The only person whose mere presence took away a nightmare. Who could peel off his bloody shirt in the shower one minute and trust him with her body's secrets the next. Who looked for a way to help him calm a black eye that they both knew he deserved.

The question now was what Eli was going to do about it.

Sliding back behind the breakfast bar, he pulled over his plate of pancakes—though keeping his attention on task instead of studying the way his oversized tee brushed Dani's thighs was bloody difficult. "Well then," he started. "It's going to be a busy day."

"Hm?" Dani wrapped her hands around her coffee.

Eli straightened his back. "Slimy things first. And failing that, I was thinking a pirate costume with eye patch would make a hell of a contingency plan." He tried and failed to capture her gaze, but with how quickly his pulse was suddenly racing, that wasn't much of a surprise. Damn. He felt like a schoolboy, sweaty palms and dry mouth and all. Which was ridiculous. He'd gone into war zones with less active nerves. "If you could condescend to join me at the fundraiser," he said after a final mental kick, "I'd love to pick up something for you as well."

Nothing. No response.

He cleared his throat. "A parrot, perhaps?"

"What?" Dani's head shot up, those beautiful intelligent eyes catching up with the conversation. "Sorry! The fundraiser. I'm flattered but…"

"But?"

She shifted in her seat. "Wouldn't it be a bit awkward? I mean, what capacity would I be showing up in? Former antagonistic roommate? Frenemy? Occasional lover? It's not exactly high society material."

Where was that coming from? Eli narrowed his gaze. "How about elite escort service?"

Red's mouth opened in indignation.

He shrugged. "You're the one who brought up high society. Do you imagine the perfection you see doesn't get some designer help?"

Dani's attention strayed to Eli's shirt, her face coloring. Yeah. He'd made his point. But then he wanted more than to win the round; he wanted *her*.

"Just come as my plus one, and we'll leave it at that," he offered.

Dani's hesitant smile sent a ripple of warmth through him. "In that case, I'd love to go," she said quietly. "Thank you."

Excellent. The exact words he wanted to hear. Except... "Something on your mind, Red?"

She shook her head a little too quickly. "Just a snag with some of my reports. Nothing to worry about."

"Then why are you worried?"

"I'm not." Dani took a swig of coffee.

Eli's chest tightened, a gray chill settling on what had been a lifting mood. She was lying to him. Either because she didn't trust him or because she'd just sunk his career. Neither boded well. His appetite suddenly gone, Eli put the rest of his half-eaten pancakes into the fridge and gave the woman a mimed salute. "I'll... I'll ask Sky to help get something appropriate for you and pick you up at six. Just let me know where you'll be."

ELI HAD ONLY BEEN in the office an hour—he'd taken a detour to procure a set of hungry leeches at what passed for Chinatown in Denton Valley—when his new receptionist, Louise, appeared at his door. In her early thirties, the woman was everything Zana had not been. Responsible. Discreet. Diligent to a fault.

"Mr. Mason, there's a Mr. Brock Talbot of Talbot Insurance at the front. He doesn't have an appointment, but given that he's from their C-suite—"

"Are you saying that he's an important bloke and I should play nice and see him?" Eli asked. The name Talbot rang a few bells from a recent online ads complaint, but Eli couldn't fathom why the firm wouldn't have gone straight to his risk management people.

"I—" Louise hesitated, plainly trying to work out what Eli wanted her to say. Dani never did that. She spoke her mind. At least until late this morning.

Eli raised a placating hand toward his assistant. "I was trying to say that I agree with your assessment, Louise. If you can make the schedule work, show him in."

Louise smiled, relief filling her features. "Very good, sir."

"Louise, wait." Eli held up a finger. "How does the eye look?"

She blinked evenly. "Which eye, sir?"

Eli snorted. HR must have reached all the way back to London to find her. "The one that's black and three times the size it was last week." He leaned forward, bracing his forearms on the desk. "If you and I are to be working together, you should know that I only fire people for telling me the truth on February twenty-ninth. You're safe at all other times."

A hint of a smile. This one would take work. "Yes, sir. In that case, it only looks twice the expected size."

"Excellent. Then please show these gentlemen to a waiting area and send in Talbot?" Eli extended the small bucket of leeches to Louise, who, once more, didn't bat an eye at the request.

Leeches thus relocated to digest their breakfast, Eli leaned back in his chair as Talbot lumbered past his threshold. Dressed in a well-tailored three-piece Armani, Talbot was stocky, barrel-chested, and—if the salt-and-pepper hair was any indication—in his early fifties. His clean-shaven jaw exposed thick jowls, but the man appeared to be in decent shape.

"Mr. Mason," Talbot jutted out his hand, not waiting for Eli to speak first. "I'm Brock Talbot. Thank you for seeing me."

Eli rose to shake the man's hand, pointing to a free chair before reclaiming his own. "Not at all. What can I do for you?"

"Actually, there's something I can do for you." Talbot's small deep-set eyes tried and failed to keep from glancing between Eli's black eye and busted knuckles. "I hope you'll forgive me just bursting in on you like this, but I'm coming from a local insurance conference and couldn't ignore the opportunity to drop by. I understand that there's a cognitive psychologist by the name of Danielle Nelson who has Mason Pharmaceuticals under investigation."

So much for keeping things under wraps. Picking up his pen, Eli clicked the top with his thumb. "I'm not at liberty to discuss internal operations," Eli said, his tone dismissive despite rising hackles. "I'm sure you understand."

"Fair enough." Talbot gave a small bow of acquiescence. "Then how about I talk and you simply listen. If the matter is irrelevant to you now, consider it a warning tale for the future. I'm a man who still believes in paying forward, and I'd like to do for you what I wish someone had for me."

Eli clicked his pen, his face stone.

Talbot sighed, rubbing his palms over his thighs. "The scam goes something like this. Ms. Danielle Nelson—an ambitious, physically attractive young woman—approaches the board of directors at major corporations with an offer to *evaluate* whatever influential executive someone on the board has a bone to pick with for a hefty sum. A hired gun with credentials. Once the target is identified and the money is transferred, Ms. Nelson makes her move. Am I hitting any targets so far for you, Mr. Mason?"

"Not at all."

Talbot smiled. "The next act in this charade happens when Ms. Nelson makes contact with the target. A trained psychologist and heister, she uses every trick in the book to worm her way into her mark's confidence. Long talks. Dinners. Private time outside the office. I didn't think I was susceptible to such tactics until I took her bait hook, line, and sinker. Though I didn't know this at the time it's the same trick that spies have used for centuries—they call it a 'honey pot' in the trade."

Talbot paused, elevating his eyebrows at him. Eli wanted to squirm, though he did not.

"Before I knew it, I was sharing more information than I'd ever intended," Talbot continued.

"What are we talking about?" Eli asked. "Trade secrets? Research and development? Proprietary code?"

Talbot chuckled. "Perhaps if she'd have been hired by someone else, it would have gone that way. But in this case, her paycheck came from my board. And there was someone there who wanted more personal information. Things that could be used to manipulate me, to write reports that had just enough truth to carry weight while skewing reality to whatever those paying her wanted. In my case, someone on the board had a family member vying for my place. And the next thing I know, there is a dossier being passed around to discuss my 'narcissistic personality and aggressive tendencies'—all with my own words twisted to back up the conclusions."

A chill passed though Eli's veins, the story hitting too many plausible notes. If Talbot hadn't been talking about Dani, about *Eli's* Dani, he would have a hard time dismissing it. But Eli knew Red. Intimately.

Just as she knew him.

"Anyway..." Talbot scratched his shaven jawline. "I consider myself fortunate that forced leave of absence is all I have to show for battle scars. For now. That woman has a dossier filled with such a delicate mix of truth and lies that the entire federal government wouldn't be able to separate fact and fiction. I hope you never meet her, Mr. Mason. But if you do—or if you have—I hope you'll see the play for what it is. I tell you, that one will have you gutted from cock to gullet if you aren't careful."

Click. Click. Click. The sound of Eli's pen filled the ensuing silence as Talbot brushed invisible specks of dust from his suit while Eli's stomach turned over. Wasn't Talbot's speech so much like the one Eli had given to himself when Danielle Nelson first walked through his door? Weren't all the warning flags waving as proudly in the wind as ever?

"My advice?" Talbot leaned forward, his sizable jowls jiggling as he moved. "Block her every way you can. If, of course, you ever cross paths. Oh, and get ready to transfer a sizable sum of money into your attorney's bank account."

30

DANI

I twirl in front of the mirror in Eli's master bath, the light jade chiffon gown flowing around my reflection. The price tag was still on it when the express delivery service dropped it off a few hours ago, and it took me an hour on the phone with Sky to work up the courage to pick the dress up. Cut in an A-line princess style, the dress falls all the way to the floor, the full-length sleeve on one side contrasting against the sleeveless bare arm on the other. Add in the single gauzy ruffle sliding down the back, and it's the most beautiful piece of clothing I've ever tried on—much less worn.

"You look nice." Joining my reflection, Eli's approving glance scans me from head to toe before nodding appreciatively. He'd not so much as asked me about my size, yet the dress fits better than anything I've ever owned. It also cost more than all the clothes I've ever owned put together.

"Please let me know if this is a rental." I run my finger over the fabric. "Like those tuxes you wear for a day and then hand back."

"It's a rental," Eli agrees readily.

"Really?"

"No." He grins at me wolfishly, but despite a much-better-looking eye, tension paints the hard angle of his jaw.

"Everything all right?" I ask, moving away from the mirror to sit on Eli's tall bed while he shrugs into a tuxedo jacket. "You look, well, bothered."

Eli's hands hesitate on his tie, then busy themselves with the knot. "What instructions exactly did you receive from the board of directors hiring you for this project?"

My neck tightens. For the two hundredth time, I wish I could rewind everything to have never promised Madison Mason confidentiality. To have never given my word. But I had. So I give Eli as much as I can short of breaking the damn commitment. "To conduct a full psychological assessment on the CEO of Mason Pharmaceuticals Denton Valley branch. You know that."

"Are you being paid for a particular conclusion?"

"What?" Heat rushes through me, and I'm on my feet at once, my fists on my hips. "Are you accusing me of being the professional equivalent of a prostitute? Because if, after everything we've shared, you still think that's even possible, I—"

"I spoke with a previous client of yours today," Eli cuts me off, his voice quiet. Even. "This person was...distraught over your conclusions. They felt they'd been manipulated into revealing information that was then unjustly used against them."

"Wyrd." Sitting back down, I let the flurry of thoughts race through me, sorting through them on the fly. Was it Talbot? Was he following me like my paranoid brain suspected? "How did they know to approach you?"

Eli's voice hardens. "That isn't the relevant part."

I swallow, Eli's quiet fury finally dawning on me. Not only had his confidentiality been compromised—an unforgivable violation that I'll have to get to the bottom of later—but whoever inserted themselves into his business managed to press all the trigger points.

"All right." Reaching into my bag of professional tricks, I pull out a steady calm voice despite my racing heart. "Let's take this step by step. I don't know who you spoke to, or even whether this person is telling the truth about being a former client—"

"His name is—"

"Stop." My hand shoots up cutting him off. "You can't ask me clients' identities, Eli." I make my voice firm enough to drown out my own temptation to ask about Talbot. "It's not only illegal under HIPAA laws, but it breaks my ethical obligation to them and to their company's board of directors. I'm so, so sorry it happened to you. I can't do that to anyone else, though."

"Hm." Eli makes a noise in the back of his throat, his hands going into his pockets as if to say *how convenient*.

I turn placating palms toward him. "I'm not cutting off your question, just the sharing-identifiers part. For the sake of argument, let's assume this person really was an evaluee." Never mind that it's my first assignment in the western US. "And they said something to the effect of me hurting their career."

"Is this the part where you assure me they lied?" Eli asks.

"No. This is the part where I tell you that they probably told the truth." I open my hands wide as Eli blinks at the assertion. Good. It means he's listening. "Most executives I'm hired to evaluate aren't nice people. Tell me, would *you* hire a psychologist to test a stellar leader, or one you had serious apprehensions about?"

Eli pauses.

"With the exception of prehire evaluations, I'm often dealing with people who are unsuited for the positions they hold," I continue quickly. "Statistically speaking, this former client, more likely than not, fell into the latter group. But it was because of the truth, not because I was out to get them."

Eli blows out a long breath. His color is still up, the tension still gripping his face, but he's listening. Thinking. Evaluating. Which is one of the things I love most about him. "What about meetings outside work?" he asks. "Casual conversations used to solicit… " He pauses.

"Solicit what?" I prompt.

Eli clicks his tongue. Thinks before speaking. "I don't know. The dirt. Admissions against interest."

"Like…facts? Or do you imagine they make up nasty things about themselves to impress me?"

"Fair point," Eli concedes. "Facts. Still, the question stands."

"If you're asking whether I let clients choose where they feel comfortable talking, the answer is yes. Some people like a claustrophobic conference room." I pause to raise a brow at him. "Others find a coffee shop or restaurant more comfortable. If you're asking whether I've had sexual relations with any of my clients, the answer is absolutely not. With one noteworthy exception that we both know about."

Getting up, I walk closer to him. Look up into those piercing, vulnerable gray eyes. "One thing that I can promise you, Eli Mason, is that I report the truth. Unbiased truth. No matter what the board *thinks* I'll do when they hire me, or the evaluee *thinks* I'll conclude when he explains away blatant sexual harassment. I tell the truth."

Eli studies me for another moment, then, taking my head between his hands, leans downs and kisses my forehead. "I believe you," he says quietly into my hair, and I can't help lifting my face up toward him, everything inside me longing for his touch. His acceptance. His trust that the things we shared last night would never leave my confidence.

Eli's thumbs drop to trace my cheekbones, the fingers trailing slowly across my skin until my thighs and breasts tingle. I close my eyes, drinking in the sensations, then my breath catches as his lips press against mine. Instantly, his kiss becomes more penetrating, more all-encompassing as his tongue surges inside my mouth.

My tongue meets his, stoking the flames, his minty taste

downright addicting. On the heels of earlier tension, Eli's sure touch is like a released pressure gauge, the potent sensations taking over the here and now until I'm lost in him. In us.

The chime of a phone message intrudes callously into our connection and Eli softens his lips before pulling away reluctantly.

Letting out a long slow breath, I rest my forehead against his neck.

"Our ride is here," Eli says. Instead of going to his truck, he leads me out to the front of the residence, where a limo pulls out front.

"Seriously?" My eyes widen.

Eli shrugs one shoulder. "I wasn't sure you could manage a tall vehicle in that dress."

Funny. But… But also special.

Once we arrive at the fundraiser, held in none other than the ballroom of the Broadmoor Hotel, Eli escorts me inside, his palm warm at the base of my spine. Despite the sound of the piano coming from the main event, I can't help stopping to admire the lobby. With its internally illuminated stained-glass ceiling, crystal chandelier, and red velvet Queen Anne chairs, I feel like an imposter.

"What was that thought?" Eli asks, turning me toward him.

"Nothing." I cringe at his piercing look. Even with hints of bruising still tracing his eye, the man looks like a walking advertisement for men's glamor. It's truly unfair. "This is just so… fancy. It's not how I'm used to living. I'm going to stick out here."

"I'm used to having protein shakes for breakfast, but—as you and your fungi have proven—a diversion now and then isn't deadly." A corner of his mouth twitches. "But just in case anyone has doubts as to your place here…" Before I ask what he's doing, Eli brushes a hand across my cheekbone and leans forward to kiss me with the same thorough abandon as he'd done in the house.

Wyrd. I should have worn a pantyliner.

Pulling away with a catlike self-satisfied expression, Eli takes advantage of my speechlessness to guide me the rest of the way into the sprawling ballroom.

Like the lobby, Broadmoor's is a work of art. In the background, a tuxedo-wearing pianist coaxes Mozart notes from the baby grand, the long walnut bar opposite the piano gleaming like a polished jewel. About thirty round tables and a draped stage at the front round out the look, a grand sign by the podium telling the guests that Denton Valley Alliance against Sexual and Domestic Abuse is affiliated with the International Society for Mental Health.

At least that organization I'm familiar with from the mental health community, the earth-shaped logo greeting me like an old friend.

"Dani!" Appearing in a beautiful pale pink dress with a sweetheart neckline, Sky gives me a welcoming smile before shaking her head at Eli. The black of his tux contrasts gorgeously with his light reddish curls, "You couldn't hold off training for one day? Or at least keeping your hands up better?"

Eli gives Dani a roguish smile, though I catch the challenging glances he exchanges with Cullen and Liam over Sky's head. Yeah, the men know Eli wasn't in training. They also seem to know better than to bring it up. At least the eye looks better now, with only a bit of discoloration in place of massive swelling. Score one for holistic medicine.

"So what's the order of march for the evening?" Eli asks the guys while his hand on the small of my back guides us toward the bar. If I thought the man looked breathtaking in a suit, the tux he wears today takes Eli's natural beauty to a new level.

"The attendance is already twenty percent over expected," Cullen says, ordering a scotch. "Including your good friend Garibaldi."

Eli groans.

"Don't worry, I think he's as interested in keeping clear of you as you are of him tonight. Do you know what you're going to say?"

"I wouldn't go mentioning black eyes," Liam says without a trace of humor.

Eli answers something I lose track of as a flash of salt-and-pepper hair in the crowd causes my heart to ice. For a second, all I can do is stare at the far end of the room where I saw that hair, while my neck tightens in memory of Talbot's hands on my throat. Then the moment passes, and I force myself to draw breath. Yes, I likely did see salt-and-pepper hair. In fact, a good half of the guests fall into that category. *The conversation with Eli earlier has simply primed the memories,* I tell myself in a professional tone. *You're seeing your fears because they're cues for access.*

Returning my attention to the conversation, I catch Liam watching me with the same humorless expression he'd had when addressing Eli. Turning my head away from the security professional, I catch Sky in enthusiastic midsentence.

"—about Mason Village. No one here is immune to a good investment opportunity, so the project hits both sides of the aisle. With it being ten days to closing on the building purchase, it's timely too."

Ten days? I swallow. It seems like it was just yesterday that Eli and I made our illustrious introductions, with him asking me if I was a stripper and me catching him planning to bulldoze over half a dozen small businesses. Yet here we are, bulldozers almost at the ready.

"We're not naming it Mason Village," Eli says with a small warning growl. Naming convention aside, however, the Trident is comfortable in this world of thousand-dollar gowns and high-end fundraisers and discussion of mowing down a whole block of livelihoods to install his vision.

"What's wrong?" Eli catches me midthought, his gaze penetrating right through me.

"Nothing." I force a smile. This evening's fundraiser plainly means a great deal to Eli—it's not the time or place to debate the morality of a major business decision. *Plus, if Madison has her way with twisting the report, Eli won't be able to close on the deal at all.* Not that I would let my words get twisted even for that—but that plainly won't stop her from trying.

Eli tilts his head, his jaw tightening. "I really, *really* dislike being lied to, Red," he says quietly into my ear.

I sigh. "When I was growing up, my parents' small business got demolished by corporate raiders. So I'm a rather biased audience for discussing plans to destroy livelihoods, no matter how grand the final project. I'm sorry. I just can't help, umm..."

"I think the words you're looking for are 'but make assumptions,'" Cullen says, his voice low. Hard. The kind that makes my skin crawl.

Sky gives her fiancé a reproving glare.

Cullen shakes his head, not backing down an inch from the sudden harshness. "Before you presume to know someone's mind, Ms. Nelson—or expect them to know yours—you might consider asking for information. That's how it works in our circles."

"Back off, Hunt." Stepping between Cullen and me, Eli pushes a lock of hair behind my ear. "No one is being pushed out except one slumlord, who's been making the lives of over two hundred families hell for years now. The affected businesses will be inconvenienced, but we're giving them discounted rent to compensate for any lost revenue, and fair leases. We've tried all other avenues, but the bastard has a crack legal team blocking all housing department complaints. Physically repossessing and rebuilding is the only way to get him out."

"Oh." The mix of relief and chagrin running through me warms my skin. Rising on my toes, I brush my lips over Eli's— onlookers be damned. "Now that I think about it, Mason Village does have a ring to it."

"Not you too, Red." Eli rolls his eyes, quickly regaining his composure as the hostess approaches to beckon him to the stage.

Taking my drink, I move toward the windows for a better view of the stage and…and yes, to get just a little distance from Cullen. Maybe it makes me a snowflake, but I'm not sure I'll ever be comfortable with the sound of men barking at me, no matter how contained their harshness is.

"Ms. Nelson." A familiar voice from behind me makes the drink slip in my hand, only a stroke of luck keeping the crystal flute from falling all the way to the floor. Brock Talbot. Here. For real. "I didn't expect to see you here. Small world, isn't it?"

My body freezes. Except instead of staring directly at the man, I look blankly at the stage Eli is now mounting to rising applause. As if ignoring Talbot might make him disappear.

On stage, Eli is thanking the guests for coming to the Denton Valley Alliance against Sexual and Domestic Abuse annual fundraising gala, the spotlight playing handsomely off his hair and shiny lapels.

"Talbot Insurance has been a significant donor for several women and children's foundations under my tenure," Talbot continues as if we're having an actual conversation. "Of course, that's over now. Thanks to you."

I say nothing. My tongue has glued itself to the roof of my mouth, and my heart is galloping so hard that I'm shocked it hasn't jumped clear out of my chest. Trying to be subtle about it, I take a step closer to the middle-aged couple to my right, my eyes already mapping a way to get back to where Sky and the others still lounge by the bar.

Talbot closes the distance, his rose-scented cologne filling my nose. "I'm happy to walk you over to your new friends," Talbot says, following the direction of my gaze. "Or, should I say, to Eli Mason's old friends. If that's what you're certain you want."

My heart pounds. "Why wouldn't it be?"

"No reason. Unless, of course, your Mr. Mason has *not* told them who you really are. What the real reason for your visiting Denton Valley might be. What fiction did you spread this time around? Are you a temp from headquarters? Or is it more of a call girl now?"

I close my eyes, my hands shaking. How long has the man been here, in Denton Valley? Since I got here? Was he truly the man I saw in the hotel, or was that at least simply my imagination?

On stage, Eli's speech is in full swing, his dulcet tones ebbing out of his speaker like music.

"What do you want?" I ask Talbot.

"An apology," he answers readily. "You caused me a great deal of trouble, Ms. Nelson. And I would like to hear you apologize for it."

Ignoring Talbot, I focus on the stage.

"The DVASDA has provided food, clothing, shelter, childcare, and other resources to hundreds over the past three years," Eli is telling his audience now. "And we'll continue to do so for as long as necessary."

"Let me make this easy for you." Talbot's hard whisper as he steps up behind me slides across my exposed neck. "You may either step out into the hallway with me now, apologize, and be back before your current mark is done babbling—or we'll turn this into a group conversation. How many people here will rush to support the little Brit's pet cause once they know his own board of directors has sent a shrink to condemn him? No one likes mental cases, Ms. Nelson. They don't look good. And all these great folks? That's why they're all here. To look good and philanthropic. Really, it's your choice."

31

DANI

*I*f anyone had told me this morning that there was something—anything—that Brock Talbot could say to make me walk off alone with him, I'd call them crazy. Certifiably insane. That was back when I thought I was the only one Talbot threatened.

Before he showed, oh so clearly, how he could destroy Eli.

"It's so good to see Mr. Mason's mental health evaluator allowed him to come this evening," Talbot whispers into my ear, his voice mimicking a conversation. "Ms. Danielle Nelson, right over there. She truly is the best when it comes to managing unbalanced tendencies. You should look her up. I personally stand fully behind Mason Enterprise's decision to seek professional help for Elijah instead of sidelining the man… Yes, yes, I saw the black eye and busted knuckles too. These young people see so much violence overseas that it's hard to integrate into civilian life…"

My mouth dries. My body is rooted in place.

"A few speeches like that to the right people here, and I'll turn Mr. Mason's whole world on its head. Investors recalculating the risk of Mason Village. The DVASDA keeping its distance. His friends asking all sorts of intrusive questions."

"Those are lies," I whisper. "Utter lies. And we both know it."

"I'm sure Mr. Mason will have no problem correcting the record, then." Talbot's smile sends bile up my throat. He's right. It doesn't matter that he'd be lying. Eli looks like he's fresh from a fight, and a few dropped comments will leave rumors circulating before anyone can cut them off.

Maybe if I'd told Eli about Talbot, it would have been different. But now…

"This is between you and me, Talbot," I say, forcing myself to meet his dark deep-set gaze. "Leave Eli Mason out of it."

"I'd like nothing better," Talbot replies, all courtesy and manners. "But the you-and-me part needs to talk. To apologize and move on."

I force myself to give the slightest of nods, though my body jolts as if zapped when Talbot puts his hand on the small of my back and guides me toward the ballroom exit, murmuring something about showing me the artwork in a tone just loud enough for the people closest to us to hear.

He takes me through the applauding crowd, and for a second, I cling to the hope that Eli's speech is somehow over, that he'll see me with Talbot and intercept us. I've no illusion that Talbot will surrender his advantage over any apology, but the conversation might provide a hint into what leverage would work. And it would buy time, would control Talbot's movements until Eli finishes his speech and gets caught up on the problem. Fuck client confidentiality. This is blackmail.

As we approach the wide arched double doors Eli and I came in through not all that long ago, Eli begins speaking again.

"Thank you to each and every one of you for your support of this worthy cause. Now I yield the stage to our main speaker this evening, one of the earliest beneficiaries of this fund, Ms. Carrie Walker." A woman in a shimmering purple dress appears at his side, and I pause to clap along with everyone else.

"Keep going, honey." Talbot's hand on my back tightens, digging into my muscles—and sending needles of thought-numbing terror pricking every inch of my skin. I glance toward Sky to see if the Tridents have possibly registered my predicament, but their attention is still on the stage.

Then Talbot and I are through the arched doorway, sweeping down the main corridor like a pair of old friends. As we approach the turnoff toward a more isolated passage leading toward the restroom, however, I dig my heels into the carpet. "I said I'll talk with you," I tell Talbot. "But there is no way in hell we're going anywhere less public."

"Funny how you had no such reservations when you were setting a trap for me." Talbot's top lip pulls back in a snarl, his ire suddenly flaring. "So don't play games now. I know you."

"No games." I raise my hands in a calming gesture. I'm a psychologist. I'm trained to deal with unstable clients. I can do this. "You wanted an apology, remember?"

He grunts. "Yes. Show me just how sorry you are about poisoning my board with your lies." He steps closer to me, his rose-scented cologne saturating the air as he invades my space. "Don't think of bullshitting me, *Ms. Nelson.* I've watched you with Mason. I know how you operate. If it's cock you want, you should have told me earlier."

Panic races through me in flashes and visions. *An executive office. A high school closet. The sound of an opening zipper. Hands on my neck.* I step away.

Talbot grabs my wrist.

"Let go of me." My heart pounds, and it takes all my mental effort to bring a calm voice to bear. How long is Eli going to be on that stage? How long until he goes to look for me? I need to stall Talbot until then. "You just wanted an apology, remember?"

"Maybe I took a page from your playbook." Talbot's mouth

warps into a snarl. "Say what you need to say. Get 'em where you need 'em. Give 'em what they want."

Thrusting me backward into the elegant golden wood paneling, Talbot presses his mouth over mine, forcing his tongue inside as I gasp.

"No—" My protest is muffled by Talbot's mouth, his breath hot and rancid as he leans into me, his erection poking into my hip. He's so much bigger than me. So much stronger. Jerking my head to the side, I chomp down on his bottom lip as hard as I can.

Talbot yelps, and I taste blood on my tongue as he stumbles back a step. "Fucking *bitch.*"

Raising his hand, Talbot backhands me across the face. Pain explodes along my cheek, and I bring my hands up to cover my head as I scream.

"Hey—"

"It's fine. We're talking."

"What's going on?"

"Sir? Sir! I'm calling the police."

Voices come at me from all sides, none of which stops Talbot from trying to push me toward the restrooms, his hand yanking up the hem of my gown to dive beneath the fine fabric. Panic turns my vision pure white, and I go feral, scratching and kicking and—

The bang on the other side of the corridor is as loud as a gunshot.

"Get your bloody fucking hands off her!" Eli's British roar fills the hallway. Within seconds, Talbot's weight is lifted from me, Eli helping him into a wall with a spinning back kick.

Talbot seems to bounce off the wood paneling, his arms wrapping around his middle. "Who do you think you—" He never gets to finish as Eli slams his elbow into Talbot's nose, bringing him down like a building demolished with explosives. Blood gushes along Talbot's face.

More voices fill the corridor, Sky flying toward me wide-eyed. "Dani, oh my God. Are you all right?"

"I'm…" That's all I can get out. I drag my gaze from her to where Eli has Talbot pinned to the expensive wooden panels, Eli's forearm pressed into Talbot's throat. The man is still conscious but turning an interesting shade of blue.

"Mason," Liam barks a warning, but the unmitigated fury twisting Eli's expression stays unrelenting.

"*Lieutenant,*" Cullen adds, and only then does Eli relax his grasp enough to let Talbot suck in air, his chubby jowls quivering with the effort as blood from his nose splashes across both his and Eli's white shirts.

"I told you that damn shrink for hire will ruin your life," Talbot says through clenched teeth as he glares at Eli. "Just as she ruined mine. You'll see."

A pair of uniformed officers appear just then, pushing through a crowd that's no longer in the mood for antiviolence messages. As they relieve Eli of his prisoner, I again taste blood. This time I'm pretty sure it's my own. A new wave of light-headedness washes over me, and I lean my hand against the wall for balance.

"Dani." Eli is beside me in an instant, brushing mussed hair from my face. "Are you all right?"

I swallow. Nod. Not that Eli takes my word for it, running his hands up and down my body as if searching for broken limbs or bullet wounds.

"It's all right," I assure him. "Nothing actually happened. I mean, not—"

"That wasn't nothing," Eli says, a muscle in his jaw still ticking.

"Would Mr. Talbot have anything to do with the security concern you called me about a few days ago?" Liam asks, coming up to us while the event host and staff try their best to herd the crowd back into the ballroom and save what's left of the ruined event. Which isn't much.

Eli's gaze narrows on me. "You had security concerns a few days ago?"

I rub my eyes. "I wasn't sure."

"You were certain enough that you called Rowen," Eli counters, shaking his head. "And this afternoon, when you gave me a bloody client confidentiality speech—you didn't think to bring it up either?"

"Eli." I wince at the betrayed look in his gray eyes, my chest tightening. "It was just some emails. I received some here and there in Boston. I thought I caught a glimpse of him, but my imagination has been running wild. That—"

"That is called stalking. And you're only telling me about all this *now?*" Eli looks equal parts hurt and furious, but the adrenaline that's been rushing through my system is beginning to crash.

"Eli." Sky butts in, snaking her arm around my waist. "Do you honestly think this is the time and place for an interrogation?"

"Reynolds—" Cullen turns to Sky, his voice low and filled with warning.

"Don't you *Reynolds* me," Sky snaps right back at her fiancé before guiding me toward the door. "Come on, Dani. I'm taking you home. Cullen can ride with the rest of the assholes."

3 2

ELI

The calming blues of the North Vault did nothing to pacify Eli as he sat with Liam at the bar while other patrons danced to a techno tune on the opposite side of the room. Kyan had pussied out of coming out to the fundraiser to begin with, and Cullen had returned to the Broadmoor to deal with the fallout of the guest of honor and a donor getting into a fistfight at a domestic violence fundraiser, right after said donor tried to assault a guest.

It was the kind of mess one couldn't have designed on purpose no matter how hard one tried. Yet, at the moment, he didn't have it in him to care that much. Dani had lied to him. Not just that morning, but from the very beginning. Even when he'd laid open his soul, telling the woman things he'd never uttered aloud, she hadn't trusted him enough with the basic facts. Like that she'd had an active restraining order against Talbot on file—Cullen had gotten that from the police a few moments ago. That she feared that very same Talbot was stalking her. That she was in danger while she lived under Eli's own roof.

He knocked back his shot of bourbon, letting the burn going

down his esophagus numb him. Sky—and Cullen's security camera setup—would watch over Dani for the night. Hell, no one was letting the woman out of their sight until…until what? She left Colorado for good?

"You know, we can do this silent-drinking thing all night long if you want," Liam started, turning his shot glass as he examined the tequila swishing back and forth along the bottom. "But if I have to watch you brood that long, I'm dragging you into the gym come morning. And I have a feeling I'll enjoy that match more than you will."

Patrons ambled into the bar behind the two men, oblivious to the mix of ire and exasperation Eli felt. He'd been clenching his molars so fervently, he doubted there was anything of them left but powder. "Dani contacted you. A few days ago."

"Yeah."

"You didn't tell me."

"Didn't know you needed to be told," Liam countered.

"*She* didn't tell me," Eli said more pointedly. That was the real crux of the problem. How could she go to Liam, trust Liam, but not trust *him*? Especially after everything they'd been to one another? Whatever that was. Bollocks. Perhaps he'd been placing more emphasis on it than she'd been. Maybe it didn't mean to her what it'd meant to him.

"And that pisses you off."

"Hell, yes, it bloody pisses me off." Eli slammed his shot on the bar, cracking the bottom. He closed his eyes and took a deep breath. Luckily, he'd killed off all the liquor inside it, and the glass hadn't shattered.

"Fine. She's got trust issues. Want to tell me about your Boston trip, Mason? How about that black eye Reynolds thinks you got in a sparring match? And let's not even get started on the whole hired-shrink thing Talbot was going on about. I think it's safe to say she isn't some temp from headquarters?"

Prick. Eli closed his eyes. "You and I aren't sleeping together."

"Don't talk yourself into a corner, Mason," Liam warned. "You don't know the last names of most women you've taken to bed around here."

"If you're going to be like that, you can just bugger off." Eli waved his empty glass at the bartender, who gave him a pity-filled look before placing a fresh shot on the bar. Yeah. Sitting with a black eye and a disheveled blood-spattered tux didn't leave much need for imagination.

"What are you going to do?"

Eli picked up the shot glass. "If I knew that, you think I'd be here with you?"

"My point"—Liam blew out a breath—"is that you need to decide if you're done with her over this or not."

"What did she ask you, exactly?" Eli didn't know why he was hunting for Dani's specific verbiage, but he wanted to hear it.

"Basically, she asked about your firewall."

"My firewall?"

"Yeah. She asked me if spam emails could get through at her hotel when they didn't get through when she was staying with you. She kept her language hypothetical and wouldn't get more explicit than that, but I did wonder what she'd been worrying about."

"What sort of spam emails?"

"She wouldn't say. I started to have one of my guys monitor the Marriott for suspicious behavior after that, but we didn't detect anything out of the ordinary."

Liam's phone beeped with a notification, and after clicking a few keys, Eli's screen lit up with a rundown of Brock Talbot's background information. Times like this were when Eli most appreciated his friends. Yes, the guys enjoyed being pains in the asses, but when he truly needed them they were there, no questions asked. Even better, they knew him well enough to anticipate his requests before he even made them.

Particularly when it came to Liam's security measures.

Brock Talbot did turn out to be the CEO of Talbot Insurance, just as he'd claimed, but Eli detected nothing on his screen that substantiated him being put on forced leave. Of course, such a detail might not show up on such paperwork. What did show up were three previous charges of sexual harassment against him, all of which had eventually been dropped. How exactly had the man made that happen?

The image of his hefty, barrel-chested frame pushing down over Dani made Eli see red, and he clenched both his hands into fists again. He'd been percolating with rage over Talbot's assault, vibrating with it, and he still wanted to pound the man to death. That said, at least a quarter of the anger was still aimed at Dani for lying to him, even if it had been through omission.

What if Eli had gotten pulled into a conversation and not noticed Dani's vanishing act? What if Talbot had taken her somewhere else? What if help had gotten there a few minutes too late?

Maybe Eli wasn't angry so much as he was terrified. Lung-freezingly terrified.

"Tell me this. Besides not providing Your Highness with an annotated history of her personal demons, has Nelson ever done anything to betray your confidence? Has she compromised your secrets? Lied to you?"

Eli stared into his empty glass. No. Dani had done none of those things. Fuck. It meant Dani wasn't at all who Eli was so pissed off at. It was himself. He'd taken her care and compassion, her kind heart and her observant gaze, and he'd failed to give her as much in return. Hadn't made her feel safe with him. If he'd failed to earn Dani's trust, that was on him, not her.

"Quit that bullshit too," Liam ordered.

"What bullshit?"

"Whatever just sparked that look of self-loathing skittering across your face." Liam leaned forward, bracing his muscled forearms on the table. "How do you think my form of recreation works, Mason? It's all about reading faces and body language. It's all about trust. And I'm telling you right now, that's a two-way kind of thing. Not lying is part of it. But being ready to trust, that's another. And being ready to listen. That takes work, not blame."

"What are you, fucking Dr. Phil?"

"The fucking part's right." Liam leaned back on the barstool. "I guess the question is whether this one is worth all that effort. And from the little I've seen, the answer is *no*."

Eli's spine straightened at that, a muscle ticking along his jaw. Liam didn't know the first thing about Dani. Hell, in some ways, he didn't know the first thing about Eli either—not when compared to how much Dani had coaxed out of him these past few weeks. The connection between them, it made Eli feel whole. The way he hadn't felt since…since never. Dani was the lifeline that held him centered on a cliff, let him leap without falling into the abyss.

And the sex they'd had together? It didn't just blow his mind. He craved it like oxygen. He craved *her* like oxygen.

He loved her.

Holy bloody hell. He loved Danielle Nelson. And he wanted her.

Heart pounding against his ribs, Eli looked back at Liam's face, catching the man's self-satisfied smirk.

"You arsehole," Eli said, shaking his head. "You sadistic manipulating arsehole."

"You aren't wrong there," Liam agreed, finishing his drink. "I'd wait until tomorrow to go over there, though. Otherwise, Reynolds might just cut your balls off and serve them with a martini."

33

DANI

"How are you doing?" Sky asks, starting up a new-car-smell Lexus SUV. "We can go anywhere you'd like. The hospital. The bar. Your place. Reno. You tell me what you need, and I'll make it happen."

I smile, watching Sky pull out of the venue garage, the rows and rows of BMWs, Mercedes-Benzes, and Audi SUVs staring back at me. "Most certainly not the hospital," I tell her, leaning back in the leather seat. "Is it strange that I'm actually all right?"

"We may have differing definitions of all right," Sky hedged diplomatically.

I snort softly. "What I mean is that Talbot has been the bane of my existence for a while now. And as disturbing as the attack was today, it also means he's in custody. Witnesses, handcuffs, charges. The whole thing. He isn't returning to finish anything tonight." For the first time since that asshole assaulted me a few months ago, I almost feel safe.

Not as safe as I always feel in Eli's arms, but still, almost safe.

"How did he get you to leave the reception hall with him?" Sky asks. "Or did he ambush you by the restrooms?"

I know she's offering the latter alternative as an out for me, since we both know it was unlikely I was going to pee in the middle of Eli's presentation, but I appreciate it anyway. Unfortunately, I still don't quite know what to say. Talbot had shouted his accusation about me being a shrink, but the last thing I need to do is confirm his rumor. To hurt Eli more than I already have. "I didn't expect Eli to get quite that upset," I say instead.

Sky gives me an incredulous look. "Are you kidding me? We're just fortunate he didn't have a grenade in his pocket, or we'd be picking our way through the rubble now. When it comes to the people they love, the Trident guys take protectiveness to its logical absurdity."

Love. I jerk my head toward my friend, my heart stuttering. "He... I..."

"That man is head over heels in love, whether he knows it or not," Sky confirms. "I've never seen him treat anyone the way he treats you. Listen, the things he said, about being upset with you over not being told something... I'm not saying it wasn't an asshole move just then, because it totally was, but it was coming from the right place."

Pulling up to an intersection, Sky makes a sudden U-turn and starts tapping an address into her GPS.

"Where are we going?" I ask, watching the nice houses and well-kept streets degenerate outside the window.

"Mason Village. The investigative journalist in me wants you to see firsthand what he's doing there. If I knew you weren't in the loop, I'd have taken you earlier, and since you didn't have any better ideas for the evening, off we go."

Unable to argue with that logic and not ready to go back to the hotel, I settle in for the ride, feeling my brows pull further together the closer we get to the dilapidated square block of businesses and residences Eli has been working to purchase.

To call our final destination crappy would be the

understatement of the century. Where the better neighborhoods in the town have manicured lawns and well-tended landscaping, this area has none of that. Everything from fast-food containers to used condoms litter the streets, and some joker with spray-paint has even tagged several places along the crumbling brick of the external structure.

As Sky circles the block, I get a full view of the broken or boarded-up windows in the residential portion, the few trees and scrubby bushes fighting a losing battle to stay alive.

"What's that?" I ask, pointing to a black-and-gold-gilded sign above the one decent-looking door. *Garibaldi Leasing.* "I've seen that before somewhere."

"Hmm. Either you're having a flashback to the Giuseppe Garibaldi in European history, or else you've had the pleasure of overhearing Eli and Cullen howling in frustration over the Petro Garibaldi who's the owner of this fine residential establishment. They've already had one deal with him go bad, and now he's fighting with teeth and claws to keep the closing from going forward in ten days. Apparently, slum lording is *very* good money, because the amount this guy spends on legal fees is insane."

I make a noncommittal sound. That makes sense, but I've a feeling I've seen the name elsewhere too. Not just the name, but the logo. A letterhead in Madison's office, perhaps? Though that seems like a stretch. "Is there any reason M—" I pivot, narrowly avoiding saying the name of a person I supposedly have never met. "Any reason Mason Enterprises corporate would have any contact with him? I thought I saw something in the offices about Garibaldi, but it might be my imagination."

Sky shakes her head. "None at all. This is Eli's pet project. He's financing it outside the company, so beyond the status and validity his CEO title holds with investors, there's no connection. Anyway, I just wanted to show you that this isn't some stomp-out-the-little-guy plan that I admit it may sound like. In fact, the businesses on the other side will probably close within a year without intervention."

Sky and I spend the rest of the evening driving around the city, but when she insists that I spend the night with her and Cullen, I beg off. I truly do feel better knowing exactly where Talbot is spending the night, and I want the morning to myself. Well, to myself and Eli. There are things I need to tell him.

I sleep longer than I expect, the physical and emotional exhaustion catching up to me all at once after Sky reluctantly agrees to drop me at the Marriott, but I wake with a sense of defined purpose. Today, Eli and I will talk. I'm ready. I'm even ready to tell him about the jerk who raped me in high school—though not even my parents know about that.

I've just finished a shower and my first cup of coffee and am ready to call Eli when a rapping at the door startles me from my plan. Ensuring that my dead bolt is in place, I peer out the peephole to find a well-dressed middle-aged woman standing with a tray of coffee and scones outside my door.

Madison Mason.

I look away, rub my face, and peer through the peephole again. Madison is still there, though now looking agitated at the delay. Wyrd. Jostling the coffee to get into her purse, the woman pulls out her cell.

"Rudy, Madison here. Double-check that room number for me… I see. It appears I'll need a key card run up to me, then… Oh, don't be ridiculous. Mason Enterprises is paying for the suite. If anyone has a right to access it, it's me. If you're feeling put-upon, go ahead and get Felix on and we'll—" I fumble to undo the locks before some poor security agent loses his job.

"Disregard," Madison says on the other side as the latch clicks open. "The person I was hoping to reach has just materialized from the elevator. Thanks so much." She hangs up in time to grace me with a carnivorous smile as I pull the door.

"Dani, dear." Sweeping past me into the room, Madison

settles the breakfast pastries onto the polished table in the work section of the suite. "We've been going back and forth so much with this dreadful evaluation, I wanted to get things settled in person. You'll forgive the last-moment meeting, I'm sure, but my schedule is such a moving target that I simply didn't know what to expect today."

"So you flew across the country on a whim?" I clarify.

"Don't be silly. I was traveling anyway, and the pilot simply made a convenient detour. Now, do sit down and have some breakfast."

My head is still spinning as I drop into a chair opposite my client. After weeks of take all the time you need, the emails I've received over the last twenty-four hours—my phone registered at least five over the course of yesterday evening—speak to some hair-on-fire emergency I simply don't see.

"Is there something specific I can help you with?" I ask, reclaiming some agency in this conversation as I silence my phone to give my client my full attention. I also take a blueberry scone. Sugar is good to get the brain moving.

"Indeed." Pulling a leather portfolio from her Gucci bag, Madison takes out a stack of neatly formatted papers, my latest report copy being at the top. "I appreciate your get-straight-to-business approach. What I'd like is to leave this room with the finished evaluation report, at which time we can terminate this project and return you home. My office will take charge of the dissemination from here on out."

I stare at her, trying to work out whether she's kidding or not. Seeing no traces of humor on the woman's face, I clear my throat and reach for my most courteous and professional tone. "Ms. Mason, I'm of course happy to discuss the findings with you, but I can't give a finished report as it does not yet exist. The final official copy will be completed for the next board of directors meeting, where it will be presented in person. You can see how it would be unethical for me to provide an exclusive copy to a single board member in advance."

Madison huffs. "You may provide copies to whomever you wish, but I'm afraid the timing of the next board meeting is no longer suitable. Elijah is to be removed from his position this Friday."

My pulse picks up, Madison's words striking into me like darts. Remove Eli? That would be catastrophic. For him. For Mason Pharmaceuticals. For the people of the future Mason Village who've needed someone to stand up for them for a long, long time now. More to the point of the present discussion, it's clear that Madison is not just hoping but full-out expecting my conclusions to fall in line with supporting her agenda.

I take a moment to weigh my words, then decide with the straight-to-the-point approach. "I'm certain you and the board have your reasons. In the spirit of disclosure, you should be aware that my report makes no such recommendation. I've updated the notes to reflect additional details about the circumstances of Zana's termination, as you requested, but the conclusion remained substantially the same."

"Then reevaluate your conclusions, Ms. Nelson." Madison crosses her thighs and pulls a sheet of paper from her pile. "Here are the key facts I recommend you focus on. You may change the wording as you like."

I read the sheet, my brows rising with every word.

Elijah Mason has demonstrated ongoing verbally abusive behavior toward his subordinates, including an instance where he cornered and harassed a young female intern. Mr. Mason exhibited a similar hostile behavior toward the evaluator, despite knowing he was being observed—which further speaks to a deficit in impulse control. In general, Mr. Mason was uncooperative with the evaluation process, often refusing to provide answers to interview questions. He frequently appeared in the office with evidence of physical confrontation on his face and knuckles, which contributed to the overall hostile work environment.

It is my professional opinion that Mr. Mason is not at present psychologically suitable for a high-power position such as the office of the CEO.

Putting the paper down on the desk, I lay my palm over it and look Madison in the eye. "Those are not my conclusions, ma'am. In fact, the request you seem to be making goes against all ethical—"

"Oh, don't talk to me about ethics, girl," Madison snaps. "Unless having intercourse with your evaluees is a new recommendation of the American Psychiatric Association, I think you're well out of your league." Clicking her phone back on, Madison turns the screen toward me.

Blood drains from my face as photographs of Eli and me together flip through in succession, the images leaving little to the imagination despite their odd angles. Any one of those would get my license pulled. Altogether, hell, I'll be lucky to escape charges of criminal misconduct. I've no idea how Madison got these, but from the setting and vantage point at least some came from that pool party drone, a few others from something a computer camera might capture. Despite my hammering heart, I still can't help staring at one stray shot with Eli's hand on my cheek, an all-consuming look in his gorgeous gray eyes gazing deep into my soul. Opening up his own. Whoever captured these stolen seconds caught us at just the right moment.

Turning the phone toward her, Madison snorts at the image in disgust before hitting Delete. "You're young, Dani." Madison's voice has a kind lilt to it. "Indiscretion is part of youth. But even so, pictures—like statistics—tell only a part of the story. Perhaps these pictures aren't showing a psychologist sleeping with her client. Maybe they're evidence of coercion? If Elijah pressured you into a compromising situation, that's reason enough not to attack your license. If that's what happened, all you need to do is—"

"Dani?" Eli's voice accompanies an insistent knock on the door. "Will you let me in, please? I need to speak with you."

Wyrd. I feel my ribs tightening around my chest, my heart lurching into a panicked gallop. Of all the times to show up…

"Dani. I know you're in there," Eli continues, a vulnerable note in his voice cracking my heart. "If you won't take my calls, please just open the door for one minute."

I glance at my silenced phone and curse silently. Madison raises a curious brow.

"Fine." There's a small sound, as if Eli is leaning his forehead against the door. "If you don't want to talk to me, just listen, all right? I—"

I'm at the door in an instant. The "maybe he'll go away if I don't reply" plan is a clear failure, and I can't let him finish his sentence, can't allow him to expose his emotions with Madison in the audience.

Opening the door a crack, I bite my lip as I take in the sight of him. "Hey."

"Hi." Eli pauses, his gaze brushing over me desperately before tightening on the door. Despite being dressed in freshly pressed slacks and shirt, he has a slightly bedraggled look with his red curls flopping impertinently onto his forehead. It makes me long to reach out and push it free of his face. But I don't. "Are you intending to not let me in?" he asks.

"Elijah, is that you, darling?" Coming up behind me, Madison pulls open the door, like Medusa herself gazing upon her next catch. "What a fortunate coincidence. Dani and I were just discussing the evaluation. I'm running point for the board on this one. Would you like to join us? I brought scones."

Eli's expressive features morph into stone right in front of me. "You're running point for the board?" he clarifies, his cool gaze flickering between his mother and me. "I was unaware."

Though the words are directed toward Madison, they hit me

in the stomach so hard that I lose my breath. Before I can recover, Eli inhales audibly.

"I imagine the discussion might progress more smoothly without my company," he says, all calm politeness as he straightens his spine and does an about-face on the carpeted hallway. "Please, carry on."

"*Eli*," I call out, stretching my hands toward him, but it's too late. Far too late.

Without turning around, Eli walks out of my life.

34

ELI

*I*t was like getting punched in the face. A dull, disorienting ringing that made the world shift about. Then the pain.

He wasn't at the pain part yet. As Eli strode out of the Marriott, all he could do was twist the scene he'd just witnessed around in his head and stare. Maybe it hadn't been Madison inside Dani's room. And if it was, maybe that was the first time she and Dani had spoken. Or met. Maybe they weren't talking about anything that had to do with him at all. Maybe they hadn't been together in this from the start. Maybe the woman he'd fallen in love with hadn't lied to him.

Climbing behind the wheel of his Jeep Gladiator, Eli rested his forehead against the steering wheel. His phone was silent. No missed calls. Was that a good thing or a bad thing? Sitting up sharply, he slammed his palm against the side door and shifted into gear. What did Dani—what did the bloody universe—want from him? Was he just so sodding wrong inside that there wasn't enough cosmic karma for him to have what others took for granted? Was there more punishment he could take to even the scales, to make himself a worthy applicant for a soul?

The phone was still silent when Eli returned home, the pile of special-order portabella heaped on the kitchen table managing to sucker punch him. They were Dani's favorite. He'd somehow forgotten he was the one who drove to pick them up that very morning, a small surprise for the breakfast he imagined they would share.

But they wouldn't share it. Because Dani, the Dani he'd been certain was real, existed only in his childish imagination. The real woman was nothing but a manipulative con artist who did exactly what she needed to find just the right spot to plunge a dagger into. And then twisted. Just when Eli thought there could be nothing, *nothing* that he and Brock Talbot could possibly have in common, reality reared its head. He and that bastard had both fallen for the same act. Grabbing the whole sodding box of the damn fungus, Eli stuffed it into his garbage disposal in heaps as great as the mechanism would take.

He grabbed his phone again, hovered over the Delete button at Dani's number, then punched up Liam instead.

"Rowen."

"Meet me at the gym."

A beat of silence. "On my way. Bring your mouth guard. You'll need it."

If there was anything for which Liam could always be counted on, it was a good fight, and his friend didn't disappoint. They didn't talk as they squared off on the blue mats, and there was neither question nor blame in Liam Rowen's face as Eli let go of all stops, delivering blows with a savageness that left no margin for safety. It felt good to sink his fist into something that wasn't a wall or a punching bag. And when he was finished trying his fucking best to crack the other's SEAL's ribs, when Eli's lungs stabbed with every breath and his reserves were empty, he kept fighting, taking every ounce of punishment Liam inflicted.

Because that blow from the hotel room, the one that felt numb at first, now it was starting to hurt.

"Keys," Liam demanded as they headed out of the gym.

"Piss off. I can drive."

"And I'm a fucking fairy godmother in a goddamn tutu." It was the most words Liam had said in a row since they'd started. He hadn't asked how things went with Dani. He'd known from the moment Eli called. "I'm taking you home where you'll get your head into getting the Mason Village deal closed."

Eli's phone vibrated, Dani's image flashing on screen.

Reaching out, Liam took the thing right from his hand and declined the call before tapping something with his thumbs.

"What the fuck—" Eli snatched his phone back, scrolling through the notifications.

Call from Red. Declined.

Red: *Eli, please pick up. I want to talk.*

You: *Mason is unavailable. -Rowen*

Incoming notifications from Red successfully blocked.

Eli twisted toward the bastard, fingers already curling into a fist.

"Stand down." Liam opened the door of his truck, got in, and started the engine. "You have her number. You want to call her, call her. But having your brains scrambled each time that phone beeps will do you no good right now. Now get in. I'll have someone drop your truck off to you."

Eli knew Liam had been right the moment he returned to his house and felt the full force of reality finally ring through him. He'd been lied to. Manipulated. It was no one's fault but his own that he'd left his guard down and he—of all people—should have known better. And to add a kick in the balls, he still loved the woman.

In the quietness around him, pain sizzled from one temple to the other. Eli clutched his head to make it stop. It didn't, though. And his head wasn't the only part hurting. He ached all over, as if whacked with some supercharged version of the flu. Or maybe an AK-47. And it was the worst in his chest, just under the ribs.

Grabbing a set of cleaning supplies from the closet, Eli went about setting his place to rights. The mushrooms were gone, but their smell was still there. Her smell was still there. So Eli cleaned the kitchen and then threw his bedding into the wash, trusting Tide to remove Dani's lavender fragrance, the lingering scent of contentment.

But of course, the second he put the linens on the bed again, all he could think of was how Dani's long red hair looked resting on the pristine white sheets. So he went digging through his closets for another set—a much darker set in black-on-black—and stretched it over the mattress instead.

The clothes were next. Whatever Dani had worn or touched was tossed into the wash, even the clean stuff. The T-shirt she'd slept in, the dress back from the drycleaners after its shower. The suit he'd worn to the fundraiser. Everything. Finally, he washed himself too—in his own shower, not the one they shared—and followed Liam's damn advice, turning on his workstation and getting the hell to work.

Mason Village was not going to close itself, and Garibaldi would have some last trick up his sleeve before the deal was done. Eli was sure of it.

35

DANI

"It was a setup from the very beginning, sweetheart," my father says, reaching out across the kitchen table to pat my hand. Behind him on the old-fashioned wood-panel walls—painted over with a soft yellow by my mother when I was a toddler—are myriad family photos documenting our life. There are so many memories there. The three of us picnicking at the Boston Public Garden before Amber was born. Amber and me, filthy in our rain-covered yard after I taught her to make mud pies. The four of us laughing at my dad's silly face created from Thanksgiving mashed potatoes.

There are Christmases in front of our little brick fireplace. First me, then Amber, learning to ride our bicycles and plant herbs and tell the edible mushrooms apart from the deadly ones.

My mom nods. "These billion-dollar conglomerates like Mason Enterprises didn't get to where they are by being worried over cracking a few heads. There's a reason when they move into a town, it's a hostile takeover, not a joint venture."

I swallow, tightening my jaw. Everything since the moment Madison Mason knocked on my door has felt like being hit with a runaway train over and over. I told my family as many details as I could without compromising Eli's privacy, but that doesn't make the conversation any easier. It doesn't make the decisions any easier either. Maybe that's why I've held off finalizing my report. I'm presenting my findings to the Mason Enterprise board tomorrow, and I still don't know what I'll say.

"Eli isn't like that." I can't stop the pang of pain I feel when I say his name, can't stop seeing the devastation in his eyes when he found Madison in my room. Can't stop hearing the deafening silence of my phone not ringing, my texts going unanswered. Still, I can't bear to have my parents think ill of him.

"You should see this whole project he has going with Mason Village," I tell them. "It's not about taking over the small businesses, it's about giving them a chance to thrive. He was a SEAL. He's all about protecting and defending."

"I never said he wasn't." My dad tops off my tea. "But Mason Enterprises isn't just Eli. In fact, Mason Enterprises wants Eli out. His ideas don't fit the business model. You were never hired to evaluate him. You were hired to fail him."

My sister huffs. "So just fail him already."

"Amber—"

"No," she interrupts. "All you have to do is tell the truth. Didn't that woman Madison give you like, the ultimate cheat sheet? It's not like anyone is asking you to change any facts, so I don't understand what your problem is."

I sigh. "Madison wants me to make a conclusion I disagree with."

"Well boo-hoo for you. Your feelings will be offended. Or no, wait, your honor will be tarnished." Slamming her tea on the table, Amber storms off to the backyard door. "If you cared so much about your honor, maybe you shouldn't have fucked your evaluee," she yells before slamming the door hard enough to rock the flimsy walls.

My mother lets out a long breath. "She's sixteen, Dani. It's a dramatic age. We're going to be fine no matter what happens. We'll find a way to be fine. This house is getting too hard to keep up with anyway. It's been past time to downsize. And with so many online schooling options nowadays, we have many places we can move to."

Each of my mom's kind words only makes the reality hurt more. I know Amber is aggravatingly self-centered, but she's also watching the very likely unraveling of life as she knows it. And it is my fault. Because I'd taken Madison's too-good-to-be-true job offer, I've managed to threaten the very foundations of both my career and my family's financial well-being. This house, where I grew up and where my mom and dad still cultivate various organic plants and herbs for the local farmer's market, my parents can't afford it anymore. The money from this project was going to pay off the house. Give Amber a chance to go to college. To lose that on top of having my license suspended and me out of a job would be devastating.

"I'll go talk to Amber," says Mom.

"I'll go." Getting up before she does, I head out the door to find my sister sitting on a little bench swing our father built ages ago.

"You're going to cost us everything tomorrow," Amber says, throwing me a hate-filled look. Her hoodie and artfully torn jeans may look relaxed, but her stiff posture is anything but. "And yet you just sit there like everything's okay."

"Nothing about this is okay, Amber."

"Yeah? But one thing *could* be. Us. Our family." She gets up and kicks some dirt with the toe of her boot. "This great guy of yours, the one who isn't even taking your calls, the one you're never going to see again—why does he get some golden loyalty ticket instead of us? Have you even told him about the pictures?"

"He's not taking my calls, so—"

"Don't bullshit me." Amber glares up at me, and I realize with a start that tears are staining her wind-reddened cheeks. "If you wanted to tell him, you'd have found a way. You know, email, a friend, whatever."

I throw up my hands. "So that he could do what? Give me some absolution for ruining his life? He's been hurt and betrayed enough without adding my guilt trip onto it."

"The man's loaded. Maybe he could take some responsibility for the mess his company got you into. The kind that comes with several zeros on the end, you know?"

"I'm *not* asking Eli for money." My voice is sharper than I intend, the anger at the suggestion getting the best of me for a moment. By the time I get myself under control, however, Amber is already walking away.

"Of course you aren't," she says without bothering to turn around. "Your dignity is so much more important than your family. You know, you had a soul when you went to Colorado. Too bad you left it behind when you came back."

36

ELI

*T*he melodic ring of the doorbell made Eli realize that he'd been working on his computer for twelve hours without looking up, and his neck hurt. He padded downstairs, then pulled open the door into the rainy evening and herded two wet women inside.

Sky and Jaz looked like a pair of drenched cats who were unsure whether to be pleased with themselves or angry at the world at large. From their snug sleeveless tanks to their leggings and curved-sole low-profile shoes, the pair were dressed for climbing—which was beyond the logic of the weather even for Kyan's sister. "Reynolds. Jazzy-girl. To what do I owe the pleasure of your dripping company?"

"To Garibaldi and your mother." Swooping past him, Sky headed for the kitchen and started rummaging through his tea cabinet.

Taking another look at the two women, Eli pulled out a bottle of whiskey and three glasses, which seemed more to the point.

"They've both joined the Death Eaters?"

"No." Pulling out a packet of Earl Grey, Sky stared at it for a moment, then exchanged it for Eli's offered alcohol. "But there is a connection. After the fundraiser, when I was showing Mason Village to Dani"—Sky winced apologetically—"she mentioned having seen the name Garibaldi before."

Eli sighed, trying and failing not to feel a pang of pain at Dani's mention. "So has everyone who's taken European history in high school."

"She saw it in Madison's office."

Eli froze. "Dani told you she was working with Madison?"

"No. She told me that she thought she saw that name, as part of a logo, when she met with someone from the Mason Enterprises board of directors in Boston. Jaz and I deduced that it was in Madison's office tonight."

Eli's brows rose. "And how did you do that?"

"Investigative journalism."

"Uh-hm." Climbing getup, no rocks in sight, and new information. He drained his glass and poured another. "In other words, I should be grateful I'm not picking you up from the police station on breaking-and-entering charges?"

"Tomato tomahto," said Jaz.

"Should I also assume that you two have *investigated* Dani's full job description?" he asked darkly, though Talbot's shouting back at the fundraiser left little to the imagination.

"You should," Sky chips in. "Care to compare notes?"

Eli sighed. "Dani is a cognitive psychologist sent to evaluate my ability to lead Mason Pharmaceuticals as CEO. I thought she was working for the board of directors, but apparently, she's been working for Madison all along."

"I think it's not that simple," said Sky.

"You call that setup simple?" Eli rubbed his face. Maybe it *was* simple. Dani was working with Madison. She'd been deceiving him all along. "Can we have this conversation some other time?"

Jaz blew out an exasperated breath. "You don't want to know what we found?"

"Not particularly," Eli said honestly. "But I have a feeling I need to."

Sky pulled out her phone and brought up the photo roll, turning it over to give Eli a better view. A pair of checks from Madison's personal account filled the screen, the astronomical amounts giving Eli an uncomfortable idea of how Garibaldi had been funding his legal defense against Mason Village.

"There's more," Jaz said, bringing out her own phone. "While sleuth senior was working out the Garibaldi connection, I did a little picture walk through his computer."

"Liam has been giving you hacking lessons?" Eli couldn't help himself.

Jaz's shoulders rolled at once, making her look like a hissing cat. "The day I let that asshole give me lessons, hell will freeze over and grow daffodils. Also, there's no reason to hack when the password is left on a sticky note beside the computer screen. Seriously. Some people are just asking to have their files rummaged through. You want to know what I found or not?"

"Again, no."

"Good." Jaz pulled up photos of a computer screen, the first email coming from a no-reply Denton PD's address. "This is an email receipt for bail," Jaz narrated. "Dated exactly six days ago. Remember what happened then?"

"The fundraiser."

"Brock Talbot getting arrested at the fundraiser," Sky clarified. "He was supposed to be held without bail, by the way. Multiple offenses and a restraining order violation. Getting him out took some very powerful legal maneuvering."

Eli rubbed his temples. "Are you telling me Madison, Garibaldi, *and* Talbot have all been in bed together from the start?"

"No," Jaz said. "I don't think anyone knew about Talbot until the whole debacle at the gala." She flipped her photo roll to the next screenshot, this one showing an exchange of emails.

Garibaldi.Petro@GaribaldiLeasing.com

B. This is your new friend. I'm waiting.

BTalbot@Talbotinvestements.com:

Can't thank you enough. Let me reimburse you for your time and more. What account would be convenient?

Garibaldi.Petro@GaribaldiLeasing.com That wasn't our agreement. If you're no longer interested in this relationship, things can be returned to status quo.

The next email had no words, just a few photo attachments. Eli and Dani leaving Mason Pharmaceuticals together. Intimate ones from the pool party. A few damn explicit ones from inside his own home. The angle on the latter ones was strange as if…as if someone had taken over a laptop camera and was snapping whatever came into the shot. This email was forwarded to Madison's personal email address.

A chill ran over Eli's skin as he flipped through Jaz's screenshots, noting the time stamps. Putting the story together. "Garibaldi sees Talbot go after my date at the fundraiser. Follows him to the PD to discover if he can be of use. Then exchanges a promise of legal defense for Talbot's stalker photos. Sends those to Madison… Who is here by morning to blackmail Dani."

Eli tried and failed not to feel a stab of pain at the words. That day in the hotel room hadn't been the first time Dani and Madison had met, that much was obvious. But that still left Dani in a position she never deserved to be in.

"Something about the timing of your mother trying to get you fired is ridiculously convenient," Sky said, getting on her toes to look around Eli's shoulder. "I mean, flying across the country on an hour's notice to stick newfound blackmail under Dani's nose? The only reason to do that is if time is of the essence and more convenient pressures have been exhausted."

"The Mason Village closing," Eli said, finishing Sky's line of thought. "Cullen and I were trying to push the date up. It was supposed to have happened shortly after the fundraiser. Want to bet that if we were to dig into the financials, we'd find Madison profiting off Garibaldi's little racket?"

"That's not a bet, that's a story." Sky's eyes flashed with predatory gleam, but the fire died out quickly. "But that type of forensic analysis takes months, Eli. The closing is next week now."

Which meant Madison was going to assemble the board to get Eli removed before then. Remove him as CEO, and all the investors would flee. No investors, no closing.

"What if you tell the board of directors that the cognitive psychologist they hired to evaluate you was being blackmailed into providing a poor evaluation?" Jaz suggested.

"Then I'd have to disclose the photographs. Dani loses her license." Picking up a pen, Eli clicked it viciously. He couldn't do that to her. He had to protect her, even now. So he would have to do something.

37

DANI

*M*y drive to Mason Enterprises is uneventful, but I'm a wreck anyway. As I circle Kenmore Square for parking and walk through the gray, overcast afternoon toward Mason Enterprises, every joint in my body clenches with strain. No matter how the day goes, it will leave ruined lives in its wake.

It feels surreal to return to Mason Towers, where this nightmare started. As I walk up to the double-door entrance, I'm again struck by the details of the corporate building. Even at just twenty-one stories, it stands out against the Boston skyline. The mirrorlike material of its silver beams and interconnected windows make it reflect what surrounds it. Right now, that's puffy white clouds in a brilliant blue sky.

The irony isn't lost on me. The exterior of this place is beautiful, and the interior's environmentally friendly design speaks to my soul. And yet it's also Madison Mason's domain.

Dressed in a formal jade-green business suit, with my hair rolled up and pinned, I try to embody the self-assurance my appearance is designed to present. But the truth is, I'm terrified. The sound of my heels changes from soft thuds to higher-pitched clicks as I enter through the glass revolving doors on the lowest level. The floor is constructed of travertine laid out in an intricate pattern that spells the words *Mason Enterprises*. It's polished to a rich shine, but I only manage to traverse half of it when I hear my name.

"Danielle Nelson."

I pivot, my stomach clenching. "Yes, I'm Danielle Nelson."

"We've been expecting you," a Latino man with dark, penetrating eyes and a navy-blue three-piece extends his hand to me. "I'm Alfonso DeJesus, one of the board of directors' sitting members. It is a pleasure to meet you."

I stare at Alfonso's hand a moment too long before shaking it, earning myself a raised brow.

"I'm afraid you've caught me off guard, Mr. DeJesus." I give him a disarming smile, though after Madison, I don't trust anyone here. "I didn't expect anyone from the board to meet me in the lobby."

Alfonso shrugs one shoulder. In his early thirties, he looks too young and fit for the position, his toned body reminding me too much of Eli's. "Actually, I'm just running late, but claiming to be waiting for you made me look better."

He's lying. But I pretend not to notice.

Turning smartly, Alfonso steers me to the gilded elevator bank and then heads past it. "Would you mind terribly if we take the stairs, ma'am?" he asks over his shoulder, the *ma'am* in it having a practiced, military-like feel. "Avoiding the elevator is the only exercise I get all day."

"By all means," I say dryly. "What floor?"

"Twenty-first."

I stop, my hand on the railing. Grateful as I am to avoid the elevator, the *I know something about you* game doesn't sit well with me either.

Realizing I'm no longer following him, Alfonso halts a few steps ahead of me, looking over his shoulder with a resigned expression. "Eli Mason asked me to escort you up." His gaze clips down to my kitten-heel shoes. "I seem to have fallen for a bit of British humor."

My throat tightens. Eli. Even now, even after everything he thinks I've done, he's still trying to protect me. Even in these small ways. From the corner of my ear, I hear Alfonso proposing a return to a more civilized mode of transportation and shake my head, picking up the pace. "The stairs are just fine," I say quietly. "Thank you."

Following behind Alfonso, I ascend at a steady pace, the exercise stalling the worst of my anxieties. Nonetheless, the twenty-first floor comes too soon, and with it a large LCD screen announcing "Mason Enterprises Board Meeting. 8:00 a.m. in suite 100."

Heading left, I follow Alfonso across a new corridor, which leads us over some of the thickest plush carpeting I've ever seen and into a conference room with heavy wooden paneling. Four other people—two men and two women—are already there, Madison's eyes narrowing in momentary displeasure at seeing me and Alfonso walk in together.

"Ms. Nelson," Alfonso says, smoothly pointing to the man at the head of the table and working his way down, "may I present Mr. Gordon Fettering, chairman of the Mason Enterprises board of directors, and the other members, Kent Bellman, Bianca Truman, and Madison Mason."

In her Donna Karan suit, Madison Mason shoots me no more than a fleeting glance at the introduction, but even that is packed with warning.

"Thank you, Alfonso," the chairman says on the heels of the introductions, directing me to take a seat at the head of the table opposite him. "Welcome to everyone. The meeting today concerns the outcome of a third-party cognitive analysis of the CEO over in our pharmaceutical branch in Denton Valley, Colorado."

He sounds precise and clinical, not even using Eli's name. Perhaps saying the last name *Mason* is considered too prejudicial. But it's still Eli. Still his name. "The evaluation was ordered with a three-to-two vote. Today, Ms. Danielle Nelson is appearing before the board to present her results. Ms. Nelson, the floor is yours, ma'am."

I stand, raising my chin despite my heart beating so hard against my ribs that I can barely hear myself over the pounding. "Thank you, sir. I'm Danielle Nelson, a certified cognitive psychologist. Over the past six weeks I've been tasked with evaluating Elijah—"

"Ms. Nelson," Madison interrupts, her gaze on her notes. "Are you in any way affiliated with Mason Enterprises or any other business tied to our interests?" *Subcontext: Step out of line and the next question will be about your affiliation with Eli specifically.*

"No, ma'am, I'm not."

"Excellent. And you had ample time to finish your evaluation?" she continues.

"I did, ma'am."

"All right. Please proceed."

Clearing my throat, I lay my briefcase on the table and extract five sealed envelopes, which I pass around to the board members. Copies of my report. Signed and dated. I wasn't going to pass them out this early, but I need to cut off my own escape route.

The chairman raises his finger. "Before anyone opens their envelope, I would like to remind the board members that the contents inside it should not be shared outside this room. Whatever the conclusions, I expect the discussion to remain civil. Yes, Alfonso."

"For the record, I would like to raise my objection to the whole evaluation process again. The Denton Valley branch has been a consistent producer and innovator. Our investors are happy with the performance. I renew my request that the evaluation be dismissed."

"If Mr. Mason is the performer you suggest, Alfonso, then I'm sure his evaluations will say as much," Kent counters. "We hired an independent professional, after all."

I keep my face straight. I'd been under the impression—which, I now realize was absurd—that my preliminary drafts were circulated to all the parties. Clearly not. Madison had wanted to control the process. And, wyrd, she did exactly that, didn't she?

"Enough. The objection is noted and overruled," the chairman says. "Ms. Nelson."

Here we go. "Ladies and gentlemen, if you could open your envelopes—"

"Actually, let's not do that," a British voice says from the opening walnut double doors, Eli striding into the room dressed impeccably in one of his finest black pinstriped suits, his head unbowed and his shoulders squared. He's a glorious army-of-one commercial, but he shouldn't be here.

He doesn't look at me. He doesn't even peek in my general direction. He just stands there before the chairman, his hands draped behind his back, as if at parade rest.

"Elijah." Madison jumps to her feet. "What is the meaning of—"

"I realize this is unorthodox and a heinous breach of etiquette," Eli tells the board, his voice a smooth, commanding baritone that fills the room, "But I've something of time-sensitive significance to deliver." The room falls silent. Even Madison becomes stationary. Eli waits another heartbeat, then pulls a sheet of paper from his pocket. "I quit."

"What?" Madison squawks at the same time that the chairman says, "Excuse me?"

"I resign as the CEO of Mason Pharmaceuticals effective immediately."

No. No, no, no. This isn't supposed to happen this way.

Gordon Fettering frowns. "I don't understand"

Eli shrugs as if the matter is of none-too-grave concern. "The fact that the board of directors saw fit to hire a *cognitive psychologist*"—Eli says the words as if discussing a particularly unpleasant venereal disease—"to evaluate my suitability as CEO is in itself a vote of no confidence. Whether or not that report contains derogatory information, its mere existence would be a black mark on my reputation. As such, I ask that it remain sealed ad infinitum. Or, better yet, shredded. There is, after all, no need to indulge in reading an evaluation of a person not in your employ."

Another moment of silence echoes through the room, blood draining from my face with each passing heartbeat. I try to catch Eli's gaze, to shake my head at him, to somehow let him know that I'm not here to hurt him, but he won't so much as look in my direction.

Madison is the first to speak, pushing the sealed envelope away from herself. "I accept Mr. Mason's conditions," she says, her voice kind. Understanding. "It is a difficult situation, and he has the right to his privacy."

Eli half bows to his mother, a show of misplaced gratitude.

Alfonso, however, is on his feet now, his palms slamming the table. "You're going to give up, Mason? Roll over and play dead without even seeing what's in here? That's a coward's way out, and I had no idea you were—"

"You're out of line, Mr. DeJesus." Eli's voice snaps with a military harshness that stops Alfonso in his tracks, though not without a flash of anger rushing over the man's tanned features.

I bite my lip, trying to follow what Eli thinks he's doing. Alfonso must be as close to an ally as he has in this group. Embarrassing the man in front of his colleagues is not going to preserve Eli's reputation...which, come to think of it, is not in grave danger from the mere existence of a confidential report. Eli's argument is stupid. And Eli is not stupid. Not by a long shot.

The realization hits me all at once, closing off my throat. It isn't his record Eli Mason is trying to protect. It's mine. Somehow, some way, Eli found out about the photos. And now he's here, taking cover fire to give me the chance to escape with my license intact. Even though I've hurt him—and wyrd, I know I have—Eli is still here. Looking out for me. Because that's the kind of man he is.

"Eli, wait," I call out to him.

At last, Eli glances at me, but I can read nothing in his face beyond sheer determination. But that's all right. Because no matter what he feels, no matter how he found out about the pictures, I know how I feel. And what I feel is love. Love for him.

The license be damned, I don't regret a moment we spent together.

"Enough of this," Madison says, her confident tone ringing out over the boardroom. "The man has resigned. That is his right. As for the report, if Alfonso insists on reading it, then out of respect for his service on this board, we can—"

"I would stop talking if I were you, Madison," Gordon Fettering says quietly, drawing the room's attention to where he'd taken it upon himself to open my report while the others had argued. Drawing the clean typed pages out into the open, the chairman turns them around for the room to see, the title crisp beneath the conference room's lights.

Mason Enterprises Leadership Suitability Report. Subject Evaluated: Madison Mason.

3 8

ELI

A cold shock zapped through Eli's spine as Gordon Fettering flipped through the report pages, the other members of the board now opening their envelopes. Reading over Alfonso's shoulder, he felt his stomach drop more with each damning line.

… pathologic need to cast false aspersions… conclusions drawn with lack of legitimate proof… Her attempts—enumerated throughout this report —to sway, cajole, and eventually coerce this evaluator into reporting not just an alternate view of documented events witnessed, but falsifying evidence to support the requested conclusion.

Twisting toward Dani, he stared into her beautiful, brave face, terror racing through him. The woman hadn't just taken a calculated risk of submitting a true account, she'd signed her own career death warrant. For him. Even when she had no reason to think they would ever cross paths again.

"Dani," he whispered, shaking his head. Trying to figure out how to turn this around before—

"Ms. Nelson." Madison's cultured voice sounded utterly

unconcerned, with only a hint of curiosity underlying the tones. "Might I ask the manner in which you were—" she pulled the report slightly away from her face, getting the paper to a comfortable reading distance," —swayed, cajoled, and eventually coerced?"

Fuck. Too late.

Dani straightened her suit jacket, speaking to the board. "Ms. Mason presented me with photographs documenting a romantic relationship between me and Elijah Mason."

"And these photographs," Madison continued in that same calm tone of a trained prosecutor. "Were they forgeries? Or inaccurate in some way?"

Eli's heart pounded against his ribs, the way Dani held her head up putting him to shame.

"They were accurate, ma'am," Dani said.

"Is this permitted by your ethics board, Ms. Nelson?" Fettering asked.

Dani chuckled without humor. "Absolutely not, sir. Which is why it made for exemplary blackmail." She pushed a strand of hair behind her ear, and Eli was sure he was the only one able to detect the tiny tremor in her hand. "That's what ultimately led to my decision to revise my report late last night. If I revised the report as per Ms. Mason's instructions, I'd not only be handing over lies but would be helping to smear the reputation of the most honest, compassionate, and honorable man I've ever met. If I provided it as it was, I'd have violated my ethics again because no matter what I tell myself, I'm helplessly biased in my evaluee's favor." Dani bit her lip. "So I pulled out the old adage: when all else fails, try the truth."

Silence settled over the room, the air heavy with tension. Madison, her mouth slightly ajar, stared at Dani. Dani stared at the chairman. The chairman stared at the report.

Click.

Eli registered Alfonso clicking his pen just as Dani did, her shoulders—which had stayed so straight and confident the entire time—flinching at the sound. Bracing his hand on the edge of the conference table, Eli cleared it in a single leap, landing just behind Dani to lay a steadying hand on her shoulder.

When Dani's fingers came up to brush his own, his heart stuttering like a boy's, he knew he wouldn't—couldn't—let go of her. Never again. No matter what happened.

Taking off his glasses, Fettering let them skitter across the table while he pinched the bridge of his nose.

"If I may," Madison started again, only to be cut off by the chairman's waving hand.

"You've said—and done—quite enough, Madison," he said flatly. "Ms. Nelson, you signed an NDA when you were retained for this evaluation?"

"Yes, sir." Beneath his touch, he could feel Dani's muscles tensing, the energy that it was taking to hold the entire boardroom in check starting to give beneath the pressure. Yet here she was. The bravest woman Eli had ever met.

"Good," Fettering continued. "That holds in full force. Especially now."

"The medical ethics board will convene—" Madison started to say again.

"There will be no medical ethics board," Fettering said, cutting Madison off at the knees. "There will be no report. There has been no evaluation. Not on Eli. Not on Madison. Not on anyone in this entire place. None of this happened. Ms. Nelson, you will send out a Myers-Briggs personality assessment test to this board, which will be filed under the notes for this gathering. And as for you, Mason." Picking up Eli's resignation letter, Fettering ripped it to bits. "Get back to work. I've had enough drama today to last me a lifetime."

HAND on the small of Dani's back, Eli gently led her out of the boardroom. From behind the closing door, Madison's voice was still insisting everything had been precipitated by a misunderstanding, and for once, Eli didn't fully disagree.

It was a misunderstanding. Of priorities. Of loyalties. Of what his soul needed to be whole.

"Walk down with me?" Eli asked.

"It's twenty-one floors." Dani looked over her shoulder. "Let me guess, you need the exercise today?"

"No. I just want the company." For a second, Eli feared that Dani would pull away, but after a heartbeat of hesitation, she motioned for him to lead the way to the stairwell. As the door closed behind them to cut off all the noise from the main landing, however, Dani slowed her steps.

"What's going to happen to Madison?" she asked.

"She will sit in a proverbial penalty box for a year or two," he answered. "Fettering knows she is a viper now, but he also knows that if the board airs too much dirty laundry, the reputational damage will hurt the bottom line with the investors. The important thing is that she can't hurt you anymore."

Reaching up to Dani's face, Eli traced her cheek with his thumb, savoring the feel of her cool skin beneath his touch. After the raised voices in the conference room, the silence of the stairway was that much more stark, Dani's soft soprano voice and lavender fragrance washing over his senses. "Sky and Jaz found photos of us on Garibaldi's computer. He'd gotten them from Talbot to send to Madison." Eli paused, his hand still on Dani's face as he asked the question whose answer he feared. "Why didn't you tell me you were being blackmailed, Red? About Madison? About Talbot? Why didn't you trust me?"

Dani's chin jerked up in surprise. "Trust you? Of course I trusted you. With Talbot..." She winced, and it was all Eli could do to keep from pulling her toward his chest. "I didn't want to think it was real. I thought I was crazy and…and that it would sound stupid."

"Never," Eli whispered, shaking his head.

"As for the rest," she took a breath, "I had given my word, Eli. Before I ever met you, I'd given my word to Madison to keep our acquaintance confidential. It had seemed like a straightforward enough request, and by the time I realized all the complications that came with it, it was too late."

Dani scraped her teeth along her bottom lip. "I'm so sorry I hurt you. I'm so sorry I worked with Madison. And I'm so, *so* sorry that I had to keep the truth to myself even when I knew what the woman had done to you. But I'm not going to apologize for keeping my word. I can't."

Bloody hell. This, *this* was why he loved her. "I wouldn't ask you to," he said, holding her gaze. "And if I hadn't been such a wanker when you tried to talk to me, I would have realized the truth. I'm sorry, Red. Can you forgive me?"

He held his breath.

Instead of answering, Dani stepped closer to him and, getting up onto her toes, covered his mouth with her own. The kiss started out soft and tentative, but within heartbeats, its intensity grew, more and more, until Eli was holding Dani with all the desperation and passion that had built up inside him. And she, him.

Eli was breathless by the time they finally pulled apart—his bulging cock made even the slightest movement excruciating—and tossed a covert glance. Bloody hell. He winced.

"Wyrd, we got a little carried away there," Dani said, plainly trying—and failing—to contain a too-knowing smile.

Eli tugged her against him. "Yes, well, falling in love with you makes one a bit keen to have you again."

She froze in his arms, then lifted her chin enough to study his face. "You're falling in love with me?"

"Fell," he corrected her. "Already fell."

"I…" She blinked several times. "I love you too."

Warmth suffused his entire system, each nerve and fiber alive and settled. His next words left him as a gruff croak. "Good to know."

39

DANI

*A*s we walk through the revolving door, Boston greets us with its traffic, and sirens, its exhaust fumes, and sprawling crowds. A group of teens strut by, discussing something *wicked awesome* as they bend around us.

"Boston is your home, isn't it?" I ask Eli.

He shakes his head. "Not even close. I grew up here when not hauled off to boarding school in London, but my real family is in Denton Valley. Speaking of family, let me drive you home."

I feel my parking voucher in my pocket. "I drove in."

"Let me drive you anyway. I want to thank your father for the leeches."

"And?" I ask. There's more. I know there's more.

He gives me a coy look. "And given that their daughter set out to Mason Towers this morning with the full intention of destroying her livelihood on my behalf, I figure they may want to throw some things at me before we can call a truce."

I shift my feet uncomfortably. Even though I'd sent home a text to say all is well, when it comes to Amber, Eli isn't wrong—there's a chance she'll literally throw something just because. My mother wouldn't, of course, but I have little faith that she'll be able to conceal the undertones of resentment she feels toward conglomerates in general, no matter what happened. Even my dad is unpredictable—he's the most open-minded of the three, but after the turmoil of the last few days he isn't in the best mental state either. The thought of having the people I care most about in the world shoot anger spears at each other right now turns my stomach.

Eli interlaces his fingers with mine. "It's not as if I've not gone behind enemy lines before," he whispers into my ear. "And for less reason. Any family who raised a daughter like you is one I want to meet."

My heart flutters as I prop open the screen door to knock on the thick oak main door of the house I grew up in. My mother has hung a wreath of orange maple leaves on it while I was gone. She's always crafty, but more so when she's anxious. And this wreath is an elaborate mix of geraniums, Shasta daisies, and black-eyed Susans.

"There's still a chance to retreat," I murmur to Eli.

"Never." His voice is confident, but his complexion is more blanched than it should be. He's nervous, I realize, but doing his damnedest not to show it. Before I can suggest we simply postpone until a better time, though, the door is yanked wide, revealing my little sister, Amber.

I hold my breath.

Amber switches her narrow-eyed gaze from me to him, a hint of color touching her cheeks as her gaze traces Eli's lithe body, his Armani suit underscoring broad shoulders and a taut waist. Standing beside him in her skinny jeans and cropped top, my sister looks, well, young. She opens her mouth, closes it, blushes scarlet. "So you're my sister's boyfriend?"

I hide my snort, though just barely. Up till now, I've never seen Amber with such an obvious crush for someone who isn't a member of an alternative band or one of the Marvel Cinematic

Universe's superheroes. Add in the lack of filter between her brain and her vocal cords, and here we are.

Eli extends his hand. "You must be Amber," he says. "I'm Mason."

She takes his hand. "I thought your name was Eli."

"My friends call me Eli," Eli agrees, their hands staying locked longer than they should. Then I see Amber's white knuckles and realize she's actually trying to play bone crush with a SEAL.

"But I'm supposed to call you *Mason?*" Amber sneers. Yep, that's my Amber.

Eli looks down at their still-connected hands. "Does it appear to you like we're friends?" he asks calmly. If I want to twist Amber's teenage head off, the attitude rolls off Eli like water from a duck—he isn't going to take Amber's crap, but he doesn't take the anger personally either. I love this man.

"Did Dad tell you that everything is fine?" I ask. Amber has still not moved aside to let us in. "You can stay in the house."

"Yeah. By some miracle. But it was no thanks to you." Amber goes to pull her hand back, but this time, it's Eli's turn to tighten his grip.

"Your sister is the bravest woman I've ever met," he tells her, his gray gaze capturing Amber's as his voice turns hard. Commanding. "Believe me when I tell you that's saying something."

He lets go of her, and Amber stumbles back, her mouth opening and closing again without making a sound. "Whatever," she says finally, disappearing into the house, but there's a note of something in it I haven't heard in some time. Respect.

"Well, don't stand there in the doorway." My mother appears in the spot Amber just vacated. "Please come in."

"Thank you, Ms. Nelson." Standing aside to let me go in first, Eli gives my mom a half bow.

My mom clears her throat. "I have lunch ready. It's not

anything like you're used to, of course, but I didn't know we were going to be hosting. I'm happy to run out to the store to pick something up, though." She looks from Eli to me. "What does he eat?"

I clear my throat. "He isn't a puppy, Mom."

"It's no problem," Eli assures her. "I've some protein powder in my car, ma'am. Shall I fetch it?"

My mom stares. "Protein powder? Why would we need protein powder?"

Eli shrugs his large shoulder. "You asked what I was used to. That's what lunch usually is. Though Dani tends to insist on— what do you call those things again?"

"Vegetables," I supply.

My mom's eyes widen. "Good God, you subsist on protein powder?"

"Hot dogs too," Eli offers helpfully. "And power bars. I have some of those in the car as well."

"Not in this house you don't," my mother declares, her fists going to her hips. "Go wash your hands, both of you."

Eli ducks his head obediently and follows me to the bathroom, lathering his hands as instructed. I nestle my head in the bend of his shoulder. Leaning down, Eli kisses the top of my head. Calm. And happy. And homey.

Lunch breaks the final ice between Eli and my folks, with Eli recounting the effectiveness of the leeches before comparing notes on edible and medicinal plants in austere environments. The conversation makes Amber oscillate between blushing at Eli and making faces at the discussion, before finally joining in with a knowledge of mushrooms that puts Eli to shame. When Eli pulls a pad from his inside jacket pocket and starts taking notes on Amber's insights, I know he's won himself a new friend.

After lunch, Eli and I amble outside to the front porch, sitting on the old wooden swing that's been there ever since I can remember. We peer out at the myriad vegetables and herbs growing beside my parents' porch steps in little terra-cotta pots, in the upraised planting boxes, and inside the full garden patch beyond that. This plot of land on the outskirts of Boston smells sweet, like hay and honeysuckle and several other aromas combined, the scents of my childhood.

But the fragrance I most enjoy inhaling is deep whiffs of Eli's fresh-grass scent as he pulls me onto his lap, the swing juddering about precariously.

"Liam texted," Eli says softly, his hand coming around me. "Talbot's legal defense is no longer funded, and now that it's safe, more accusations from women are coming in. He's going to be behind bars."

I close my eyes, pressing into him, the safety of his presence penetrating my skin—but Eli pulls me away.

"Your father told me you aren't one to stay in one placc long. But what would you say about giving Denton Valley another go?" He swallows, his strong face so very vulnerable. "With me. Together."

I trace my fingers along his hand, waiting for my mind to go into overdrive with the proposition. But it doesn't. Maybe because so much of Denton Valley isn't foreign to me any longer. Or maybe because being beside Eli just feels so very right. Plus, I really can do my job from anywhere. "I'd like that," I say, meaning every word. "I'd like that very, very much."

Smiling with a mix of triumph and relief, Eli seizes my hand and kisses the palm. "Good. Except there is one wrinkle. I might be renovating the guest room. So you'll have to do with sharing my room. And bed."

"Uh-huh." I bring a hand up to his forehead and push back one of the misbehaving curls. "And when exactly is this renovation starting?" I ask.

Eli pulls out his phone. "Oh, in about five minutes."

I roll my eyes and brush my lips over his, pulling away more quickly than I wish in deference to being on my parents' front porch in broad daylight. Denton Valley is looking better and better with every second. As if to underscore my unspoken thought, Amber comes barreling out of the house, the screen door slamming shut with a loud bang behind her. Seeing Eli and me—or, more accurately seeing Eli and nothing else—she stops in her tracks, color rising along her neck.

"Hey," she says.

"Hello, Amber."

She sticks her hands into her pockets. "So… Do you want to get a beer or something?"

"What?" I jerk up in Eli's lap. "You're sixteen. You're not getting a beer with Eli or anyone else."

The red on Amber's neck creeps to her face, and I feel a bit bad. I didn't mean to embarrass her, but *seriously*.

"Amber, make sure you weed the herb garden and clean your room," our father calls out loudly enough to be heard through the open window, sealing the final nails in the coffin of my sister's humiliation.

Sliding his hands under my knees, Eli slips me aside and leans forward toward Amber, his forearms braced on his knees. "You're sixteen?" he clarifies.

"Sixteen and a half."

"Does that mean you have a driving permit?"

Amber bites her lip. "I have a license, but Dad is worried about me driving the car."

Of course he is. It's our only one. If Amber crashes it, things won't go well.

"He says his nerves can't handle it," Amber adds quickly.

"Well, I'm a bit of an adrenaline junkie," Eli says, his tone so serious that it's starting to make me nervous. "And there's something I need help with. So I'll make you a deal—help me with my little errand, and you can drive."

Amber's face lights up then falls just as quickly. She isn't stupid. She knows what a damaged car would do to our family. "I don't think it's a good idea. Dad might need the car."

"We'll use mine." Eli waves away the concern. "But this isn't a free ride. I need that help."

"Really?" Amber's face lights up. "I mean, deal."

"Wait. What? Where are you taking her, Eli?" I demand.

"That's between Amber and me, Red," Eli says impertinently, tossing my sister the keys to his Mercedes SUV rental. "See you in a bit."

A bit turns out to be no less than three hours—with only the regular proof-of-life phone calls to my parents stopping them from calling out a search-and-rescue party. Every time Amber calls, her voice sounds a little more giddy, her answer a little more evasive. By the time the pair returns—with Amber in the driver's seat—I smell a rat.

"Where were you?" I ask, noting the new Oakley sunglasses Amber is now wearing.

"Parking lots. Lots of parking lots," she tells me.

My mother clears her throat, tapping on her own glasses in question.

"The sun was getting into Amber's eyes," Eli says smoothly. "It was a matter of safety, ma'am. I hope that's all right. You'll especially notice the difference in the winter, when the snow starts reflecting the rays."

Amber kisses our mom's cheek. "He was very good. I think I can parallel park better than you now. Call me for dinner?"

"Where are you going?" my mom asks as Amber trots up the stairs.

"Science paper. Call me for dinner?"

My parents exchange incredulous looks.

Amber pauses at the top landing, leaning over. "Eli?" she calls.

"Mason," Eli calls back.

"Three point four?"

"Three point five."

She sighs and starts to her room. "Fine."

I cross my arms. "Start talking, *Mason*."

"I might also have told Amber that if she has a 3.5 GPA by winter holiday—and if it's all right with your folks—she can come out to Colorado. Try out some different cars. Learn different road conditions. All normal things." He shifts his weight, his hands going adorably into his pockets as he meets the gazes of the three adults. "What? It's not like I promised to take her to the grenade range."

"There are grenade ranges?" I ask.

Eli brightens. "Of course. Want to go?"

"No," Mom, Dad, and I all answer at the same time, Eli shrugging his shoulders in a *your loss* kind of way. I snort and then, just to be contrary, raise my brows at him. "Plus, I said I'll come with you to Denton Valley in this nice July weather. I never said I'll stay there for the winter."

"Yes, about that." Eli shifts his weight. "Amber and I discussed it at some length. We decided that there was only one thing to do about that little problem."

Reaching into the inside pocket of his jacket, Eli pulls out a tiny powder-blue velvet box and lowers smoothly to one knee. With the door still open behind him, I can see the sun dipping into the skyline along the horizon, transforming the heavens into a myriad of crimson, orange, and lavender.

My body freezes... Wait. He can't be... He isn't...

"Danielle Nelson, I know being around me hasn't always been a picnic, but..." He flips the box open, a large diamond solitaire surrounded by a circle of smaller diamonds glimmering and shooting prisms of colors around the rough cedarwood of the entryway. "If you'll let me, I'll do my best to shear off the rough edges. You make me a better man, Red. I love you, and I wish to spend the rest of my life with you. So...will you marry me?"

My vision becomes fuzzy as tears spill down my cheeks. "Eli, I…" I trail off as a sob erupts from my chest. I want to say more, but can't. The emotion I feel overwhelms me, consuming my soul entirely.

"Amber said you'd like the rose-gold setting," Eli says into the silence. I hadn't even noticed the rose gold due to the sheer numbers of diamonds encrusting its surface. "So if that's the problem, you know, it's all her fault."

I chuckle, Amber, the nosy busybody, echoing the sound from upstairs. "I love the rose-gold setting," I assure him. "And you too. I love you too." My gaze lifts from the ring to Eli's gray eyes. "Yes," I whisper into the breathless silence. "Yes. My answer is yes."

Rising, Eli slides the band onto my finger, the cool metal fitting perfectly. From Amber's room upstairs, the notes of a bridal march fill the house in none too subtle a salute. Giving his new younger sister a thumbs-up, Eli steps closer to me, laying his wide hand on my cheek.

And then we're kissing. Deeply and desperately. Bidding goodbye to the old world and starting anew. Together.

EPILOGUE

Six Months Later
Dani

 open my eyes long enough to hit snooze on my alarm. The bed is just too cozy to crawl out from, and Eli won't be back from training with the guys at Liam's for another twenty minutes. Even living together, I still can't figure out how Eli manages to do everything—run Mason Pharmaceuticals, train, volunteer at the Rescue, manage side real estate acquisitions and still spend time with the people he cares for. The man functions on four hours of sleep a night.

I, however, do not. Just as I flop onto my pillow and let my eyes drift shut, my alarm goes off again. I startle, realizing that I'd fallen all the way asleep. Wyrd, I keep doing that lately. Maybe the late-night sex is starting to cut too much into sleep. Or else it's the magical Colorado winter, with so much pristine snow.

Reaching for my cell phone, I check messages. Poor Sky. Her wedding is this Friday, and the groom and groomsmen are all still trying to kill each other this morning.

Sky: *I never thought I'd be googling "best tux to offset a black eye."*

Me: *No worries. I keep leeches around just for that now.*

In the past months, I've seen more black eyes than ever since Eli talked me into helping out with some mental health needs for Garibaldi's old slum residents while they stayed at a shelter, waiting for Mason Village to be built. What was supposed to have been a weekend-long endeavor has morphed into a full-time project that I'm spearheading. I'll return to executive evaluations eventually, but being able to help people directly is too rewarding to stop now.

I know firsthand the value of having someone to discuss past demons with now, having finally confided in Eli about my high school rape. Turns out that burying memories and healing from them are two things worlds apart. I've always known that professionally, of course, but it's different when it's personal. And I am healing now. With Eli's help, I've even told my parents what happened, and we've given Liam a green light to see if he can track down the senior who'd done it. There's no news yet, but if anyone can find the bastard, it's Liam.

As Eli predicted, Madison has been lying low since that board meeting. She still has her position on paper, but Eli says she can't make a single move without the chairman himself signing off on it. As for Eli's father, that's going to take some time to settle. Eli is starting to talk about the abuse, but there's a long way to go. For now, the fallout from Madison's machinations is casting enough taint on Eldridge to make him retreat into the shadows and lie low for a bit—and when Eli is ready, we'll confront the man together.

Getting out of bed, I head downstairs, a blanket of white snow greeting me out the window. Having been raised in Boston, I know how much a winter wonderland can transform the landscape, but Colorado outshines Massachusetts. Or maybe it's living with Eli that makes everything feel more potent. More alive.

I walk into the kitchen at the same time Eli does, carrying in several packages.

"Mushrooms?" I ask hopefully.

"Clothes." He sets them down as I shake my head. My growing wardrobe has already taken over half of the walk-in closet and keeps expanding. None but two of the items were actually purchased by me. Deciding that I wasn't adequately equipped for the Colorado weather and getting tired of hearing I was too busy with work to go shopping, Eli hired a professional stylist to do it for me. The woman was a genius, but took the order to *"set her up with an appropriate wardrobe"* to its logical absurdity.

"You know, I did somehow manage to not walk around naked before meeting you," I tell him.

"Hmm…" A glint flashes in Eli's eye. "Then you should most certainly do more naked walking now that we're together."

Well, I walked into that one, didn't I?

Raiding the fridge for eggs and veggies, I start prepping everything for a morning omelet and frown. Something about the ingredients seems off.

"Does this smell strange to you?" I ask, bringing my mixing bowl to Eli.

"It smells like vegetable and a fungus coated in egg. So yes."

Getting up on my toes, I nip Eli's ear. He's fresh from the shower, his fresh-grass scent mixing with a male musk and men's cologne.

"Stop that," he groans, and I look up to find his gray eyes have turned utterly molten.

"Stop what?" I ask innocently.

"Stop nibbling on me like I'm your own personal dessert. You're making me bloody horny, and we both need to get to work."

"Mmm?" I rub my hand down his perfectly defined chest and

drag it over his sternum, his six-pack of abs, and finally over his pulsing cock.

"To hell with work," Eli mutters, my thighs dampening at his words. He suckles along the side of my neck, hastily moving my hair out of the way. Each day we're together, he seems to learn my body better and better, always searching for new ways to drive me out of my skin with need.

Turning in his arms, I crush my lips against his, every fiber of my body craving more and more of him. "Take me," I gasp. "Right here. On the barstool."

Eli's hands close around my hips as he lifts me effortlessly onto the seat. In short order, he's stripped off my sleep tank and pajama bottoms, groaning appreciatively when he sees that I skipped pulling on some panties last night. "You've got an evil streak in you," he whispers, running his thumb over my bunching nipples, my breasts full and achy and so, so sensitive.

"Do I now?" I breathe.

He rips off his sweatshirt, then ravages my mouth with his tongue. He's just made my moan echo against the kitchen cabinets when my cell phone rings on the counter.

"Bollocks," he swears, leaning down far enough that he can draw my nipple into his mouth with gusto. When he releases the puckered peak, he moves his exceedingly dexterous hands between my legs, pushing two fingers into me at once as his thumb brushes my clit. "Don't answer that."

"Oh..." I make a noise that comes out as half hum and half keen, but then I catch a glimpse of my screen. Denton Primary Care, where I had my physical yesterday. My stomach tightens. They said they'd only call if lab results strayed out of norm.

Reading my face, Eli looks at the phone. "Answer it. Right now. Put it on speaker." His military voice, hard and demanding. The kind I used to resent before I learned that it came from a place of love and concern.

I draw a shaking breath.

"It's all right." Pulling me closer, Eli takes my phone from the counter and clicks Answer. "Danielle Nelson's cell. This is her fiancé, Eli Mason, but Dani is right here as well. You're on speaker."

"Thank you, Mr. Mason," the melodic, professional voice says on the other end of the line. Doctor Bailey-Thorne herself. Not a staff member. Not someone from billing or lost and found or any other mundane thing. "This is a confidential call. May I speak to Dani directly?"

Eli rubs a small circle on my back. "There's a HIPAA privacy release on file for me. You can go ahead and speak freely."

"Yes, please do," I say quickly. "Eli can hear whatever it is."

Doctor Bailey-Thorne clears her throat. "I really think you might—"

"No, I'm sure. Whatever is wrong, please just say it."

"There's nothing *wrong*, Dani." The doc's voice gentles. "This is more of a congratulatory type of call. I'm looking at your lab results here. You're pregnant."

Eli drops the phone. Then scurries to drag it off the floor again. "Doctor, can you say that again?"

"Your bride-to-be is expecting."

"No," I tell the doctor. "No no no. You have something wrong. I told you, I wasn't. I'm, *we're* careful."

"Dani, sweetheart, I know what you said. But your urine sample doesn't quite agree. That's why I'm calling."

"But…" I'm on birth control. Have been for years. Had I forgotten a dose somewhere with all the flying between across the country and moving? No. No, I couldn't have. "How is that possible?"

"Well," the doctor hesitates. "It typically involves intercourse while—"

"That's all right, Doc." Eli pulls the phone closer to himself. "I'll take care of explaining how babies are made. We'll, um, call you back. Or we'll call an OB. I mean… Uh, th-thank you," Eli

Mason, the most articulate man I've ever met, stutters into the receiver before disconnecting the call.

For a long moment, we simply stare wide-eyed at each other. Then, as if we're choreographing a dance, we look down at my bare belly together. My hand and his meet over my navel, fluttering over the flat expanse with the lightness of a bird's wing.

"Holy fuck," he utters. "We're going to have a baby."

It's then that instead of pure astonishment, I feel a wave of warmth in my chest. We are. Yes, yes, *we* are.

And somehow, even though this is brand-new and monumentally terrifying, I know it will be glorious.

You've finished Eli's book, but there are more Tridents to get to know. If you enjoyed this book, you may also like the other stories in the TRIDENT RESCUE Series.

If you are reading this in ebook version, continue on for a FREE preview of ENEMY LINES.

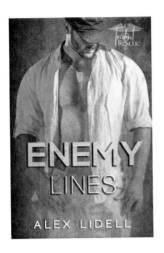

Kyan Keasley. Reckless, broken, and heart-stoppingly gorgeous.

AVAILABLE HERE IN KINDLE UNLIMITED.

OTHER BOOKS BY THIS AUTHOR:

TRIDENT RESCUE (Writing as A.L. Lidell)
Contemporary Enemies-to-Lovers Romance
ENEMY ZONE (Audiobook available)
ENEMY CONTACT (Audiobook available)
ENEMY LINES (Audiobook available)
ENEMY HOLD (Audiobook available)
ENEMY CHASE
ENEMY STAND

IMMORTALS OF TALONSWOOD (4 books)
Reverse Harem Paranormal Romance
LAST CHANCE ACADEMY (Audiobook available)
LAST CHANCE REFORM (Audiobook available)
LAST CHANCE WITCH (Audiobook available)
LAST CHANCE WORLD (Audiobook available)

POWER OF FIVE (7 books)
Reverse Harem Fantasy Romance
POWER OF FIVE (Audiobook available)
MISTAKE OF MAGIC (Audiobook available)
TRIAL OF THREE (Audiobook available)
LERA OF LUNOS (Audiobook available)
GREAT FALLS CADET (Audiobook available)
GREAT FALLS ROGUE

GREAT FALLS PROTECTOR

SIGN UP FOR NEW RELEASE NOTIFICATIONS at https://links.
alexlidell.com/News

ABOUT THE AUTHOR

Alex Lidell is the Amazon Breakout Novel Awards finalist author of THE CADET OF TILDOR (Penguin) and several Amazon Top 100 Kindle Bestsellers, including the POWER OF FIVE romance series. She is an avid horseback rider who believes in eating dessert first. She writes as both Alex Lidell and A.L. Lidell.

Join Alex's newsletter for news, bonus content and sneak peeks: https://links.alexlidell.com/News

Find out more on Alex's website: www.alexlidell.com

SIGN UP FOR NEWS AND RELEASE NOTIFICATIONS

Connect with Alex!
www.alexlidell.com
alex@alexlidell.com